MELPOMENE'S DAUGHTER

BOOK THREE

Also by Cassandra Page

Lucid Dreaming

The Isla's Inheritance trilogy
Isla's Inheritance
Isla's Oath
Melpomene's Daughter

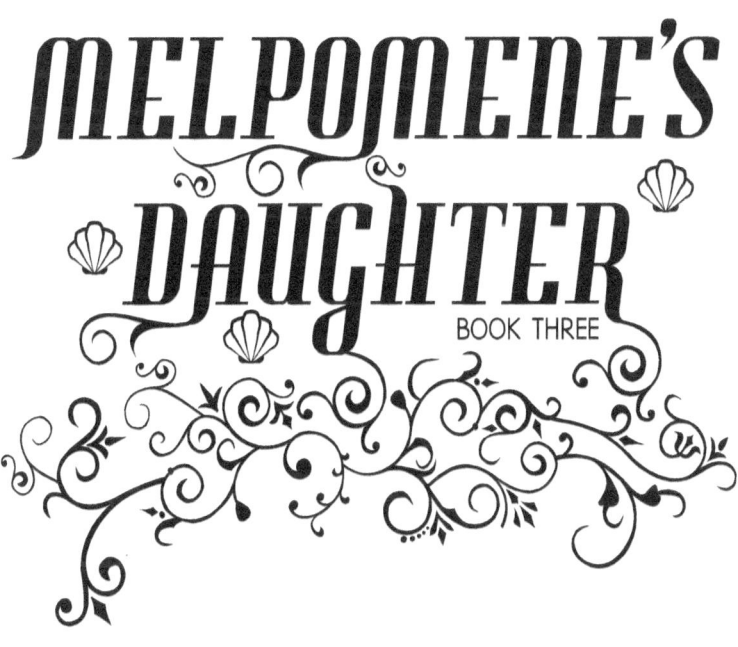

MELPOMENE'S DAUGHTER

BOOK THREE

CASSANDRA PAGE

www.cassandrapage.com

Cassandra Page
www.cassandrapage.com

Cataloguing-in-Publication data available from
the National Library of Australia www.nla.gov.au

ISBN: 978-0-9944459-7-1

Formatting and cover design by KILA Designs
www.kiladesigns.com.au
Cover images: ©Shutterstock

To my readers. Because, without you,
I'm just talking to myself.

CHAPTER ONE

When Aunt Elizabeth nagged me about getting a job, I doubted this was what she had in mind.

I stood behind Talbot's cottage, coppery autumn sunlight drifting down from the artificial sun above. An artificial sun I'd accidentally created two months before. I was inside the *sidhe*, the magical land under the hills— or perhaps in another reality accessed via portals into the hills. I wasn't clear on the physics. Either way, it was where Canberra's *duinesidhe*, or faeries, lived.

Before me was a wide space. The cottage was at the far end of the eclectic village, so there was nothing but grass between the back of his home and the cliff-like boundary of the *sidhe* beyond. I stared at the field, biting my lip. The amount of space I had to fill was daunting.

"You can do it," Jack murmured beside me. I glanced at him, reassured by the trust in his wide sapphire eyes and, visible only to me, in his aura. "Here." Our fingers brushed as he handed me a piece of paper.

Sketched on the paper in my cousin Ryan's distinctive artistic style was a fantastical tree. He and Talbot had spent hours working together on the picture, with all the intensity and desire for accuracy of a police sketch artist and his witness.

Talbot's requirements were very specific.

I closed my eyes and pictured the drawing in my mind—the spiralled trunk that reminded me of seashells I'd found on the beach as a child; the large, flat leaves shaped like hearts; the huge, spreading branches; the flowers like tiny points of light.

When I was sure I had the image right, I *pushed*, projecting it outward and onto the empty field before me.

For several heartbeats, nothing happened. Someone shifted nearby. An anxious whine sounded in the back of a throat.

Then the *sidhe* took hold of the idea, pulling it from me like a child sucking juice through a straw. My knees trembled, but Jack was ready. He caught me around the waist and helped me stand. I gritted my teeth and concentrated, brows furrowing, eyes scrunched closed.

Timber creaked, and irregular thudding arose from around us as the ground shook. Talbot swore.

Silence fell.

Jack spoke quietly, his breath tickling my ear. "It is done."

I opened my eyes and stared. Even though I knew what the tree was meant to look like, my jaw fell open as I looked up … and up.

The tree towered, the leaves of its domed crown glimmering like emeralds, lit all around with gently glowing flowers. Talbot sprang forward into the deep shade beneath the boughs, bare feet whisking through the grass as he dodged clods of displaced earth. He reached up and plucked a bloom from a low-hanging branch, inhaling deeply, his dark-skinned nose twitching in his pale face. When he smiled, I sagged with relief. Jack grinned.

"Here," Talbot said, returning to my side and placing the flower in my palm. "Smell it."

The bloom was a soft pink, radiating gentle light like a Disney fairy. I sniffed it, the pollen tickling my nose. "Strawberries. And musk."

Talbot beamed. "It's perfect."

"Have you checked the other colours?" Each type of flower was meant to smell different, a cornucopia of delights for a *puca* such as Talbot. Like the rest of his species, he was a shapechanger; his other form was a long-eared hound dog. He collected scents the way I collected beads for the charm bracelet that glittered on my wrist.

"Not yet," Talbot said, turning back to the tree.

"Can we finish up here first?" Jack said, indicating me with a tip of his head as he gave the *puca* a significant look.

"It's okay," I protested, although the waver in my voice undermined me.

"You need to rest."

"Well, how about I rest in the shade of Talbot's new tree? Just till he's happy he got what he's paying for."

Jack pursed his lips, but I frowned at him until he relented and we set out across the grass. I leaned on his shoulder. Making changes to the *sidhe*, a place made of magic, wore me out—even for a half-blood *aosidhe*, one of the ruling fae race, making changes had a price.

Jack led me to the huge trunk. I sank down into the soft grass with a grateful sigh, leaning against the bark.

"Would you like to take some energy from me?" he asked, looking down at me.

"No."

"You should."

"I won't." We'd had this argument before. I believed taking emotions from others, feeding on them like some storybook psychic vampire, should be reserved for emergencies. I'd prefer to never have to do it at all. Jack, on the other hand, didn't like to see me suffer.

He was a good boyfriend.

The thought made me smile as I gazed up at him. He looked even more mysterious than usual in the green twilight beneath the tree. His golden hair, tapered chin and large eyes suggested his elfin heritage while still being close to human; the long, pointed ears on the other hand weren't even close. In the outside world, the human world, he concealed them under bandanas or hats. Here in the *sidhe* he was able to leave them unhidden.

I preferred them that way.

"What are you smiling at?" he said, sitting beside me.

"You." I leaned forward and kissed him softly, enjoying the warmth of his lips against mine, his hand curling in my hair.

We both jumped when footsteps thudded above. I looked up. Talbot walked along a broad, low branch, bare toes clinging to the wood. "I've got peppermint and chocolate, and this white one here, what's this? It smells fresh, like your skin, Isla."

Jack scowled, but I couldn't help laughing at the *puca's* enthusiasm. "It's moisturiser. Try the darker brown one. It's coffee. My favourite."

"Wonderful!" Talbot dashed away.

MELPOMENE'S DAUGHTER

"This is such a weird idea," I murmured to Jack, running my fingers over one of the trunk's curves. The upward spiral narrowed as it grew, like a giant unicorn's horn. Or a *karkadann's*. I'd never seen a real unicorn, but the *karkadann* I'd met a couple of months ago were similar in appearance to the mythical creature, if more bloodthirsty.

"There is a tree much like this in one of the Old World courts. Talbot used to serve there, before he escaped to Australia."

"How many *duinesidhe* here are refugees from Europe?"

"Maybe half." Jack looked away, expression grim.

Regret made me wince. "You're safe now." He'd had to kill his *aosidhe* master to free himself and his sister from continued enslavement and torture. The idea my boyfriend was a murderer didn't bother me as much as it would have a few months ago. My mother's people weren't the kind, noble high elves you read about in children's books: they were vain, cruel and self-centred. Although I'd only ever met the one, he'd lived up to everything I'd been warned about—and Jack wasn't the only one with blood on his hands. I shuddered. Jack hugged me tighter, his preternatural warmth easing the sudden chill.

A voice from beyond the field cried, "What is *this*?"

"Bloody *aosidhe*!" bellowed another.

"They don't sound happy," I murmured.

"Stay here." Jack leapt to his feet with an energy I envied. But, before he could stride away, I caught his hand and pulled myself up after him.

"Like hell." I lifted my chin.

He gave me a stern look. I didn't budge. Sighing, he shrugged, staying in front of me as we emerged from the tree's shade. A small crowd had gathered at the edge of the impressive herb garden behind Talbot's home. Several of the *puca* and hobs I knew by appearance, although not by name. Among them stood several rock-like creatures.

"Can we help you?" Jack's voice was cool.

"What has she done now, hob?" A creature made of granite glared at me, eyes fierce. He was about four feet tall, and almost as wide. One blow from his fist would crush bone. "First the sun, now this? She's taking over the *sidhe*."

"Isla—" Jack emphasised my name slightly "—created this tree at Talbot's request. She is not taking over but helping out, Scree."

"A helpful *aosidhe*?" Scree laughed, the hard, gritty sound of rocks grinding together.

"Indeed." Jack's eyes narrowed to dangerous slits. My heart leapt into my throat—I recognised that look. "You may recall that barely two months ago she saved our home from invasion by Everest."

"Everest would not have been here if not for her." Jack's sister, Evie, stepped forward, pushing her hair behind her ears. I was able to look at the scar running across her face without flinching now, even at the twisted knot of flesh where her left eye should have been. Evie had every reason to hate the *aosidhe*.

"Evie..." Jack's voice was reproachful. His emotions shifted from defiance to sadness, his aura to the grey of sheeting rain.

I hated seeing him stuck in the middle.

Ignoring the way he stiffened in protest, I stepped out from behind him, concentrating on walking without swaying on my feet. "Talbot asked me to help. As a service to him."

"It's true," Talbot called from above our heads, drawing closer but staying aloft. His aura was a nervous greenish-yellow, his face paler than usual with fear. He resembled a dog frequently whipped by its master—terrified of confrontation. "I asked her to. And I'm paying her for her aid."

Throughout the crowd eyes widened. Scree, sensing he was losing ground with his audience, pounded a fist into his hand with a cracking sound. "It's an *aosidhe* trick."

"I swear to you, it's not," I said softly. The feeling of the oath settling around me made everyone shiver. Like all *duinesidhe*, when I swore an oath I was bound by it.

"I'm sorry, I should have warned everyone," Talbot mumbled, studying his dirty feet.

Scree's mouth clattered shut. I looked past him to the rest of the crowd. "I'm happy to help the rest of you with your homes too, if there's anything you want that you can't make for yourselves or buy in the human world. Just let me know."

"If you do," Jack added hastily, "you can arrange it through me in the first instance. We can discuss the terms of the trade."

I rolled my eyes at him. He and I had argued—one of our first as a couple—over whether I should accept Talbot's offer of payment for the tree. I'd told him I should create it for free because Talbot was my friend. He'd argued that *duinesidhe* society worked on a barter system. Even the *aosidhe* traded with each other, if not with what they called "the lesser races". Those they just enslaved.

A few *duinesidhe* in the crowd exchanged speculative glances. Others said nothing, expressions unmoving and auras mistrustful. Scree stomped away, the ground trembling with every step, Evie on his heels.

When the rest of the crowd began to disperse, Talbot leapt down from the tree, landing easily in the soft grass. "Sorry about that."

"Don't worry about it. The important thing is that you're happy with the tree." I forced a smile. I'd been dealing with *duinesidhe* suspicion of me for months, but it wasn't getting any easier. Blending in with them was impossible—when I was in the *sidhe,* my skin glowed faintly, a visible reminder that my mother was a member of the race they all hated. Sometimes being able to see people's emotions wasn't even a little bit awesome. "Have I satisfied the terms of our deal?"

"I'm very happy." Talbot bobbed his head. His brown eyes were bright with enthusiasm and he clutched a rainbow of tiny flowers in his hand. "Although the moisturiser scent is new, it's otherwise just like I remember."

"You get credit for that," I said, giving Jack a grateful look as he slipped a supportive arm around my waist. The dizziness was slowly receding. Still, I wanted a nap. "It was your description that let me picture it so vividly."

Talbot blushed, fumbling in a pocket with his free hand. He pulled out a battered envelope, folded in half. "Here. Two hundred dollars, as agreed."

"Thanks," I said, stuffing the envelope into the back pocket of my jeans. Although the money wasn't much, it was enough to cover my board for a couple of months. My aunt wasn't charging me or my cousins a lot, but she was adamant that—since we'd finished school—we needed to contribute to running the household. Dad was still subsidising my board, but now I was eighteen it was a point of pride for me that I help.

How would I tell her I'd earned the money? I bit my lip. "Excuse me?"

We spun back to where the crowd had been. A single figure remained on the trampled grass—the towering figure of a *powrie*, an ogre-like creature dressed in ragged, unwashed clothes that barely fit his huge frame. His hair was greasy, his teeth uneven. Some of them were missing, probably lost in long-ago fights.

I'd met him before.

"What do you want, Gall?" Jack took a step forward, shoulders tensing beneath his T-shirt. He hated *powrie* almost as much as he did pure-blooded *aosidhe*. He'd told me before that they were only capable of hatred and violence.

And he didn't even know Gall had tried to kill me.

Gall took several steadying breaths, nostrils flaring. I studied his aura. His emotions were the scarlet of rage, tempered by fear and—was that hope? "I wanna make a deal with your *aosidhe*."

"For what?" The hob thrust out his jaw.

Gall's red-tinged eyes flicked between Jack and me as he gnawed at a ragged fingernail. "What is it?" I said, trying to keep my tone calm despite my fear. I didn't want to provoke him.

"You can change the way people feel." Gall scowled. He'd learned that the hard way.

I nodded.

"Change me."

I blinked. "To what?"

"I don't wanna be angry no more. No one likes me. I break stuff. I can't help it. They just make me so *mad*." He clenched his huge hands into fists the size of soccer balls and took another deep breath. He was struggling to control his rage—at me, at Jack and, for all I knew, at the inoffensive fence paling behind him.

I glanced at Jack, and he shrugged faintly. His eyes were wide with shock.

"I can do what you're asking," I said slowly. "But I'm not sure if the anger will come back again, or how quickly." I'd never taken all of an emotion from a person before, down to the source, afraid it might be like pulling a plant out at the roots—that the feeling might never come back. Which, of course, was exactly what Gall was hoping for.

"If it comes back again, you take it again."

"You're sure?"

"Of course I'm sure," Gall snarled, stepping forward. Before we could react, he shook his head as though shaking away an annoying fly. "Sorry. Can't help it."

"Okay."

"About payment—" Jack began.

"Helping Gall is in everyone's best interests, Jack." I gave the hob a reproachful look.

"I will pay," Gall said.

Jack raised an eyebrow. "You do not have money."

"Not money. This." The *powrie* pulled a twist of chequered fabric from his belt and unwrapped it gingerly. Glittering within the folds of material was a bright blue opal.

"May I?" I asked. He nodded and I took the gemstone carefully from the cloth, turning it over in my palm. It was maybe an inch long by half an inch wide. The back was a warm brown, but the front ... to call it blue was too simple. Green, red and yellow played through its heart, glittering as I turned it in the light.

"I got it in Queensland. Traded a dwarf for it. He dug

it out of some ironstone, polished it up real good."

I looked at Jack. "A dwarf?"

"Like Scree," he murmured. His gaze didn't waver from the *powrie*; his muscles remained tense, as though he expected a sudden attack.

I kept my face still, trying to hide my surprise. All the pop culture descriptions of dwarves had struck far afield of the truth, if Scree was typical of his race. He was basically a walking boulder. There wasn't a beard or even a single stray hair—at least not anywhere I'd seen.

The glittering stone in my hand drew my gaze. I placed it reluctantly on the scrap of fabric. "I can't take this."

Gall's lips thinned and he took a slow, angry breath before answering. "Why not? It's good."

"Too good. It's too precious." I didn't know how much it was worth. I guessed thousands of dollars.

"Don't care. Take it!" He thrust the stone at me.

Jack touched my shoulder. "If you are going to help Gall, you should take the stone. Otherwise he will owe you an unspecified debt, which makes *duinesidhe* … nervous."

Gall nodded emphatically, his big hand taking my palm and slapping the gemstone into it, fabric and all. The piece of material resembled a handkerchief. I wrinkled my nose, hoping it was clean. It seemed unlikely.

"Okay." I wrapped the opal and tucked it into another pocket of my jeans. "Did you want to do this now?"

The *powrie* nodded again, fear tricking into the scarlet in his aura. "Will it make me cry?"

"No, it won't," I said. Although Jack looked puzzled, Gall's question made sense to me. When he'd tried to kill me, acting out of friendship with Jack's sister Evie, I'd struck back, filling him with fresh sorrow I'd taken from a friend. I'd heard later that Gall had wept for days. Afterwards, I'd promised Evie not to tell Jack what she'd done—more for his sake than hers. By extension, my boyfriend was also unaware of the *powrie's* attack on me.

Given the suspicion with which Jack eyed Gall as I reached out and took one of the *powrie's* giant hands, that was definitely a good thing.

"Will it hurt?"

"I don't know," I admitted. He didn't seem troubled by my answer, which saddened me. What kind of life had he led, that the fear of sadness was worse than the fear of pain? "Ready?"

When he nodded, I concentrated on the raging scarlet saturating his aura, underlying and seeping into everything else. My nervousness returned. What would happen to the *powrie* without the emotion that defined his personality? Should I even be doing this? It was the little flare of hope in his aura, a guttering candle nearly extinguished in the sea of rage, which convinced me. I should at least try.

I drew Gall's anger into myself, swift as thought. The emotion came freely. It was scalding, like bitumen on a summer's day; coppery, like arterial blood; enervating, like too much coffee. My weariness evaporated. My heartbeat accelerated, pounding in my ears. My hand clenched around Gall's. I'd taken the surface emotion. He smiled serenely. The hope blossomed brighter.

I'd absorbed anger before. I'd even done it from a *powrie*. However, I'd never tried to take *all* of it, to rip it out and cauterise it so it could never come back. Now I dug deeper with the fingers of my power, finding the heart of his rage. I tugged on it. At first, it didn't budge.

It was like trying to pull a sword from a stone when your name wasn't Arthur. I used some of the new energy infusing me to chip away at the fury's core.

Finally, grudgingly, the emotion shifted.

A crack juddered through me, felt rather than heard, and the flow of rage began anew. But to call it rage was to describe the sun as "a bit warm". The feeling was pure, molten. Dangerous. It burned into me until I was full to bursting. I was sure my skin would fly off and char into ash. Whimpering, I tried to stop it. I released Gall's hand, hoping that would break the flow. The rage kept coming. Standing at the foot of a dam as the floodgates opened might feel similar. The feeling crashed into me, a thundering wave.

I lifted my face to the sky and screamed.

"Isla!" Jack grabbed my arm, recoiling with a cry. "You are burning up!"

Through stinging eyes, I looked down at my arm. It was glowing, not just the faint firefly glow I always got in the *sidhe*, but a vivid light, like staring into heart of a fire.

If I didn't release some of this energy, I might explode— just like Everest had. "Jack. Help me."

"How?" His voice was desperate.

"I don't know," I cried.

"You need to release some of the energy before..." His voice broke.

I looked at Gall. He hadn't moved. A faint smile tickled his lips and his eyes crinkled at the edges, an unaccustomed expression on his hard face.

I could have just done it. He couldn't have stopped me. But... "Gall. Do you want to be beautiful?"

"What?" He blinked as though seeing me for the first time. His pupils narrowed to pinpricks as he peered into the light around my face. "Um."

"Yes or no?" My voice was high, scared.

"Yes?"

I snatched his hand, my limbs leant preternatural speed by the power roaring through me. Then I stared at him, picturing him changed.

I'd never altered a living creature before. It was as easy as playing with wet clay. Horrifyingly easy. As the *sidhe* had done when I willed a tree into existence, Gall's body now did. I visualised his hair clean and smooth, free of knots. His teeth even and white. His nose, crooked from a badly healed break, straight once more. His eyes wider, with blue irises instead of beady red ones. His back straight rather than hunched.

Each change drew some of the inferno from me. It was almost bearable. Almost. So I made cosmetic changes, giving Gall a clean set of perfectly fitting jeans and a T-shirt, some dark leather boots, and, for good measure, a manicure.

I dropped his hand when I was done. His new face was drenched with sweat, his even teeth clenched. "Did I hurt you?" I asked, eyes widening with remorse.

He shrugged the question off, staring at his trimmed nails with wonder. "What did you do?" Now he was no longer snarling, his voice was a pleasant baritone.

"I hope you like it," I said. "If not, I could make changes..."

He ran his hands over the new jeans. "They fit! Clothes never fit. I need to see." He turned, striding back into the village. Beyond Talbot's house, wondering voices arose.

"You're welcome," I muttered under my breath. Except

MELPOMENE'S DAUGHTER

I couldn't blame Gall for charging off. Under the circumstances, I'd need a mirror too.

I turned to Jack, who was staring at me like he'd never seen me before. His aura was the plasma-purple of shock.

"What?"

"I never … I did not think you would use the power on him."

"You told me *aosidhe* could change the *duinesidhe* too, remember? The first time we came here."

"I thought you would use it on the *sidhe* itself. Make more changes." He gestured around us.

"What, and have the mob come back?" I shook my head. "Not without permission."

"You could have changed yourself," he said. I imagined myself six inches taller, with glowing eyes and hair that never tangled. My family might notice. "Or stored it in that opal for future use."

I touched his cheek. My hand still glowed, but I was relieved to see it was no longer enough to cast a shadow in the afternoon sunlight. "Why does it bother you that I used it on Gall?"

"He is a *powrie*," Jack said shortly. "He does not deserve it."

An idea struck me. "Jack, next time … what about Evie? If she agreed, could I give her back her eye?"

His sapphire eyes widened. "Yes. I think maybe you could."

CHAPTER TWO

"She said *no*?" Sarah stared at me with wide, blue-green eyes, the bottle of milk paused halfway to her coffee cup. She still wore her rumpled supermarket uniform, having just finished her shift; she managed to make it look good.

"Sort of." I shrugged, tearing little pieces off a blank sheet of paper on the counter. Although the energy I'd taken from Gall no longer pained me, I was still twitchy. "She said next time I took the rage from a *powrie* and had energy to burn, to let her know and she'd consider it. I think I could have at least healed the scarring with what I have left, but she didn't want me to."

"Wow. What an ungrateful mole." My cousin scowled.

"She might be afraid of the pain. Jack said being altered like that hurts quite a bit."

"It didn't bother Gall?"

I nodded. "It did. I just think he's used to being hurt. It's sad, really."

MELPOMENE'S DAUGHTER

"What did Jack say about Evie?"

"Not much. He wasn't happy though. He's gone back there now to talk to her about it. Are you going to pour that milk before you spill it?"

Pulling a face, Sarah splashed some milk into her mug. Some of it spilled anyway. "Are you sure you don't want one?"

"I do, but the caffeine wouldn't do me any favours right now." The pile of confetti beneath my hands grew.

"There's Mum's decaf." The corner of Sarah's lips twitched as she grabbed a sponge.

"Wash your mouth out." I puckered my lips as though I'd eaten something sour. "It tastes like something scraped off the floor of a coffee factory. One where the workers walk around barefoot."

"Gross." Sarah picked up her brew and headed for the sliding door leading to the back deck.

"Exactly my point." I swept the paper into the recycling bin and followed.

The autumn sunshine was brighter than the *sidhe* had been. The trees and larger shrubs around the edge of the yard were all natives, bottlebrushes and eucalypts, and they remained blue-green in defiance of the season. Beyond the fence, the leaves on the neighbour's fruit trees were starting to turn a brilliant red the colour of Sarah's hair.

The trees didn't have a blond streak in their fringe, though.

I suddenly wondered whether Talbot's tree would shed its leaves. He hadn't specified whether it should, and I hadn't considered it when I'd willed the plant into existence. Whatever the answer, I hoped the *puca* was happy with it.

"I still think you should tell Jack what Evie did," Sarah

said, sitting at the outdoor setting and putting her feet up on an empty chair. Her black terrier, Hamish, appeared from behind a shrub, mulch clinging to the fur of his belly, and trotted across the yard. He could sense an available lap from fifty metres.

I shook my head. "I swore not to, remember?"

"There's no way to wiggle out of it?" She frowned. My cousin had strong views on people trying to murder members of her family. I could understand that—I felt the same way.

I began to braid my hair before the breeze tangled it into knots. "If I told him, I'd get really sick. Maybe even die. The only way I could is if she gave me permission."

"Like that's going to happen." Hamish leapt onto Sarah's legs. She began to pick the pine chips from his fur with her free hand.

"Exactly." I sighed. "In her defence, she attacked me just after Jack swore his oath to serve me. When she found out, she thought I was trying to enslave him like their previous master had."

"Well, a normal person asks before reaching for the kitchen knife. I'm just saying."

"I don't think any of the *duinesidhe* count as normal."

Sarah raised an eyebrow at me, sipping her coffee. "Well, that explains *you* then." Her eyes twinkled.

"Hey!" I laughed.

"No one else I know created a new species of tree today."

"Heh. True."

We sat there in silence for a few minutes. My gaze strayed to the garden shed Ryan used as his studio when the weather wasn't too hot. I didn't go in there anymore. My powers had awoken when I turned eighteen; since then, being in the presence of cold iron made me want to throw up—and even brushing against it blistered my skin. The shed's back shelf overflowed with iron sculptures my father had given me over the years. Still, despite my reaction to them, knowing they were there made me glad. You never know when an *aosidhe* is going to turn up and start threatening your family.

Besides, if Aunt Elizabeth discovered they were gone, she'd want to know why—and I *so* didn't want to have that awkward conversation.

"Is Ryan home?" I leaned forward to scratch Hamish behind the ear. He tipped his head and pressed into my fingers.

"Yeah, he's working on something," Sarah said. "He's got that wild-eyed look. You know, like he's had another vision."

"Dammit," I muttered. "Let's hope it's of something good this time. World peace or rain for drought-stricken farmers. Something like that." Ryan's last vision painting had been of Everest's eventual self-immolation. When he'd died, Everest had been trying to enslave me the same way Evie believed I was enslaving Jack ... but knowing that didn't stop the nightmares.

"Um, Isla?" Sarah's voice pulled me from my thoughts. I looked up at her and frowned. Her aura was a sickly yellow, shot through with purple swirls that made my heart skip a beat. She read the expression on my face and scowled. "You're reading my aura again, aren't you?"

"It's hard not to. It's right there!"

"Well, stop it." Embarrassment suffused the other colours like a blush. "I thought that siren taught you how to not see auras."

"Yeah, but I can't do it all the time. I have to concentrate.

What are you worrying about?"

"I said stop it!"

"Sarah!" I sat back in exasperation. "Stop trying to change the subject. Just spit it out."

She set her mug down on the glass tabletop beside her. "Fine. All right." She took a deep breath. *Uh oh.* "Dominic came past the store today."

"Dominic as in my ex Dominic?" My heart fluttered in my throat, a curious mixture of guilt and nerves. He may have dumped me, but it had been my fault.

"We don't know any other Dominics," Sarah pointed out.

"How did he seem?"

"It's hard to say. I only got to talk to him for five minutes while I was ringing up his groceries."

I knew there was more to it, or she wouldn't be so anxious. "But?"

"He said he doesn't remember much about that day. You know. He thinks it was a fever dream." Everest had kidnapped Dominic and taken him into the *sidhe*, using him as leverage against me. The magic of the place had overwhelmed Dominic's unprotected mind. It had taken me two days to undo the emotional damage it—and I—had wrought.

"That's probably for the best."

"He asked me out." Her words came out in a rush. I stared at her, feeling as if my chair had dropped out from under me. Her wide eyes pled with me not to be angry with her. "I'm sorry. I didn't say yes or anything!"

I studied my fingernails and took a deep breath. When I spoke, my voice was steady. "Did you want to? Say yes, I mean?"

"No, of course not." I looked up and she wilted. "Yes. But I won't."

"He's been single for a couple of months. I have a boyfriend. And he's a nice guy." *All true,* I reminded the butterflies in my stomach sternly. "He deserves a girlfriend who can be honest with him about her life."

Sarah winced. We'd had so many arguments about my reluctance to explain the stranger parts of my life to Dominic that I'd lost count. On Valentine's Day, suspecting I was having an affair with Jack, Dominic had threatened to break up with me and I'd panicked, manipulating his feelings so he would trust me.

It had made him vulnerable, much easier for Everest to kidnap.

Although I'd set things right, Dominic had then broken up with me, and I doubted he'd ever trust me again. Especially not when I started dating Jack shortly after—he thought that was proof I'd been cheating on him all along.

"So you think I should say yes?" Sarah said, hands knotted together in Hamish's fur. He grumbled uncomfortably.

"If that's what you want to do," I said around the lump in my throat. "Just don't set up any double dates with me and Jack. Awkward." I wrinkled my nose.

Relief suffused her aura and, shoving the dog from her lap, she lunged forward to give me a hug. "You are the best cousin ever, did you know that?"

"I know." I grinned.

Sarah downed the rest of her coffee and disappeared inside the house to put her mug in the dishwasher—and no doubt to call Dominic. Hamish followed. I sat back and stared at the treetops, watching them dance in the wind. Given I'd started dating Jack right after Dominic left me, I wasn't in a position to judge the haste with which he'd asked her out. But my heart still ached as I recalled how happy we'd been together. At least at first.

I sighed. If I were being honest with myself, there'd been a lot of anxiety too. Jack had introduced himself to me three weeks after Dominic and I went on our first date; my preoccupation with the hob and his—my—world had been part of Dominic's and my relationship almost from the start. Our friend Natalie had called me out on it at Sarah's birthday party; she'd seen my interest in Jack, and my jealousy of the girls flirting with him, before I'd realised it myself.

I wasn't built for love triangles.

Dominic and Sarah would make a cute couple. The only thing that surprised me was that he was willing to ask her out after everything that had happened. I would've thought her involvement in the events surrounding his kidnapping would have made him suspicious of her too. Unless—

The thought made me sit up straight in the chair, hands clenched into fists. Dominic wasn't the sort of person who would ask Sarah out to get back at me. Was he?

The idea of a double date suddenly seemed like a good idea, no matter how awkward it would be. I could read his aura and make sure his feelings were genuine.

"Isla?" Ryan called from inside the shed, his voice echoing against the steel walls. "Can you come here for a sec?"

Great. Could this day get any worse? I grimaced, heading down the path, and stopped a couple of metres away. The steel in the walls didn't bother me—something about the manufacturing process diluted the iron's toxic effects even as it hardened the metal. Still, I could feel the nauseating effect of the iron sculptures from here. "I'm not coming inside."

"Right." My older cousin appeared in the doorway.

Dishevelled ginger hair stuck up on the top of his head and bags smudged the skin under his eyes. His aura was a sad, dull silver.

"You look awful," I said, and then winced. *Good one, Isla.*

Ryan didn't seem to notice. He rubbed his forehead. Freckles stood out on his pale skin. "I haven't been sleeping. And I've got a rotten headache."

"*Aislinge* vision?"

Ryan's visions revealed themselves through his drawings and paintings. Other *aislinges*—human seers created by the *aosidhe*—had their individual abilities manifest in different ways. Everest's Shannon had been able to envision the locations of people and places, but as far as I knew, she'd never been able to see the future as Ryan did.

Ryan nodded grimly. "I tried to ignore it. I didn't want to paint it. But the dreams got worse and worse." His hands shook, and he added in a croaking voice, "I didn't have a choice."

"I'm so sorry, Ryan." Tears of remorse burned the back of my eyes. I swallowed hard. I hadn't meant to make him into an *aislinge*, and now I had no way to undo it.

"That's not what's bothering me. Here, let me show you." He ducked back inside the shed and returned within moments, holding a large sheet of paper. He'd drawn a picture in black ink, which glistened in the afternoon sunlight. Ryan's hands shook, distorting the image. I gently took it from him.

The picture was of a headstone. Its edges were still sharp, as though newly cut, and there was no grass growing on the dirt before it. A fresh grave. But the headstone was blank.

"Whose is it?" I whispered.

"I don't know. Believe me, I've tried to see. I have. I just can't."

Gnawing at my lip, I stared at the picture. All of Ryan's previous visions—of my mother, an attack on Dad's farm, Everest's impending death—had been tied to me, as though his power was only attuned to things I'd care about. If the vision was of a *duinesidhe's* death, such as Jack's or my mother's, I doubted they'd have such a prosaic human headstone. But my human family, my friends...

"Shit," I said.

"Yeah." A change in Ryan's voice made me look up. His frown had eased. "As soon as I showed you the painting, my headache went away," he said with relief.

"Good." Then what he'd said sunk in. Cold seeped into my bones. "Oh god. The *aislinge* magic was forcing you to tell me about the vision."

He nodded slowly. "I thought that might be the case. It makes sense, right?" His nose wrinkled. "It wouldn't do for an *aislinge* to withhold their visions from their master."

"I'm not your master!" My hands crumpled the edges of the drawing.

"I know," he said, smiling, "but maybe the power doesn't agree with us. Don't worry about it. I don't mind, normally. I'm a much better artist than I was six months ago. I'm actually making some sales. The visions are like having an overzealous muse with ulterior motives. That's better than no muse at all, right?"

"I'll have to take your word for it," I muttered, looking back down at the ink drawing. My stomach swooped. Someone was going to die. Someone I cared about.

Or I was.

"Jack, I need you," I whispered.

The drawing had been dried, smoothed out and rolled up. I clutched it in one hand, leaning against a tree in the park across the road from our house. The sun sank low on the horizon and the playground was empty, children called home for dinner. This park was where Jack and I had met during the first couple of months of our friendship. It was where I'd been when I found out Dad was in a coma ... and it was where Evie and Gall had tried to kill me, before Sarah saved me, wielding an iron candlestick as a weapon. As I stood there now, my heart fluttered with remembered fear.

"I need you, Jack," I said again, feeling like an idiot. But Jack didn't have a phone in the *sidhe*. One of the benefits of his oath of service was that whenever I called him, he knew.

At least, it benefited me. I wasn't sure how he felt about it.

Within minutes, he was striding along the path towards me, wearing long denim shorts and a plain blue T-shirt. A bandana pulled his hair back and concealed his long ears. When his gaze settled on my face, he increased his pace. "What is wrong, Isla?"

I tried to smile. It didn't feel convincing. "What, can't a girl just miss her boyfriend?"

"You saw me only hours ago."

"So?"

He laughed, but his eyes drifted to the paper in my hand. "Has your cousin had another vision?"

"Yeah." I unrolled the sheet to reveal the ominous drawing.

Jack stared at it for several minutes while I twisted my hair through my fingers, studying his face. His features stayed still, his forehead smooth—but his emotions swirled the greenish yellow of apprehension.

"I wish I had your poker face," I blurted.

"Learning to control my expression is one of the benefits of having been a slave to a monster like Cacodaemon," he said, voice low as he turned the paper from side to side as though changing the angle might reveal some new detail. "Expressing disapproval when your master orders you to facilitate his latest depravity results in your death. Or in your sister's torture." He glanced up at me. "Fortunately, he could not read my emotions." Although it hadn't stopped Cacodaemon from torturing Evie.

He fell silent again. I tried to keep still, but my frustration and panic built inside me like a scream.

"What do you think?" I demanded finally.

"It is a gravestone."

"Well, thanks for that," I said sarcastically. He raised an eyebrow at me and my cheeks burned, but I didn't look away. "It means someone close to me is going to die, doesn't it? Or I am?"

"You are not going to die," Jack said, his voice firm with conviction.

"How do you know?"

"I will not let it happen." He re-rolled the picture and handed it to me, then wrapped his arms around my waist protectively. I leaned into his shoulder with a sigh. He was the same height as me, but his body contained a quiet strength and grace, like a big cat. It made me feel safe.

MELPOMENE'S DAUGHTER

"Jack?"

"Yes?"

"If I did die, and Ryan couldn't tell me his visions anymore, what would happen to him?"

"You are not going to die," he repeated.

"*If* I did—"

"He would be freed of his role as *aislinge*, and would go back to being a regular human. In the same way that any oaths you held would be undone."

I exhaled with relief. But my brain only gave me a few heartbeats to enjoy the feeling before turning, rat-like, to gnaw on my other concerns. "Is there anything we can do to stop it happening? The death, I mean?" Tears stung the back of my eyes. "What if it's Dad? Or Sarah?"

His silence was answer enough.

"Crap," I said, crushing the picture in my hands before burying my face against him and letting my hot tears soak his shirt.

CHAPTER THREE

Jack stayed for dinner. He didn't say it, but I guessed he didn't want to leave me alone, in case the headstone-precipitating incident happened straight away. I wasn't sure what he planned to do about it. On the other hand, if anyone was determined enough to change fate, it was him.

Aunt Elizabeth hummed around the kitchen, wooden spoon in one hand. She'd chased us—Jack, Ryan and me—out onto the balcony when we tried to help. Sarah had gone out on a date with Dominic.

That happened fast, I thought, rattling my ice in the bottom of my glass. I leaned against the railing, while Jack stood a careful distance behind me. Because he was a full-blooded *duinesidhe*, steel affected him the way iron did me—with nausea and burns. Anxiety prickled my skin every time he got into my car.

As for pure iron ... I'd seen what iron could do to a hob. Moray's skin and bone had melted like butter. He'd died instantly. Gratitude that I was half-human surged in my chest. Although I hadn't been fond of Moray in the ten minutes or so I'd known him, I still shied away from the memory of the iron bullet hissing inside the cavity of his skull. Being less vulnerable was a relief.

Nausea tightened my throat. Turning, I put my drink on the table, not wanting it anymore.

"Isla showed you the drawing?" Ryan slouched in a chair, looking rumpled.

Jack nodded.

"Thoughts?"

"None that Isla and you have not already discussed. There was no extra detail in the vision that you have failed to render? Some clue that may be of use in determining the, ah, subject of the painting?"

Ryan shook his head, sitting up straighter and folding his arms. "Nope. Believe me. I tried to see more. Nearly gave myself a nosebleed doing it. That's all I got. The headstone and the freshly dug earth in front of it."

Jack's lips thinned. Before he could speak, the glass door behind him slid open and my aunt leaned out. "Dinner's ready, kids."

"Kids?" Ryan muttered, but shoved his chair back and stood, heading inside.

Aunt Elizabeth chattered as she brought bowls piled with butter chicken and white rice over to the kitchen table. I steered Jack to Sarah's usual spot, trying not to think about what she might be doing right now. Ryan surprised me by setting the table; when he pulled out the good silverware with a knowing wink—rather than the stainless steel we'd normally use—I heaved a sigh of relief. That could have been a disaster, and it hadn't even occurred to me to head it off.

"This smells amazing, Mrs Blackman. Thank you," Jack said, taking the cutlery from my cousin with a grateful nod.

My aunt smiled, brushing an auburn lock back behind her ear. The colour was darker than her original ginger; now that she was starting to go grey, she dyed it. "Why, thank you. I confess the sauce is from a jar. But I did add a few extra spices."

Jack waited until we all started eating before doing so himself. His large eyes flickered to my hand movements as I ate. Was this the first meal he'd shared with a human who didn't know what he was? I gave him a reassuring smile. Aunt Elizabeth's reaction to Jack had been mixed at first—she liked Dominic, and Jack's insistence on head coverings inside the house offended her old-fashioned notions about hats indoors—but he'd won her over with his impeccable manners.

She'd told me once, when her son was out of the room, that she hoped some of Jack's charm would rub off on Ryan. I'd bitten my lip to avoid laughing.

"Isla told me you managed to find her some work?" Aunt Elizabeth said, smiling at the hob.

Jack nodded, glancing at me with wide eyes. I hadn't warned him about this. I swallowed a mouthful of scalding rice. "It's just casual," I rasped. "But I have some money for you."

"What sort of work is it?"

I sipped my juice to soothe my throat and buy myself time to think. "Landscaping." It was hardly even a lie.

Her eyebrows shot up. *Damn, should've lied.* "I thought you didn't like gardening."

"It surprised me too." I studied my bowl as though it

contained a secret vital to national security. The sauce was only a few shades darker than the blazing orange of fear. "The actual plant maintenance is someone else's job."

Aunt Elizabeth opened her mouth to ask another question but, before she could, Ryan started describing his last shift at the supermarket. Looking surprised, my aunt let him steer the conversation as we ate. Jack spoke seldom and kept his answers short but polite.

The phone rang, saving us from the awkward situation. Muttering about telemarketers, Aunt Elizabeth stood up to answer it, and Ryan leaned over to whisper, "You owe me."

"I know." Should we tell Aunt Elizabeth about my secret heritage? Nana, her mother, had told her and Dad many tales about the fae when they were children. Aunt Elizabeth never talked about them. Dad said she'd always assumed they were only stories. He'd known better.

If I declared I was half-human, my sensible bank manager aunt would probably want me to see someone about my mental health.

At least until she saw Jack's ears.

I tipped my head to the side, staring unseeingly at the wall. What did it say that Sarah had insisted I should tell Dominic my big secret, but it never occurred to either of us to tell her mother?

Ryan's elbow nudging my side dragged me back from my growing unease. When I glared at him, he nodded towards Aunt Elizabeth. We could see her through the open door to the lounge room, standing with her back to us. She pressed the phone handset to her ear with a white-knuckled grip. Her shoulders trembled.

I blinked, realising what I was seeing. Slate grey hung in her aura, the colour of storm clouds. The trembling shoulders—she was crying silently. I glanced at Ryan and he shook his head, hands clutching the table as though it was the only thing stopping him from drifting away like a child's balloon. The fear in his eyes when he'd shown me the drawing of the headstone was back, immobilising him.

Bracing myself, I stood and slowly made my way to my aunt, feeling as though the air had thickened around me. I clenched my fists and fought down the panic. Who was she crying for? Was it Dad? Or Sarah?

When I brushed Aunt Elizabeth's arm, she turned to me. Tears glistened in her eyes, wet her cheeks. "Please hang on a moment," she said to whoever was on the phone. Then she muffled the receiver against her shoulder and turned to face Ryan and me. "I'm sorry, kids. Nana has died."

Relief flared in my chest, smothered immediately by shame and remorse. I hugged my aunt tightly. "I'm so sorry."

"It's okay." Her voice was hoarse with suppressed tears. "I'm going to take this call in my room. You kids finish dinner."

None of us had any appetite. I put Aunt Elizabeth's bowl in the oven, on the slim chance she'd still be hungry when she got off the phone, and cleared the table.

"Was this the same Nana I met?" Jack murmured, wiping the table as I rinsed the other bowls.

I nodded. "The one who killed Moray. I don't even know if I have a grandmother on my mother's side."

He grimaced. "I should have thought of that. It was a silly question."

"Not so silly." I gave him a weak smile. "Ryan and Sarah have grandparents on their father's side. They're still in England too, like Nana is. Was."

MELPOMENE'S DAUGHTER

"I wonder what it was," Ryan muttered. He sat at a stool, elbows leaning on the counter, watching us clean up with glazed eyes. His freckles stood out, bruises on pale skin. Under other circumstances, I'd needle him for not helping, but his aura sparked with shock, like a power cable lying in a puddle of water. "What killed her?"

"You think she was killed?" I froze, dishwasher half-open.

He locked gazes with me. "Why else would I have seen a vision of her grave?"

His words rang a note of truth in my soul, a sombre, funereal chord. I tried to argue anyway. "You might've seen it because it affects me. And she was old. It could've been natural causes."

"She was only in her sixties," he said, looking down.

I followed his gaze and realisation shivered across my skin. He was looking at his hands. His painter hands. I hesitated for a heartbeat, then reached across the bench and took his fingers in mine. "You're not responsible for her death."

"I know." He snatched his hand away and stood so abruptly the stool toppled backward. Timber clattered on tiles. I wasn't sure why he bothered lying to me—he knew I could see the guilt swirling in a fog around him.

Maybe he was lying to himself.

Before I could think of something to say to make it better, he growled, "I'm going for a walk." The front door slammed behind him.

Jack walked around the counter and righted the stool. "Was Ryan close to your grandmother?"

I shook my head, wringing out the dishcloth and hanging it over the tap to dry. "None of us were. Aside from Dad and Aunt Elizabeth, I mean. Obviously."

"His reaction was … vehement."

"He's blaming himself."

"That does not make sense." He took my hand and we headed out onto the porch. I didn't turn the light on. The idea seemed disrespectful somehow.

"Welcome to human nature." Leaning against him, I looked up at the stars. The night air was cooling fast, but his chest was warm against my back. I pulled his arms around my shoulders like a shawl.

"Are you also blaming yourself?" His breath tickled the back of my neck.

"I … I'm not sure. It depends how she died."

"Then what are you feeling guilty about?"

I turned, gazing into his face from centimetres away. The kitchen light was behind him, casting his expression into shadow. "Can you read emotions now, Jack?"

"No. I know you. What is bothering you?"

My throat ached; I had to force the words around a lump that had settled there. "I was relieved," I confessed in a whisper. The heat of a blush blasted across my cheeks, as though I stood before an open furnace. "My first reaction when I heard it was Nana was relief it wasn't Sarah. Or Dad."

"You and your grandmother did not get on."

"I reminded her of my mother. She assumed I was an evil *aosidhe*." My tongue tasted sour with remembered bitterness. "When she arrived in Australia, Dad was still in a coma and she thought I was behind it."

"And after she found out you were not?"

"She still never trusted me." Memories of the confrontation at Dad's bedside came flooding back. She'd said

34

some hateful things about me, about Dad. I'd lashed out with my power, which was barely under my control, and knocked her to the ground with an emotional assault. Even after I undid the damage—more or less—she hadn't forgiven me. Her last words to me, as she'd boarded her flight back to England, were to guard against the evil in my soul.

Sarah got a farewell kiss.

"It seems to me," Jack said slowly, "it is only natural for you to be grateful that the one who died was not someone dear to you."

"But I—"

"Shh." He kissed me to stop me talking, just a peck, but my heart leapt in my chest, a magpie taking flight. "Are you glad she is dead?"

"What? No. Of course not!"

"Then you have nothing to feel ashamed of."

I opened my mouth to argue, but closed it again. In the shadows, I glimpsed the ghost of a smile on his lips.

Movement inside the house drew our attention. Aunt Elizabeth was returning the phone to its cradle, shuffling like a sleepwalker. I hurried inside, Jack following more slowly.

"Where's Ryan?" she said.

"He needed some air. I put your dinner in the oven if you want it."

She smiled, rubbing red-rimmed eyes as though they ached with grief. Maybe they did. "Sweet girl. But no, thank you."

"Do you want anything? A drink of water?"

"Stop fussing," Aunt Elizabeth said, although her tone was gentle. "I'll be fine. I called your father. He's going to drive in."

"Now?" I blinked. His farm was an hour away and it was late.

She nodded. "He can sleep on the couch. We need to organise our flights to England for the funeral." She added softly, "And he doesn't want to be alone right now."

"Do..." My voice rasped in my throat. I swallowed and tried again. "Do they know what happened? To Nana?"

She hesitated, and my stomach twisted. "Not yet. The police are investigating."

"So it wasn't natural causes?"

Aunt Elizabeth frowned. "They don't know, Isla." She was hiding something from me; I was sure of it. But when I glanced at Jack, he shook his head. My shoulders drooped. He was right. It would be cruel to pursue it further. And I couldn't ask her what I really wanted to know—whether Nana's death was related to the *duinesidhe*.

"Okay," I said. Jack took my hand.

I'd find out soon enough.

CHAPTER FOUR

The house still smelled of breakfast's bacon and toast when Dad called my cousins and me into the lounge. Aunt Elizabeth was in the study, booking tickets online; Dad glanced over his shoulder before gingerly closing the door after us.

I sat beside Sarah on the three-seater couch Dad had slept on the night before, eyebrows raised at his furtive air. My second cup of coffee was warm in my curled hands. "That's ominous."

"Your aunt doesn't think we should tell you the truth about what happened to Mum." Dad stuffed his hands in his pockets. He looked tired. We'd all stayed up late the night before, reminiscing about Nana. Or rather, Dad and Aunt Elizabeth reminisced and the rest of us listened. Jack left late, and I'd fallen into a sleep full of restless dreams.

But—although his eyes were puffy and his shoulders slumped with weariness—Dad didn't just look tired. He looked old. The crinkles around his eyes and mouth seemed deeper than before, and the golden morning sunlight illuminated his hair, now more silver than red.

My heart ached as I studied him.

"I don't agree with her, obviously," he said. "Although she'll read me the riot act, you need to know. Especially under the circumstances." His gaze met mine.

"You mean because of who I am? What I am?" I said. Hands trembling, I set the coffee cup on the table in front of me. Guilt made my heart ache.

He grimaced. "Who, pumpkin. Never what."

"So what was it?" Ryan slouched in the single seat. His walk the night before hadn't improved his mood. I wasn't brave or cruel enough to ask him if he still felt his muse was worth the cost of these little glimpses into the future.

"She was strangled." Dad's voice caught on the last word. "They found her in her back garden, clutching a pole. They think she may have struck her attacker with it before she was … before she died. It's being tested for DNA."

"The pole was iron?" Sarah guessed. Tears glittered in her eyes, making them shimmer like the opal hidden in the bottom of my jewellery box.

"I don't know yet. I couldn't think of a way to ask without sounding peculiar. But I think it probably was, yes. She hated all *duinesidhe*, not just the *aosidhe* nobles—she would have kept something handy just in case." His eyes met mine. "But, even if it was iron, that doesn't mean her attacker was *duinesidhe*. It could've been a regular human scumbag, and because she had iron close to hand that's what she used. If I was attacked at the farm it's even money I'd defend myself with iron too."

"Nana had a history with the *duinesidhe*, though," I said. "She killed Everest's hob, Moray."

"I thought Ariel was his hob?" Sarah said, a frown marring the lightly freckled skin of her forehead.

"Ariel was the one who came with him in February. Moray was the one he sent here back in November, the one who tried to kidnap Dad."

Ryan sat up straight. "Ariel escaped after Everest died, didn't he? Did he know Nana was the one who—"

"Yes," I croaked. Breakfast sat in my stomach, a greasy lump. "Everest found out, so Ariel would've known."

"Well, that was careless of you." Ryan's eyes were hard as ice.

"I didn't tell him! He tortured it out of one of Moray's accomplices. Then cut off his head." My voice dropped to a whisper and I stared down at my clenched fists. "I still should've warned her."

Dad reached over, brushing my hair back from my face. "Don't think like that. You couldn't have known this would happen."

"I should've guessed. Ariel was furious when he found out Moray was killed."

"Even if you had warned her, would it have made a difference?" Sarah pointed out, curling her fingers around one of my fists. "Uncle David said she had iron around the place for self-protection. If Ariel was crazy enough to risk that to get revenge, what could Nana have done differently?"

I shrugged, biting my lip. *She could have run.*

"Anyway, even if it was a *duinesidhe*, there's another possibility." Sarah glanced at Dad, and then back to me. "It might have been your mother. Melpomene."

A shiver ran down my spine. Dad shook his head vigorously. "No. She wouldn't do that."

"Can you be sure?" I said, trying to keep my voice gentle. "You did piss her off before you left England. Maybe she's trying to lure you back over there to capture you."

"Language," he chided, voice soft. His heart wasn't in it.

"Well, you *did*." The only reason I existed, a half-blood *aosidhe*, was because Dad had trapped Melpomene with an oath to love him, an oath she'd escaped by having me. The idea that my gentle father would rob someone of their free will still made me squirm—although, in his defence, she'd first manipulated his emotions to make him fall crazily in love with her. He hadn't been able to bear the thought of losing her, so he trapped her instead.

The situation pretty much defined poetic justice.

"It doesn't make sense, though," Ryan pointed out. His anger had softened. "Nana's been living in the same house for decades, and your mum presumably knows where, given she was with Uncle David for almost a year. If she wanted Nana, she could've killed her any time."

"That's right," Dad said, too quickly.

"Maybe it wasn't her." I sat upright in my seat as a terrible thought gripped me. "But Dad, you admit you brought me to Australia to get us both away from her, in case she wanted revenge. You going back over there ... even if she didn't organise to have Nana killed, do you honestly believe she won't take advantage of it?"

Dad kneeled on the carpet beside the couch and gazed at me. This close, I could see how bloodshot his eyes were. Had he slept at all? When he spoke, there was pain in his voice. "No, I don't think she would. It's been eighteen years. Why would she bother, after all this time? Why would she care?" As he spoke, the grief in his aura at Nana's death was tinged with an older sadness, less raw but just as deep. He believed Melpomene didn't love him anymore, and mourned it.

"I'm scared something will happen to you," I whispered, blinking tears away before they could fall.

"I'm not. And at least you'll be safe here."

I clutched at his hand, his callused fingers. "I want to come with you." Beside me, Sarah gasped.

"You can't." He shook his head.

"I can look after myself, Dad."

"I know you can, pumpkin. Unfortunately, my concerns about your safety aren't the only reason you can't go. Return tickets to London are about three grand each. I can't afford to bring you."

"I ... I could get a loan." Even as I said it, I knew it wasn't possible. I didn't have a real part-time job, not one that provided pay slips. No bank would approve it. Aunt Elizabeth was a bank manager, and even she wouldn't.

Dad was shaking his head. "No, Isla. I need you to stay here. Safe."

We all jumped when the door opened. Aunt Elizabeth walked in, holding a sheaf of papers. "I got us flights via Melbourne and Dubai, leaving tomor—" She stopped, taking in the scene with narrowed eyes. "This all looks very serious."

"Isla wanted to come to the funeral." Dad stood quickly, his gaze drifting sideways and his mouth turning down at the corners. His poker face was as bad as mine, and my aunt read his guilt just as easily as I did.

Her gaze hardened. "You told them, didn't you? After I asked you not to?"

"Brothers never listen," Sarah murmured with a sideways glance at Ryan. Then she bit her tongue under her mother's withering glare.

I barely heard them argue. All I could think of was my father, heading back to England, and the enemies awaiting him.

Dad left soon after, to drive back to the farm and pack. As soon as his jeep grumbled out of the driveway, I grabbed Sarah by the elbow and dragged her to my bedroom. "I need your help."

"With what?" She gently freed her arm and sat on my bed.

"Can you go out to the shed and get something iron for Dad to take with him? I would, but..."

Sarah pursed her lips. "He won't be able to take anything in his carryon luggage. Kim told me she had her hand lotion confiscated last year when she flew to Vietnam for the holidays, if you can believe that. No way they'll let him take an iron crowbar with him."

"For his suitcase then."

"It'd have to be something small. They have weight limits—"

"That's fine!" I snapped, and she glowered back. I wilted. "Sorry. I'm just so worried about him. He doesn't see Melpomene as a threat to him. He's still so in love with her."

"Can't you, you know, fix that?" She wiggled her fingers in a way I guessed was meant to be mysterious.

"I offered to. Unfortunately, he's not even willing to admit she made him love her. *Because* he loves her."

"Talk about your rose-coloured glasses," Sarah said. I nodded, and she continued, "So why not just do it to him anyway? It's for his own good."

"I can't."

"Sure you can. You fixed Dominic up." Her cheeks flushed pink as she said my ex-boyfriend's name. When I raised an eyebrow, she looked away, scooping up my long-limbed plush bear, Mister Monkey. She rubbed the fuzzy black fur on his nose with her thumb.

"After Dominic, I promised myself I wouldn't use my powers on people without their permission unless it was in self-defence." I sat beside her on the bed. "So will you do it? Get some iron for Dad to take? The shed is stuffed full of things he's given me over the years. There's got to be something small you can find that looks legit. Maybe that chunky iron pendant he made me? We could make it look like he's taking a gift to someone in London, in case his bag gets searched."

"Okay. I can't make him agree to take it though."

"Leave that to me."

"But you just said—"

"I won't need to use my powers. A guilt trip will work just fine."

She laughed and leaned back against the wall, Mister Monkey hanging from one hand.

I gazed into the toy's glass eyes, told myself not to be a wuss, and took a deep breath. "So, how was your date with Dominic?"

"Good."

"*Good* good?"

Her blush told me everything I needed to know.

I reminded my stomach, which churned uneasily, that

I was happy for her, and concentrated on keeping my tone light. "He's an excellent kisser, isn't he?"

"Oh, god, yes!" she blurted. Then she bit her lip. "Sorry."

"For what?"

"Having the sensitivity of a brick to the face?"

I squeezed her hand. "Sarah, I just want you to be happy. Although if you marry him, I hope he can forgive me because I totally expect to be in your bridal party."

Her laugh was high with embarrassment. "Marriage? We've had one date."

"I know. I'm just planning ahead."

"What about you? Can I be in your bridal party when you marry Jack?" Her blue-green eyes twinkled with mirth.

"Of course," I said solemnly. *Do the duinesidhe even get married?* There were so many things I hadn't discussed with my boyfriend, so many things I didn't know about what he expected from our relationship.

I realised with a start I didn't even know how old he was.

"Hey." Sarah poked my arm. "That wasn't meant to make you gloomy."

"I'm not gloomy."

"Isla, you may be able to read auras but I can read your face like a picture book."

"It's just that Jack and I haven't talked about it. The future, I mean."

"Relax," my cousin said, dropping Mister Monkey and standing. She stretched, cat-like. "Worst comes to worst, you can always order him to propose and he'd have to do it. Half your luck. Anyway, I'm going out to the shed to find that pendant before Uncle David gets back."

I frowned after her, mind whirling.

44

MELPOMENE'S DAUGHTER

My heart ached as I watched Dad carry his suitcase out the front, the muscles in his arms bulging at the weight. "Do you need a hand?" I asked.

"I'm right," he grunted, lifting the bag down onto the footpath and raising the handle. It clicked into place. "It's all this iron you made me pack."

"One tiny thing." I walked on the grass beside him as the suitcase rumbled along the path. If I hadn't seen Dad put the pendant—a crude rose he'd fashioned during his early experimentation with ironworking—in with his toiletries, I might have suspected it wasn't there. Under all the clothes he'd packed, as well as the reinforced plastic case, not even a hint of nausea betrayed its presence. "I wish you'd take more."

"I'll be fine."

"Promise me once you get out of airport security you'll put it in your pocket, and keep it there." I clenched my fists so he wouldn't see them shaking.

"Isla..."

"Promise me!"

"Is everything okay?" my aunt called from inside the house. The screen door banged open. Ryan tugged his mother's suitcase through the door; it rattled across the sill until I thought it might topple over, and then thudded down each of the stairs. Distracted, Aunt Elizabeth resumed chiding him to be careful.

"This would be a lot easier if you hadn't packed your entire wardrobe," he grumbled.

I turned back to Dad and whispered, "Promise."

Dad steadied his suitcase before wrapping me in a tight hug that smelled of shampoo and his morning coffee. His breath tickled my ear. "I promise, Isla."

"And if you see Melpomene, run like crazy," I added, trying to muster a smile.

"That's your mother you're talking about."

"I know."

We fell silent as Aunt Elizabeth and Ryan stopped beside us. My aunt checked her suitcase over for damage before breathing a sigh of relief. Ryan clenched his teeth.

Sarah appeared from the house, a carryon bag slung over each shoulder. I hurried to her side, taking Dad's before she collapsed under the weight. It was heavy, stuffed with everything he thought he'd need for twenty-two hours of flights: quarantine-safe snacks, a book, his passport and wallet, clean socks and jocks, a toothbrush and toothpaste. "Thanks," my cousin said, brushing her streaked blond fringe out of her eyes. "How are you coping?"

I shook my head and didn't answer. If I did, I'd burst into tears.

"He packed it, right?"

"Yeah."

"He'll be fine."

"Come on, girls," my aunt called. "The cab's here."

The taxi's engine purred as it slid to a halt in front of my family. Sarah and I held the carryon bags while Ryan and Dad hefted the two suitcases into the boot. They barely fit. Aunt Elizabeth slid into the front seat next to the driver, and Dad clambered in the back, taking possession of the bags.

"Call us as soon as you arrive," I said, my voice trembling just a little as I leaned in to give Dad a kiss on the cheek. "I don't care what time it is here."

The cabbie bit back a laugh, amusement rippling through his aura. "Are you going to set him a curfew too?" I gave him a dark look and he turned to gaze back out the windshield, telling the glass, "It's meant to be the parents scolding the teenagers to not have wild parties, not the other way round."

Aunt Elizabeth's eyes widened as she looked between me and her children. I don't think the idea of wild parties had even occurred to her. "You aren't—"

"Don't worry about us," Sarah said with a twinkle in her eye, closing her mother's door before she could reply.

"And don't worry about us either." Dad's gaze locked with mine.

As the taxi pulled away, a cold lump of fear settled in my throat. I couldn't speak for my aunt, but I knew I was going to worry every minute Dad wasn't on Australian soil.

CHAPTER FIVE

*J*ack and I spent the rest of the day exploring Mount Taylor—the small mountain close to our house. We knew the area where the entrance to the *sidhe* hid, so we wandered across the other side. Autumn had chased away summer's oppressive heat, replacing it with glorious daytime weather, cold nights and the occasional spectacular thunderstorm. Today was one of the good days; from the top of the mountain, we looked down into the valley to the west, drinking in the vivid blue sky with its puffs of cloud, and the russet-and-gold foliage of autumn trees that glowed as the sun dropped towards the horizon.

Jack let me talk myself out, waiting until I started to go in circles before distracting me with a kiss. There was something electric about the feel of his lips on mine, so earnest and pure. When I looked at his aura, the red of love gleamed soft as rose petals. He ran his finger down my cheek, sapphire eyes glowing in the slanting sunlight, and my heart thumped like a galloping *karkadann* in my chest.

Maybe that was the difference between Jack's kisses and Dominic's. Jack loved me. Dominic had cared, but the relationship had never progressed to the point of love.

I bit my lip, wishing I hadn't recalled my ex.

"What is wrong?" Jack said, running a warm finger across my lips.

"I'm hungry," I said, looking away towards a couple walking their dog up the trail. "It's almost dinner time. Do you want to come over? I'll make you the very best in macaroni and cheese."

"If you wish."

"I wish."

"Very well." He smiled, taking my hand. Our fingers curled together as though made for one another.

When we turned the last corner on the walk home, I groaned. Dominic's car was in front of the house, its engine still ticking as it cooled.

Jack blinked. He recognised it, of course—we'd borrowed it to go out to Dad's farm when Moray attacked. A *puca* had crushed Jack against the bonnet, burning him on the steel. It's the sort of memory that stays with you. "Shall I leave?" he asked, letting go of my fingers.

I snatched his hand back again. "No way. You're my boyfriend, and if Dominic is going to date Sarah, he needs to get used to that. To us."

Jack nodded, although his dubious expression echoed the sudden nerves roiling in my stomach.

My ex-boyfriend looked up from his position on the couch as I walked in, his expression neutral. However, the emotions in his aura shifted from dislike to hatred as Jack closed the door behind me. The only external sign of the change was his chocolate-brown eyes narrowing slightly.

"Hi, Dominic." Guilt and sadness warred in my heart as I looked at him. I didn't regret my decision to leave him. To do anything else would've been even more unfair. But remorse at the way Dominic had been used, first by me and then by Everest, hung around my neck—a millstone made of lies.

"Hey." He slouched back on the couch, hands in his pockets, and looked at me.

"Are you guys staying in, or...?"

"We're going to a movie. Sarah's just getting changed." He looked away. "Don't worry, we won't cramp your style."

"I wasn't worried." I hesitated before turning to Jack. "Can you give us a minute?"

Jack nodded, walking into the kitchen and closing the door behind him. It gave us the illusion of privacy, although I knew the hob's keen ears would still be able to hear us.

I sat on the single couch and leaned forward, trying to meet Dominic's gaze. He looked at me out the corner of his eye. "I wanted to say I'm sorry. For everything that happened."

He grunted. "You should be."

"I know what you think—" his eyebrows shot up into his hairline "—but I didn't cheat on you."

"Does it matter what I think?"

"To me, it does," I said. "If you're going to date my cousin, I ... I was hoping we'd be able to stay friends." His sharp laugh cracked the icy exterior of my remorse, but I swallowed the angry words dancing on my tongue. "Okay, well, if not friends then polite acquaintances. I

MELPOMENE'S DAUGHTER

just want to make it easier for Sarah. None of what happened was her fault."

"No. It was Jack's."

I thrust out my jaw and took a deep breath. He made it sound like I was some weak-willed bimbo who would do whatever a boy asked me to. "I made my own decisions."

He glared at me and pressed his lips together.

"Just promise me one thing, Dominic."

"What?"

"That you're not going to hurt Sarah to, I don't know—" it felt stupid to say it, but I made myself go on "—to get back at me."

His eyes widened and he ran a hand through his dark hair. "You're serious! You really think I'd do that?"

"I know how angry you are at me."

"You think you're so special, don't you, Isla?" Acid dripped off his words, so sharp I could almost smell it. "Well, you're not. We only dated for, what, three months? And I'm not some asshole who sets out to ruin his ex's life, no matter how much of a bitch she's been."

My mouth fell open, shame burning my cheeks.

Sarah hurried into the room, eyes wide. "Is everything okay in here?"

"Just peachy," Dominic said, flashing his teeth at me in a grin. The expression didn't reach his eyes. "Isla and I were just catching up."

"I thought I heard raised voices." She looked from him to me.

I forced myself to smile. "It's fine. Just clearing the air. We're done now. Right, Dominic?"

"Right." I wished I couldn't read his aura right then. I might have believed he meant it.

Jack waited in the kitchen until Dominic and Sarah were clambering into his car. Then he poked his head into the lounge room. "Are you alright?"

I shrugged. "I should've kept my mouth shut. You heard how it went."

"I did not seek to." His pale cheeks reddened faintly. "I would have gone outside, but the screen door has a steel frame. So..."

"I wasn't complaining." I stood with a sigh and crossed the room, kissing him on the cheek. Then I slipped past him into the kitchen and opened the pantry. He followed me, sitting at the counter. "I figured you'd be able to hear."

"Do you believe him when he says he does not intend to harm your cousin?"

"Yes. I think so. Oh, I don't know. I think he likes her, but I couldn't tell for sure. His aura was so full of hate for me." My voice wavered a little.

"Do you want me to follow him? To make sure of his intentions?"

"Seriously?" I blinked, hands full of ingredients. Then I shook my head. "What if he saw you?"

"When I first discovered you, I followed you for several days without you seeing me. I am very good at it."

"Don't remind me. It makes you sound like a stalker." I softened the words with a smile.

"I can be one when I have to be. When it involves the safety of the *sidhe* or the happiness of my girlfriend."

His words melted me to my toes—until I realised what he was saying. "Hang on, you thought I was a threat to the *sidhe*?"

"I thought there was a chance you might be. Until I realised how special you were."

His words reminded me of Dominic's accusation. I tore open a new packet of macaroni, and swore as little tubes spilled across the bench. "Not that special."

"You are unique."

"Yeah, yeah, the only half-breed *aosidhe* in the world."

"That is not what I am referring to. I am talking about *you*, Isla."

More toe melting. I gazed back at him. "You're pretty special too."

His smile was like sunlight, evaporating my anxiety about the argument. "So do you wish me to follow Dominic? Or have Welkin do it?"

I winced at the mental image of the loud *piskie* following Sarah on a date. He'd be just as likely to wolf whistle if they kissed, or make inappropriate comments to her when no one was watching. Sometimes I thought the little faerie had a bit of a crush on my cousin, and I was sure he'd be unkind to Dominic given the chance. Dominic hadn't exactly been kind to me, and I admit I was tempted, but if Sarah found out... "No, let's just leave it alone, okay? He'll get over it eventually. Besides, I deserve some of what he said."

"No, you do not."

"I do." I turned on the gas hotplate and ran some water into the pot. "It was unfair of me to assume his motives in dating Sarah were about me. I just can't shake the feeling something awful is about to happen. It's making me cranky."

"I had not noticed."

I frowned at Jack, wondering whether he was being sarcastic. His expression was innocent.

"I just need to keep busy until Dad gets home. Do you

think the *duinesidhe* will have much work for me to do?"

"I am certain of it."

Jack was right.

The first time I'd entered the *sidhe* I'd noticed the eclectic nature of the construction. Although their styles ranged from Greek to Australian bush, from mundane to fairy tale, most of the buildings were made from either natural materials or those readily available in the human world: timber, bricks, plastic, canvas and even fabric. Steel and iron were, of course, notably absent.

That week, I kept busy upgrading *duinesidhe* houses from unusual but mundane structures into buildings more suited to the magical place in which they'd been built. The only limitation on what I could achieve was each *duinesidhe's* ability to describe what they wanted. The yurt I'd noticed on my first visit, made of patched scraps of fabric its owner had scavenged from charity bins throughout the city, I transformed into a greenish-brown material that changed colour, blending into the surrounding grass as the sun moved across the sky. A Greek-style house made of white-rendered concrete studded with chips of ocean-coloured tiles I changed into gleaming marble with patches of opalescent rock that shimmered like the Aegean Sea. Peeking through tiny windows, I changed the interior of a *piskie's* tree-trunk home from rough-hewn timber to interlocking rosewood and golden oak, which swirled together in a cloud pattern.

Each day I arrived home, exhausted, satisfied and

with a pocketful of banknotes. I'd wait only for Dad's daily call to let us know they were okay before falling into bed and sleeping a dreamless sleep.

On Friday morning, I woke in a good mood, humming as I hopped into the shower. My heart soared. The day before, I'd upgraded Scree's underground home to one walled with glossy black-and-red granite, laid out in alternating squares. The dwarf's distrust had thawed enough to let him approach me after seeing the work I'd done for some of his neighbours. He'd been suspicious at first, but after I finished his renovation, he'd beamed a smile at me, revealing teeth like slivers of calcite.

My hands stopped, tangled in my hair and covered in suds, as I realised the only member of the *sidhe* who hadn't approached either Jack or me to ask about having work done was Evie. Although maybe she and Jack had discussed it and he wasn't ready to reveal what she'd said. I doubted it would be polite. Her continued dislike for me was an ache that wouldn't go away.

Someone knocked on the bathroom door and I sighed, quickly rinsing. "I'm almost done!"

When I emerged from the bathroom, dressed and with damp hair coiled under a towel, I froze. Sarah and Ryan were waiting in the corridor, their faces pale and their auras an identical tumult of grief and horror.

The brush in my hand clattered to the floor from nerveless fingers. My dread returned, swooping in like a leather-winged *sluagh*, a faerie of fear. "What?"

Sarah wrapped me in her arms. She sobbed once, before swallowing hard.

"It's Uncle David," Ryan said. "He's disappeared."

CHAPTER SIX

"He—what?"

My cousins guided me to the lounge room. Sarah sat beside me on the couch, her eyes wide and sympathetic.

"Mum called while you were in the shower," Ryan said, easing himself into the other chair as though he was worried I might fly apart at the seams if he moved too suddenly. Maybe I would. "Nana's funeral was yesterday, their time. Uncle David was there, but he never made it to the wake."

"Why not?" I whispered, barely able to hear myself over the odd ringing in my ears.

"They don't know yet. Mum's reported it to the police. They won't do anything much till he's been missing a full twenty-four hours."

"What time is it there now?" Sarah said, squeezing my hand.

Ryan glanced at his watch and frowned. "Eleven o'clock last night. I think."

"So not till at least tonight, our time."

He nodded.

"It doesn't matter," I blurted. My cousins stared at me and I lifted my chin. "What can the police do? He was taken by my mother."

"You can't know that…" Sarah said, her voice soothing.

"I do!" My hands curled into fists on my knees, and my throat burned as though I'd swallowed fire. "I knew something bad was going to happen if he went over there. I just *knew* it. They probably killed Nana to draw him out, and now she's got him. Melpomene."

Ryan nodded. "I think you're right." Sarah's gaze flew to him, her mouth falling open. "Why else would I have had the vision of the tombstone? It wasn't just about Nana's death. It was that her funeral was a trigger for something else to happen. For the *aosidhe* to kidnap Uncle David."

"Maybe he just got lost," Sarah said, her voice soft with doubt.

"He grew up in London, remember? I'm sure it's changed, but not so much that entire streets would've moved. How could he get lost?"

My heart ached at the sense in Ryan's argument. Sarah bit her lip as she looked at me. "Do you want something? A cup of tea?"

"Coffee, please." I sat on the couch, Ryan my silent companion, as Sarah went into the kitchen to make me a drink. He handed me a box of tissues as a tear slipped down my cheek.

The front door burst open, slamming against the wall. Ryan and I jumped. Sarah swore in the kitchen, something clattering to the floor. Jack stood in the entryway, looking around wildly, hands held in a guard position in front of his torso as though expecting a fight. When he didn't see one, he dashed to my side. "Is everything okay? I came as fast as I could."

Ryan's eyebrows shot up as he stared at Jack. "How did you know?"

"A sworn hob knows when their master needs them," Jack said, his gaze unwavering on my face. He took my hands gently, his fingers curling around my fists and easing them flat. "What has happened?"

Ryan explained what we knew. It wasn't much.

"And what are we going to do?" Jack's question cut through the haze of my shock and grief like a knife through butter. Like iron through an *aosidhe*. The question galvanised me.

"We're going to England," I declared. "We're going to save him."

There was a stunned silence as I looked between Jack and Ryan, daring them to argue. "Um, how?" Ryan said finally.

Sarah appeared beside him, putting two mugs on the table. Steam wafted from them, carrying the usually delicious aroma of fresh-brewed coffee. Now it turned my stomach. "Ryan has a point. Flights are expensive."

"I've got money," I said. "A few grand, by now."

"How?" Sarah squeaked.

"*Duinesidhe* home renos pay pretty well, it turns out." I'd been willing to do the work free, but was suddenly grateful to Jack for insisting I be paid for my time. "Enough to pay for two tickets one way." Sarah and Ryan exchanged a look I recognised: they were gearing up for a fight. I grimaced. "Sorry, guys. I need Jack to come."

"I cannot." Jack sat back on his heels, his eyes wide and mournful.

I stared at him. "What?"

"I cannot fly in an aeroplane. I can manage being engulfed in the steel of a car for an hour, perhaps a little longer. An aeroplane would … well, the pain would kill me."

"Even if you didn't touch the steel?" I hated the pathetic whine in my voice, hated more that I was asking him to do something that would hurt him so badly.

"Even then. *Duinesidhe* have tried to fly before. They go mad."

"Then I should go," Ryan said quickly.

"What? No way!" Sarah scowled.

"I'm her *aislinge*. What if I have another vision and need to tell her?"

"Email a photo." Her tone made Scree's gravelly voice seem soft and melodic by comparison.

"Some details don't show up in a photo."

"Then use Mum's camera instead of your phone, you idiot!"

Their words pierced my head like elf shot. I stood, hands pressed to my temples, and stumbled from the room. They fell silent for a moment, allowing me to hear Jack's soft footfalls following me.

Out on the balcony, I fell into his arms, crying. My words were barely intelligible. "It's her. I'm sure of it. Jack, I need to get over there."

"I know." He stroked my hair. "You should go without me."

I looked at him. His face wavered before my eyes. I knuckled away my tears. "Seriously?"

"Yes. If that is the only way you can go." I didn't need to read his aura to see the strength of his reluctance, though—the tightness of his jaw and the shadows in his eyes practically shouted it.

I bit my lip, my desire to run to my father's rescue warring with my growing realisation that, without Jack, I'd have no idea how to navigate the treacherous *aosidhe* politics. Without him, I'd be in hot water up to my neck faster than I could blink. Possibly literally, if the stories about how vicious my mother's people were proved to be true. They had from what I'd seen so far, with Everest—

"Everest!"

Jack blinked. "Pardon?"

"He sailed here. Could we do that?"

He tipped his head to the side, running one hand over the tip of an exposed ear. He'd come here in such a rush he'd forgotten to grab a hat. I hoped none of the neighbours had seen him as he ran up the street. "He sailed here in a yacht. Where would we find one?"

I gnawed on a fingernail. I might have enough cash to get a couple of plane tickets, but a chartered yacht? I'd need to work for years to earn that kind of money. "What happened to his?"

"If Ariel went back to England and killed your grandmother, as we suspect—"

"—he would've taken it with him. Dammit."

"Damn what?" A small, piping voice made us turn to the outdoor table. Perched on the padded back of one of the chairs was a fairy-like creature no taller than my palm was long ... and I knew this firsthand because, two days ago, he'd lain down in my hand like it was the most comfortable bed in the world, lapping blood from a tiny pinprick in my thumb.

In the past six months, my life had grown weirder

than I could ever have imagined.

"Hi, Welkin," I said tiredly.

He narrowed sky-blue eyes and ran a hand through hair as gold as sunlight. "What's going on, Isla?"

"Her father has been kidnapped, probably by the *aosidhe*. We are trying to figure out how to get to the Old World so we can attempt to rescue him."

The *piskie's* diaphanous wings beat slowly as he thought over Jack's words. "Get *you* there, you mean. Isla can fly. Right?"

Jack gritted his teeth, nodding. Even though we'd just been discussing the same thing, my boyfriend's dislike of the little fairy probably made the words less palatable coming from him.

"I need Jack to come with me. I don't know enough to get Dad back alive." I sat on the chair so my face was almost level with Welkin's. "Unless you can fly?"

"In an aeroplane? Not so much. I could get there in a week or so, the old-fashioned way." He ran a hand along the shimmering edge of one wing, his tiny eyes on mine. "Meet you there?"

"Isla." The note of caution in Jack's voice made me look at him. When I did, he shook his head, eyes rolling to give the *piskie* a significant look.

I almost smiled, despite the leaden feeling in my chest. Did he really think Welkin's help was worse than no help at all?

"There might be another way." Welkin smoothed the front of the tiny doll's outfit Sarah had given him a few weeks ago.

"What's that?" I sat up straighter. Even Jack looked curious.

"The *sidhe* tunnels that go under the ocean."

"There is no such thing," Jack said, putting a hand on one slim hip. "They only go under land."

Welkin shook his head. "That's not what I hear." Jack crossed his arms and scowled, and the *piskie* did the same, jutting his little chest out in mockery. It struck me how similar they were. If Welkin were our size, he could be Jack's winged brother. "You land *duinesidhe*, you stop at the water's edge. You don't even talk to the water *duinesidhe*. We air fairies don't have that luxury. We pay attention across land *and* sea."

"Jack found me a siren teacher a couple of months ago." I raised an eyebrow at the *piskie*.

"Oh." Welkin tipped his head to the side but didn't apologise. "In which case, I guess Jack should be willing to admit that since there are *duinesidhe* in the ocean, there might be *sidhe* tunnels there too. Maybe he can admit the possibility there are things he doesn't know?"

"Have you ever seen one of these underwater tunnels?" The hob's voice was cool.

"Well ... no."

"Then how can you be sure they exist?"

"I hear stuff."

"If they do exist," I said, looking between the two of them, "won't they be filled with water?"

"That shouldn't be a problem." Welkin's smile had sharp edges, making me uneasy. "Besides, look at it this way—what choice do you have if you want to get Jack there quickly?"

Movement inside the house caught my eye. My cousins stood in the kitchen, peering out the glass sliding door. Sarah waved, looking sheepish. I beckoned them out.

MELPOMENE'S DAUGHTER

"We didn't want to interrupt," she said as soon as she slid the door open.

Her black terrier, Hamish, followed her out the door—but he stopped short when he saw the *piskie*, darting back inside. Ryan nearly tripped over him. "Bloody dog! What's got into him?"

"He's scared of Welkin." Sarah sighed.

"Well, he shouldn't have shoved his big hairy face so close to me last time," the *piskie* said, patting the copper pin sheathed at his belt. "I thought he was going to eat me."

"You bully." She frowned at the *piskie*, but her lips twitched with mirth.

"Me?" Welkin squeaked. "I've seen the biscuits you give him as treats, Red. I'm not much bigger. I didn't want to take the risk."

Ryan pulled a beanie from the back pocket of his jeans and handed it to Jack. "I thought you might need this."

"Thanks." Jack pulled the hat down over his hair and then arranged each of his ears flat on his head, out of sight. It looked uncomfortable, but whenever I asked Jack, he waved the question off.

My cousins sat at the table and Welkin flitted to Sarah's shoulder, curling a hand in her red hair. He may have sworn himself into my service—in exchange for two drops of my blood a week—but he doted on my cousin. She and the *piskie* got on as well as Jack and Welkin didn't.

I cleared my throat and everyone turned to me. "This is the best plan I can come up with," I said, folding my arms and leaning against the railing. "Sarah and Ryan, you guys will both fly over. On an aeroplane. Welkin will fly under his own steam, so to speak, and meet you there a few days later."

"What about you?" Sarah's expression was solemn.

"Jack and I will try and bargain with the sirens or whomever we need to, to get access to the *sidhe* tunnels under the ocean."

"You're going to *swim*? No offence, Isla, but I remember you at the school swimming carnival."

"Hopefully we'll be able to bargain for aid there too," I said, my cheeks burning. I remembered the carnival too. I *could* swim, sort of; however, it involved a lot of flailing and splashing and not a huge amount of forward momentum.

Ryan leaned forward. "Won't that take, like, forever? You're talking about swimming across the entire Pacific—"

"Actually, that would put her on the wrong side of the Americas," Sarah said. "She'd need to go via the Indian Ocean and the Atlantic."

"I think my point still stands," he snapped. "It's a long freaking way."

"The tunnels don't work the way travel in our world does," I said, interrupting the argument. "They sort of fold space, make it shorter. When we tracked Aghi down, we walked through tunnels from here to the Tarlo River National Park in a few hours. It would've taken the same amount of time to get near there on the highway, and then we'd still have had to navigate back roads and hike to where he was."

"Even so, it would take weeks. Months, even."

"Ryan is right," Jack said reluctantly. "If the water tunnels work like the land ones do, it would take far too long for you to reach the Old World and set out after your father. I cannot allow you to suffer that sort of delay for me."

I curled my fingers through his. "It's not just for you,

Jack. I need you there. It's for me, too."

"Aww," Welkin murmured. Sarah shushed him.

I ignored the interruption. "I'll make you a promise. If we talk to the sirens and it turns out that either it's going to take forever or it's not possible, I'll fly over. We should know within a day or two, so I won't be far behind Ryan and Sarah. And Welkin will be able to help me when he arrives."

"How will you pay for the extra ticket?" Ryan asked.

"I'll sell the opal I got from Gall. Or spend a few more days doing renos for the *duinesidhe*, if they need any. Whatever it takes."

"Do we have a plan then?" Welkin said, kicking his legs.

"We do."

Sarah and Ryan spent the rest of the day packing, while I drove out to the airport and paid for their tickets with cash—I hadn't yet had time to bank the money I'd earned from the *duinesidhe*. What was left over I exchanged for pounds, giving half to my cousins and tucking the rest in my purse. As all three of us were dual UK–Australian citizens, we had passports for both countries, so at least we didn't have to worry about trying to sort out documentation. The perks of being born in England and then moving to a Commonwealth country, I guess.

Not that I was planning to enter England via traditional means.

When Aunt Elizabeth called that night, Sarah answered the phone. I waited, wringing my hands, to see whether there had been any news about Dad. When my cousin met my gaze and shook her head, I sighed and slipped off to my bedroom, not waiting to hear her explain that she and Ryan were flying over. I was sure my aunt would have some pointed questions.

I was wrapping my passports in cling wrap and stowing them in a waterproof bag when a tap at my door made me turn. Ryan stood in the open doorway.

"Do you think my not having an entry stamp on my passport could cause problems when I get there?" I said.

"Only if you do something that might land you in trouble with the cops." Ryan paused, and I looked more intently at him. He was gnawing the corner of his lip so hard I wouldn't have been surprised to see blood.

"What's wrong?"

"I had another vision."

I put the bag down with shaking hands, my skin going cold all over. "Dad?" Was he already dead?

"No. Well, sort of." My face must have shown how I felt, because he quickly added, "Don't worry, I think it's good news. That you're on the right track with the ocean thing."

Relief flooded through me, turning my knees weak. I sat on the edge of the bed before I fell. Then I realised his hands were empty. "Where's the picture?"

"I haven't drawn it yet. I will. I just wanted to tell you, so you'd know."

"Tell me what?" I said, swallowing my impatience.

"Well, it was of this sort of underwater grotto. There wasn't a huge amount of light, but I could see seaweed and the shape of the rocks." His hand moved through the air, seemingly unconsciously, sketching a ragged shape.

"And there was something in the middle. A manmade shape, like the handle of a broom or a rake, only not made of timber."

I exhaled a long, trembling breath. Ryan was right—it sounded as though Jack and I would be able to find passage through the *sidhe* ocean tunnels after all. "Thank god."

"Yeah," Ryan said. "Anyway, I'll just finish packing and then I'll sketch it for you."

"I don't think you need to."

"Yeah, I do."

His tone warned me not to argue, so I bit back my advice about getting an early night. He was older than I was; he wouldn't take being mothered very well. "Thanks for telling me straight away," I said instead, turning to retrieve the opal from the jewellery box. It might come in handy. "I needed to hear that."

"I know." He flashed me a tired grin before disappearing up the corridor.

CHAPTER SEVEN

Ryan gave me the drawing in the kitchen the next morning, the pads of his fingers still stained with blue and green smudges. A dark line marked his freckled forehead, as though he'd scratched an itch with discoloured hands.

"Did you sleep at all?" I murmured as my grip closed around the edges of the paper.

"A little," he mumbled, avoiding eye contact as he turned towards the bathroom. "I'll sleep on the plane. It's fine."

I placed the sheet on the bench and gazed down at it, my nose tickling with the scent of recently used fixative. The grotto, sketched in pastels, looked much as he'd described—the perspective was from outside a jagged cave entrance whose mouth looked uncomfortably like teeth. Inside, on either edge, dark tongues of seaweed trailed up from the sea floor, casting faint shadows from an unknown light source. In the middle, jammed into a rock in a way that reminded me of Excalibur, was a shaft of grey material—some sort of metal. I was pretty confident it wasn't steel or iron, though, for two reasons: the lack of rust speckling the substance, and my assumption that the location was somewhere inside the *sidhe* rather than in the earth's real ocean. Jack had mentioned several times that the *sidhe* didn't react well to the presence of iron. I'd never quizzed him on it. But the memory of my comatose father—contorted with a seizure because I'd brought the metal too close while the elf shot was still lodged in his breast—flooded my mind.

The idea of the entire landscape reacting that way while I was inside it made my skin prickle.

Sarah shuffled into the kitchen, her fringe sticking up like she'd slept in a haystack. "Hey," she grunted, looking over my shoulder at the picture. "What's that?"

"Ryan had a vision yesterday. Underwater scenery is in my future."

"Oh." She sounded disappointed, and I raised an eyebrow at her. I didn't have to wait long. "I was just … I was thinking, why don't you fly over with us? Jack can just as easily come via the underwater tunnels without you as with you."

I shook my head, stepping to one side so she could shuffle towards the kettle. "There are things I can do that Jack can't. I have more to barter for passage with."

"Like what?"

"I don't know. Maybe the sirens need some home renos done too?" I glanced down at the picture again. "This is proof we're on the right track."

She frowned. "If you say so."

"You don't agree?"

"The image doesn't show you and Jack emerging safe from the Thames, does it?"

I bit my lip. Sarah was right. All it proved was that Jack and I would *try* to pass through the underwater tunnels. Not that we'd make it out the other side.

She saw my look and grimaced. "Hey, I'm sure it will be fine. Just promise me you'll be careful, okay? I don't want to have to explain to your dad when he turns up how we lost you too."

"I promise."

A half-hour later, the doorbell rang. When I opened it, Natalie stood there, one hand on her hip, the other swinging her car keys in a slow circle. "Hey, Isla," she said without enthusiasm as I opened the door.

"Er, hi?"

Sarah rushed down the hall. "Thanks so much for coming!"

"No worries," Natalie said.

"I asked Natalie to look after Hamish while we're gone," my cousin explained to me. It hadn't even occurred to me to figure out who would mind Sarah's dog. She turned to our old school friend. "He's out the back. I'll just go round him up."

"Do you want a drink or anything?" I offered.

"No thanks," Natalie said in a flat voice, sitting on the couch and picking up one of Aunt Elizabeth's week-old, trashy magazines.

Frowning faintly, I looked at her aura. Annoyance jangled there, a riot of clashing colours. "Natalie, if you're worried about looking after Hamish—"

"It's not that."

I searched my mind for an explanation. I hadn't seen

70

her much in the last couple of months. She'd started university and a new lifestyle—if coming out of the closet could be described that way—and I'd started dating Jack. She still caught up with Sarah at the gigs my cousin did with her band, Drakeford, but I hadn't been going to those as much.

Hell with it.

"Have I done something wrong?" I sat beside her on the couch, turning to face her.

"What makes you say that?" she said, not meeting my gaze.

"You seem mad at me."

She slapped the magazine closed and looked up, her pale blue eyes boring into mine. I sat back, surprised. "I was just talking to Dominic," she said.

"What did he say?" I rasped, stomach churning.

"He told me about your conversation with him a few days ago."

"Let me guess. He said I accused him of trying to ruin Sarah's life to get back at me?"

She hesitated. "Something like that. Is it true?"

"Sort of." I glanced away. "I asked him to promise he wasn't."

"He's pretty angry at you."

"I noticed. Although I do love how he's going around bitching to everyone else about it." I couldn't keep the bitterness out of my voice.

"He wasn't bitching. Well, not exactly. I ran into him and asked how things were going with Sarah. He said they were good, despite what you were assuming." She made air quotes as she said the last five words.

It sounded like bitching to me, but I bit back the words.

"I'm not proud of that conversation," I admitted instead. Fresh shame as the memory surfaced burned my cheeks. "I only asked because I care about Sarah. I would hope my friends would give me the benefit of the doubt."

Natalie contemplated this, head to one side for a moment, before nodding. "That's fair enough. I probably would have done the same thing in your shoes, I guess. Sorry."

"It's okay." I smiled at Natalie. She was the most tactless of my friends, but her candour also meant she was always ready to admit when she'd done something wrong. I realised with a pang how much I missed her and the other member of our high school group, Kim. When we returned from England, I'd have to make more of an effort, rather than becoming completely wrapped up with Jack and the *duinesidhe* once again.

"I do think he really likes her though," Natalie continued, leaning back into the couch. It dwarfed her tiny frame. "From the way he was talking."

"That's all I wanted to know. I wish he'd just told me."

Her lips curved into a smile at the exasperation in my voice. "You're really alright with them dating?"

"Yeah, I am. Mostly. Dominic may not spit on me if I was on fire right now, but I do like him. I'm sorry things didn't work out between us. And he and Sarah would be a cute couple."

She leaned over to nudge me with her elbow. "So how are things going between you and Jack?"

"Good. Great."

She frowned. "Are you sure?"

"Of course."

"Then why do you seem..." she waved her hand vaguely "...sort of off?"

"My dad went missing in England. Didn't Sarah tell you? That's why we're going away."

"Didn't Sarah tell her what?" my cousin said, walking into the room holding a squirming Hamish. His eyes were fixed on the lead in her other hand as though it held the key to everlasting happiness. Maybe, for him, it did. His scrabbling claws came close to catching in the haematite necklace I'd insisted she wear. She'd used it to great effect defending herself against Ariel, and it was innocuous enough she'd be able to take it on the plane.

"About Dad," I said.

"Oh." She grimaced. "No, I didn't. I thought it may be something you didn't want to share."

"Well, I wouldn't post it on Facebook or anything, but I don't mind Natalie and Kim knowing."

"Right. Good to know."

Natalie stood and hooked one arm under Hamish's belly, taking him from my cousin. Then she used her free hand to punch Sarah on the arm.

"Ow!"

"You should've told me. Seriously. I came in here all crotchety about stuff, and Isla had this big situation going on. I feel like an A-grade cow now."

"What stuff?"

"Uh. Nothing." Natalie's pale face turned pink. "Where are his bowl and blankets?" she asked quickly.

Sarah gave Natalie a dubious look and glanced at me. I shrugged, smiling. "I'll just get them," she said, hurrying from the room.

I stood, giving Natalie an appraising look. "Dominic hasn't told her what I said to him?"

She shook her head. "He didn't want to hurt her

feelings."

I thought about that, scratching Hamish between the ears. His eyes didn't budge from the lead. *Dominic must really like Sarah after all. Otherwise, wouldn't he have tried to set her against me?* "Damn. I seriously owe him an apology. I should call him."

"I wouldn't. Just give him time." A note of caution in her voice made me bite my lip. Just how angry had Dominic been when they talked?

"Okay," I said. "But if you see him, can you let him know I'm sorry? About everything."

She nodded. "I will. And I'll make sure that when you get back from England he'll take your call."

"How?"

She gave me an impish smile that made her look less like a china doll and more like an overgrown *piskie*. "I'll nag him until he says yes. I'm a champion nagger."

Once Sarah had organised the rest of Hamish's luggage, we walked them both out to Natalie's car, lugging two canvas bags full of doggy things: as well as bowls and blankets, there was a huge bag of dried food and his favourite squeaky pig. Sarah trapped her squirming dog in his car harness and buckled him into the back seat. He regarded her with mournful eyes. Pouting, she kissed him on the top of his shaggy head. "Be good, boy."

He yelped when she closed the door, as though saying goodbye.

Natalie slid into the driver's seat. "You guys travel safe, okay?" She started the engine. "And Isla, when you find that dad of yours, tell him he needs to learn to stay out of trouble."

"I really will."

MELPOMENE'S DAUGHTER

I spent the rest of the morning pacing—when I wasn't checking and double-checking whether Sarah and Ryan were ready. Eventually Ryan growled at me to go away and even Sarah started to look annoyed. The hands on the elegant timber clock in the lounge moved with stubborn slowness. We'd booked a taxi, so I couldn't even keep myself busy driving them to the airport.

Given the anxiety I radiated, it wasn't a surprise when Jack arrived earlier than we'd organised.

"Is everything alright?" he asked, coming into the kitchen. I threw myself into his arms, inhaling his clean, green scent.

"I'm just stressing," I mumbled into his shoulder. "About Sarah and Ryan. About Dad. It's so unfair I can't change my own emotions."

"Is there anything I can do to help?" He ran his fingers through my ponytail, separating the tangles with gentle, deft movements.

"You're doing it right now." I sighed, feeling the tension ease from my limbs. How did he do that?

"Are you ready to go?"

"I'm not sure," I said. "What does one pack for undersea adventures? Other than a swimsuit?"

"Do not worry too much about clothes, Isla. We will be in the *sidhe*. You will be able to conjure up whatever we need."

"Oh. Right." I knew Jack meant his words to be reassuring, but the idea of both our fates depending on me using a power I'd only started practicing in the last week made me feel sick. I spun out of his arms, nervous energy driving my movements. "Hey, let me show you what Ryan drew."

Jack studied the drawing with intent sapphire eyes,

committing each detail of it to memory. I did the same—even if I wrapped the picture as I had my passports, I wouldn't be able to unpack it once we were in the underwater tunnels. It made more sense to leave it at home.

The other thing I was leaving was my phone. It wouldn't work in the *sidhe* and I wouldn't be able to use it in England. After paying for the airfares I couldn't afford to activate global roaming on my account, which meant it would just be an expensive piece of plastic. Still, the idea of not having it in my pocket made me feel naked.

The thought of checking in on Facebook from under-water midway across the Atlantic made my lips twitch with amusement.

The honk of a taxi made me jump. Jack caught my hand and smiled at me. "They will be fine."

"And us?" I squeaked.

"We will be fine too."

CHAPTER EIGHT

*M*y feet ached.

Over the past couple of months, I'd grown a lot fitter, a result of spending much of my time walking with Jack instead of taking my little car. But I wasn't used to walking for hours at a time. It had been my decision to leave the car at home rather than subjecting my boyfriend to a long drive. Also, I wasn't wild about leaving the vehicle parked on a random stretch of coastline for an unknown amount of time. I reminded myself of my reasons as I took each trudging step through the monotonous *sidhe* tunnels, ignoring the twinges of pain as my usually comfortable walking shoes rubbed against my heels.

Most *sidhe* tunnels looked the same—as though they'd been burrowed through the earth by a giant worm, their sides made of dirt compacted by the force of its passage. I wondered as I ran my eyes over the largely featureless walls whether the inside of a regular earthworm's tunnel looked the same—lots of smooth brown, gritty to the touch, marked by occasional features. With an earthworm, I imagined those features might include tiny specks of rock, or the thin, pale tendrils of roots reaching down through the soil for the nutrients the worm leaves behind.

Here, however, the features ranged from seemingly mundane cracks in the walls, leading into an impenetrable darkness our torch couldn't pierce, to strange growths of glowing pink fungus like something out of a twisted Barbie doll accessory line. In one place, we passed drawings that looped across the entire top of the tunnel, resembling Aboriginal cave art I'd seen on an excursion to Gudgenby Valley in high school. However, the colours popped here in a way they never would again on the faded walls in the real world rock shelter: bright white, vivid burnt orange, deep grey. I recognised the distinctive shapes of a platypus and kangaroo, and what I guessed from the shape of the head was probably a dingo. I doubted it was a cattle dog, which it also resembled— although, given I didn't know the origin of the art, I couldn't rule it out. Just because it looked like Aboriginal art, that didn't mean it was.

I glanced surreptitiously at my watch, not for the first time. We'd been walking for four hours. Ugh.

"Did you want to stop for a rest?" Jack was kind enough not to say "another rest".

I grimaced, willing my legs to keep moving. "I'm not sure that's a good idea. If I stop now, I may not start again."

He looked at me critically. "Are you limping?"

"No."

"Yes, you are. Stop for a minute."

Grumbling, I sank down onto the curved slope of the

tunnel floor. This far out from the *sidhe*, no one had taken the time to fill in the bottom part of the cylinder with a flat path, which made walking tricky and sitting awkward. I shifted around, trying to find a comfortable position, but gave up with a sigh.

When Jack picked at my shoelaces, I batted his hands away. "Don't."

"Why not?" His eyes were wide, earnest.

I didn't want to admit I was worried my feet would be sweaty, so I shifted away from him and slipped my sneakers and socks off each of my faintly glowing feet. Small red blisters glowered at me, one on each heel. Looking at them seemed to make them hurt more—or maybe that was exposure to the cooler air of the tunnel.

"I can heal them for you," Jack said.

"Uh, no."

"Why not?"

I rolled my eyes at him. "Because when you heal me, you take on the injury—"

"I heal faster than you."

"—and also, you have to *lick* me. There is no way on this earth I am letting you lick my feet."

"No way at all?" Did I imagine the twinkle in his eye? I shifted my torch, a small jar stuffed with glowing gems that resembled flecks of quartz, and peered at him. The corner of his mouth twitched with a smile.

Nope, not imagining it. My cheeks burned and I hoped he couldn't see them—although I was pretty sure my hope was in vain. "No way. Not when my feet are all sweaty and gross," I said instead.

"Fair enough. Then use the *sidhe* energy to manipulate your body. Heal yourself."

I remembered Gall's sweat-drenched face after I'd rebuilt his body, his grimace of pain. Butterflies swarmed in my stomach. "Won't it hurt, though? I mean, I'm already hurting. Why not just leave it?"

"It does hurt," Jack admitted. I wondered which *aosidhe* had changed him, and grimaced. Given his previous master's … predilections … it wouldn't surprise me if he'd altered his servants for the fun of it. "But the pain is only temporary, for the most part."

"For the most part?"

"Yes. If you made a change that left nerves exposed, or forced bone through flesh—"

"Oh god!" I curled my knees up to my chest, ignoring the twinge from my blisters as they scraped across dirt, and stared at him in horror. "Did Cacodaemon do that to you?"

"Not to me. To others." Jack looked away down the tunnel as though it were an interesting landscape instead of more of the same boring tunnel we'd been looking at for hours. "I am sorry. I should not have mentioned it."

I stared at his profile for several heartbeats: those sombre, wide eyes I could drown in; the loose golden hair, which fell past his ears like water over stone. His skin was smooth, flawless. He didn't have scars, not even the tiny scars on his hands that most people get from everyday use.

Evie, on the other hand… She'd gained her scar as a result of Cacodaemon torturing her with iron. Knowing that the *aosidhe* could have healed her afterwards, if he'd bothered, somehow made what happened to her much worse. Were his servants—slaves—so valueless to him that he didn't feel the need to mend what he'd broken?

Or did he enjoy the sight of his own handiwork?

"I'm glad you killed him," I growled, surprising myself.

Jack looked at me with sad eyes. "I am too. And yet…"

"And yet," I whispered. Being grateful for the death of another living creature—even one as wilfully evil as Cacodaemon had been—felt awfully like the first step to becoming such a creature myself.

"You should heal yourself," Jack said finally, breaking a silence that may have stretched on for seconds or minutes. I wasn't sure. "Aside from anything else, do you really want to walk into salty water with wounds on your feet?"

I looked down at the blisters. They hadn't burst, but we probably had another hour of walking to do. They might.

Don't be a chicken, I told myself. Then I grimaced and ran a fingertip over my heel, willing the skin to smoothness.

A bone-deep, searing pain spiked through my heel, tearing a groan from my lips as the blister under my fingertip receded into the skin, like a gross movie running in reverse. The pain felt as though I'd stepped on a shard of glass—but as soon as the blister disappeared, the feeling abated.

I had to force myself to do the other foot.

My hands shook as I pulled my socks back on. "I don't know how Gall just stood there while I made him over. It must have been like being eaten by fire ants."

Jack shrugged. "He has probably had it done to him before, many times. The *powrie* are used as soldiers by the *aosidhe*. They are often the subject of, uh, enhancements."

"And I guess their masters wouldn't take kindly to a soldier blubbering with pain."

"Not usually, no."

"That's awful."

He shrugged one shoulder as if to say *that's how it is.* I would have been offended at his reaction, but Jack hadn't been idle in the face of a cruel master: he'd given him a stiff drink laced with iron filings. By all rights, Jack should have died when his master did, but he'd managed to outlive Cacodaemon by precious seconds— seconds that had freed him from the oath and allowed him to recover.

Dark thoughts gathered close in this empty place. I shuddered, trying to shake them off.

When I had re-laced my shoes, I scrambled to my feet, wiping my hands surreptitiously on my jeans. Jack stood much more gracefully. "More walking," I grumbled.

"Yes." He curled his fingers around mine. "I confess, as much as I wanted you to travel with your cousins, I am pleased you are here."

"I'm pleased I'm here too," I said, squeezing his fingers. "Besides, admit it. You would've been worried half to death if I'd gone over there without you."

"That is true. You would have found your way into all sorts of trouble without me to keep you in line."

"Hey!" I protested before the amusement in his voice registered. Then I chuckled. "Anyway, I came with you to keep *you* out of trouble."

"I do not get in trouble," he said in a bland tone. I raised an eyebrow at him and he grinned. "Well, perhaps some trouble. However, so far this journey has been remarkably trouble-free. I take the credit, of course."

"Ha." I shuddered, remembering the last trouble we'd been in on a journey through tunnels much the same as these. A haunt of *sluagh*—a flock of bat-winged, shriek-ing nightmares—had chased us all the way back to the

Canberra *sidhe*, assaulting us with artificial, heart-stopping terror. The real terror would have been bad enough.

Jack's keen eyes caught my tremor and he squeezed my hand. "Are you okay?"

"Just reminding myself to be grateful for how boring this walk has been so far."

"Boring is safe," he agreed.

Just over an hour later—not that I was counting—we reached a junction in the tunnel. We'd passed these from time to time, places where side passages branched off, leading who-knew-where. But this one smelled briny.

"I think this is our stop." I inhaled deeply, my lips curving in a relieved smile.

Jack gave me a curious look—sometimes I forgot he didn't have much in the way of modern idiom—and nodded, leading me down the new passage. Its walls were closer together, as though it had been burrowed by a smaller worm. A baby, perhaps. But the scent of seawater and the faint feeling of air movement held my claustrophobia at bay.

At least we weren't crawling.

Sunlight streamed in from ahead, increasingly illuminating our way. I slid the torch into my bag. Jack pulled a scarlet bandana out of his back pocket and wrapped it around his ears, pinning them back to the sides of his head with the ease of long practice.

We paused at the portal, peering through the wavering surface at the world outside. Our view was framed by a ceiling and walls of smooth, eroded rock, while the ground beyond the tunnel was coated with white sand and studded with large, flat stones. Farther out, we could see sea spray flinging itself into the air as waves crashed on distant rocks. Everything shivered as though we looked through a heat shimmer.

"The tide must be out," I said. "This entrance would be underwater at full tide."

"What makes you say that?" Jack said, squinting.

"That piece of seaweed there." I pointed to a bedraggled strand of dirty green clinging to the wall outside. "If the tide was in, would it come through the portal?" A mental image of seawater crashing in around our legs, our waists, made my palms sweaty. My feet shuffled with the urge to dive through the exit.

"No. If it did, the ground here would be wet." He scuffed the dry dirt underfoot with his shoe.

"Then how does the ocean smell get through?"

He shrugged. "It just does. Are you ready?"

"Yes. Let's get out of here."

A brief, dizzy sensation brushed over us as we stepped out of the portal and onto the sand. I'd started growing used to that feeling of being yanked from one reality to another. Thankfully, I didn't get the gut-wrenching nausea Sarah experienced when she'd come into the *sidhe* with me. One of the perks of being a half-breed.

It was cool in the shallow cave. An insistent wind blew in, ruffling my shirt and tangling the end of my ponytail. I narrowed my eyes to slits as we walked into the sunlight, uncomfortably bright after so long in dimness. Damp sand crunched underfoot.

The portal nestled in the side of a headland, under a looming overhang scoured away by the tide. The cave's walls, on the other hand, were only a couple of feet deep, just sufficient to obscure our exit from any watching eyes on the nearby beach. How did the locals explain the edges' peculiar resistance, given the centre was worn away? Did they even notice it? I shaded my eyes and peered to my right; there was a single person on the strand, an older man who examined the ground at his feet with great focus. Looking for seashells, maybe.

Jack walked over to the rocks and studied the churning surface of the water as though he expected to see a siren emerging from the foam with a shark-toothed grin. Maybe he did.

"How do we find them?" I crossed my arms and gazed past his shoulder at the sea.

"There are ways to send a signal. We will come back tonight after dark, when there is less chance of being observed."

"Then what are you looking for now?"

"Sometimes they—or other things—find you. They react to the resonance of the portal being used." His voice was flat.

"Ominous." The tiny hairs on the back of my neck stood to attention.

"It can be."

CHAPTER NINE

"Right then," I said brightly, shaking off the sense of impending doom and setting out for the beach and the inevitable walkway that would lead us over the dunes. "Let's go get some food. I'm starving."

"You are sure there will be food here?" Jack replied.

I glanced back. "Of course. I don't know where we are exactly, but it's somewhere on the south coast of New South Wales. I've never seen a town yet that didn't have a little fish and chip shop. And fish on the coast is *way* better than the stuff you get in Canberra."

It turned out we'd emerged in Tomakin, a small town south of Bateman's Bay, only a twenty minute drive from where I'd stayed with Sarah, Ryan and Dominic when we'd come down to the coast a couple of months ago. After getting directions from a passing local, we found the general store. I was horrified to find they didn't have fish, instead buying a box of potato scallops, wrapped in white butcher paper. I also purchased a bottle of water from the glass-fronted refrigerator, feeling foolish for not packing one before we left.

I peeled my purse out of cling wrap to grab ten dollars from amidst the small stack of pound notes. The bubblegum-chewing girl behind the counter raised an eyebrow, but didn't say anything.

Warm box tucked under my arm, I led Jack back to the small, sheltered beach near the headland where the portal had emerged. We found a spot against the outcrop where the wind was less fierce, and sat on the sand to eat.

Jack regarded the bumpy yellow-brown discs in the box with a faint frown. "You say this is potato?"

"Uh huh," I said. "Careful, they're hot." I tore a strip of white paper from the wrapping and handed it to him. "Wrap that around the bottom half."

"And what has been done to the potato?"

"It's been battered in, well, batter. And deep-fried. Like chips, only better."

"I must admit it does smell good." I watched his expression as he nibbled the edge of the scallop. He beamed at me, and I grinned back. "Delicious. Although they taste like they would not be very good for you."

"Oh no, they're absolutely terrible." I laughed. "But I'm planning on doing a lot of swimming over the next week or so. I'll work it off. Besides, this is my last chance at carbs before switching to a seafood diet. Maybe it's a good thing they didn't have fish after all."

Although the coastline ran roughly north to south, our beach curved in the shape of a crooked finger, the headland at its tip facing east. After eating, we walked hand in hand to the lookout at the top of the headland and sat at a gaudily coloured picnic table to watch the sun inch towards the horizon behind a nearby hill. Behind us, painted in warming hues as sunset approached, the ocean continued its timeless dance with the rocks.

"Pretty view, is it not?"

The voice made me jump. There'd been no telltale crunch of approaching footsteps on gravel. Jack glowered as he regarded the stranger.

A short man—no taller than me or Jack—stood just out of reach. He wore long, loose-fitting jeans and a dark hoodie. Bright green eyes the colour of a fern's new growth gazed from his pale face, framed by the hood covering his hair.

My boyfriend stood so swiftly the breeze of his passage brushed my cheeks as he positioned himself before me. "I am Jack," he said, in his formal way.

"I am Perrin." The man's reply was equally formal. I looked harder at his face, picking out the fine tracery of wrinkles that marked a hob without a master.

The hood. Right.

The two hobs eyed each other. I stood, feeling left out. "I'm Isla."

Perrin glanced at me before his eyes returned to Jack. "Who is your master?"

"That is not any of your business." Jack crossed his arms. I couldn't see his face, but his shoulders were rigid with indignation and his aura was wary.

Perrin's aura, on the other hand, jangled navy blue with suspicion. "It is if you are here on behalf of an *aosidhe*. I will protect my people."

"We are no threat to you or your people."

"And why should I believe you?" Perrin's jaw worked as though he was grinding his teeth. Maybe he was.

MELPOMENE'S DAUGHTER

Oh, for the love of... I stepped forward to move between the two men, imagining myself wading through a cloud of testosterone. "Like I said, hi, I'm Isla—"

"Isla—" Jack put his hand on my shoulder, voice tense.

"—and I'm his master, if you must call it that. I usually call him my boyfriend." Behind me, Jack groaned. I ignored him, locking gazes with the other hob. I had his full attention now. "As you can see, I'm only half *aosidhe*. We're just passing through, and I swear we won't harm you so long as you don't try to harm us."

Perrin's eyes widened at this onslaught of information, and he shivered as my oath settled over both of us. His hostility and suspicion evaporated. "He is your boyfriend?"

"Yup."

"And your non-*aosidhe* half is...?"

I'd thought it was obvious, but bit back a sarcastic retort. "Human."

He blinked. "I have never heard of such a thing."

"Isla is unique." Jack placed a hand lightly on my arm. I curled my hand over his, conscious of Perrin's stare shifting to our interlocking fingers. His expression was unreadable even as his aura exploded with electric purple. Was an *aosidhe*—even a half-*aosidhe*—and a hob showing affection for one another so shocking?

I cleared my throat, breaking the awkward silence. "Anyway. We're here to look for undersea *duinesidhe*. Are they your people?"

"Of course not," Perrin said. I raised an eyebrow and he elaborated, "The seafaring *duinesidhe* have separate courts."

"With *aosidhe* rulers?" My stomach tightened with nerves at the thought. We'd never secure passage if we had to deal with my mother's people.

"No. Merfolk rulers. They threw off their *aosidhe* oppressors centuries ago," he said, his tone admiring. "If I may ask, what are you hoping to achieve in contacting them? They will not react kindly to you."

A mental image of the Little Mermaid danced in my mind, and I pushed it away. If these merfolk had been able to overthrow the powerful *aosidhe*, they wouldn't be anything like a cuddly Disney character. Also, the name Ariel reminded me with a pang of the vengeful hob I suspected of killing my grandmother. I licked my lips, tasting salt from the potato scallops. "We want to barter with them for passage through the undersea tunnels."

"If there are such things," my boyfriend muttered.

"Of course there are," Perrin said. Jack stiffened behind me, fingers tensing on my arm. I breathed a quiet sigh of relief that Welkin wasn't with us. He would have been insufferable. "Where are you trying to go?"

"The Old World," I said.

"Sailing would be safer." Perrin tipped his head to the side. A strand of dark hair fell forward over his eyes. He brushed it away with an irritated flick of his fingers.

"But not faster, and timing is kind of important."

"Why?"

I nibbled the inside of my lip, studying Perrin with narrowed eyes. Now his astonishment had faded, his emotions were a mixture of curiosity and—when he glanced at Jack—smug superiority. Because Jack was sworn to me, or because he hadn't known about the tunnels? Either way, I still wasn't sure whether to trust the strange hob. On the other hand, getting him offside by not answering the question would probably make the situation worse.

"An *aosidhe* has abducted my human father," I said finally. "We're going to get him back."

Perrin stared at me for several heartbeats. Did I make the wrong decision? Then he beamed a smile at me, as bright as the sun emerging from heavy clouds. "I admire your courage. You are completely mad, of course. But brave. And unique, as Jack says. I have never heard of an *aosidhe* caring enough to be inconvenienced on behalf of another. At least, not unless they are sworn to that person."

"Uh, thanks?"

"You are welcome." He bowed from the waist, a shallow inclination of the torso, then turned and pointed behind us, to the east. "See that island, off the next headland?" We nodded. "The humans call it Barlings Island. A pod of sirens often comes into the shallows there, to hunt fish or steal the bait from fishermen's lures. That is the best place around here to find seafolk."

Jack and I walked to the low log fence marking the edge of the headland, Perrin trailing behind us with his hands in his pockets. The small island—maybe seventy metres long—was at the other end of a long, sweeping beach with several optimistic fishermen spaced out along its length. The orange light of the setting sun bathed the island's forested sides, but also revealed the creeping tide slowly burying the jagged rock bridge connecting the island to the next headland. "We're going to get our feet wet getting over there," I muttered to Jack.

Behind me, Perrin barked a laugh. I glanced at him and he met my gaze, green eyes dancing with mirth. "Forgive me, but that is pretty funny. The entrances to the undersea tunnels are all underwater. You are going to get wet on this side, regardless. The sirens could show you where the nearest entrance is, if you can convince them. However, you are going to need to hold your breath on the way down. I hope you are a good swimmer."

"There is no place within the *sidhe* where the undersea and land tunnels connect?" Jack said.

Perrin shook his head. "They were destroyed long ago. Even their locations have been lost to memory. The merfolk guard their kingdom jealously."

I hugged my arms to my chest, trying to hide the shiver that ran through me. We'd assumed I could use my *aosidhe* magic to either modify the *sidhe* to be more hospitable to us, or adapt our bodies to the *sidhe*. But we were going to have to swim under our own steam to get to the tunnels—all before I could make any changes. In the freezing ocean. In the dark.

Jack wrapped an arm around my shoulder. "Are you cold?"

"A little," I said, forcing the words around a knot in my throat. "It's getting chilly." Jack met my gaze, his eyes sympathetic. Although he knew me well enough to see the lie, he didn't say anything. I turned back to Perrin. "Thanks for your advice, Perrin. We should be out of your hair before dawn."

"Good luck." He gave us another half-bow before striding down the slope towards the town. At the base of the hill, a tall, bulky figure stood up from behind a parked van and fell in beside him. A *powrie*? He'd brought backup. I couldn't blame him, really.

Scuffing loose gravel with the toe of my sneaker, I waited until the pair disappeared from sight among the houses. "Jack, how are we going to get to the tunnel entrance? What if it's a two-minute swim? Or five minutes?

I can't manage that."

Jack looked away towards the island. His face was increasingly in shadow as the sun kissed the horizon. "You will have to make the changes to our bodies before we speak to the sirens. We will need to be able to breathe underwater. Flippers would also not go astray."

I frowned. "Maybe I could magic up some diving suits."

"You could, although it would be safer if the changes were to us rather than to our equipment. A breathing device can be removed, and if you are unable to react swiftly enough..."

"So you're thinking, what, gills?" I said, laughing a little.

He nodded. "And webbing between our fingers and toes."

Eek.

"What if I get it wrong?" I whispered. "We looked at fish during biology, but I don't know how gills work. What if—"

"You will be fine," Jack said with a confidence I didn't feel. He took my hand, warm fingers curling around my frozen ones, and tugged lightly to start me walking. "The first thing we need to do is buy some meat as an offering for the sirens before that store closes."

CHAPTER TEN

The tide had crept forward during our second trip to the general store, inching towards the portal entrance with watery fingers. We waited until a surging wave retreated before darting forward, our shoes leaving divots in the wet sand behind us.

The tunnel was warmer than the cool evening air, but I still couldn't shake the lump of ice in my gut. The creeping realisation that I hadn't really thought through what this journey entailed made my throat close over. A journey through the ocean, an environment almost as hostile to humans as outer space. What was I thinking?

Ignoring Jack's expectant gaze, I closed my eyes and leaned my forehead against the curved wall, conjuring in my mind an image of my father. His crinkled, laughing eyes, so much like Sarah's. His hair, once bright red, now speckled with silver. His ready smile and callused hands, pocked with tiny scars from various mishaps around the farm.

I was doing this for Dad.

Straightening my spine as though it was one of Dad's iron rods, I opened my eyes and looked at Jack. The stargems in the glass jar he held cast gentle shadows across his cheeks, making him look more fay than usual. "Okay, let's make a list. Gills first. Only we still need to walk to the ocean on the other side of the portal, so we need to be able to breathe air as well. We need to be amphibious. Like a lungfish." A memory tickled my brain. "There's a Queensland fish with lungs that can also breathe through its gills. A barramunda, I think it's called. But—" I swallowed hard "—I don't know the exact biology. Jack, we're talking about massive changes to our bodies."

"It seems to me the best thing to do is not to overthink it." He brushed the hair back from my face. "Tell the *sidhe* what you need, and let it provide."

"It seems?" I squeaked. "You don't know for sure?"

"Well … no. I do not have your particular talent. But I assure you no *aosidhe* I have ever met has been a child of science. They just decided what they wanted and then did it."

That made sense. If it worked for my mother and Everest, why wouldn't it work for me? Also, it's not like I knew a lot about dentistry, and I'd still been able to change Gall's teeth without any problems. The lump of ice thawed slightly. "So, you think we need webbing for our fingers too?"

"Yes. There's also the matter of the cold. Perhaps changing our clothes to something more suitable would be appropriate after all."

"How about I do that first? As a sort of dry run. No

pun intended."

Jack laughed softly.

I stared at his outfit—jeans and a plain T-shirt—and thought about what we needed. I'd web our hands, but decided on flippers for our feet. Once I had the image firmly fixed in my mind, I projected it onto Jack's clothing.

I'd had my eyes closed when I conjured Talbot's tree, and when I changed Gall I'd been half-blinded by the inferno of his rage. I stared now as Jack's clothing writhed and shrank, growing glossy and smooth as it compressed around him, hugging the contours of his body. The colour shifted to black with cobalt blue lines running down the outside of his arms and legs, and in a V shape across his torso and back, matching a photo I'd seen of a wetsuit on Facebook. For visibility underwater, I guessed. His sneakers changed to black dive boots, and a pair of open-heeled flippers like ones I'd worn snorkelling as a child shimmered into life over the top of them. Only his were plain black, not princess-themed as mine had been.

Without pausing to overthink it, I made the same change to my own clothes—although my wetsuit high-lights were green rather than blue. Jack ran his gaze over me appreciatively. Realising how tightly the suit clung to my chest and hips, my cheeks burned with embarrassment. He raised a hand to his face to hide a smile. Determined not to be outdone, I stepped forward and trailed my fingers across the fabric on his chest. It was smooth under my fingertips. "That looks good on you," I murmured.

Jack shivered, his eyes darkening with sudden feeling that made my head spin. Curling a hand in my hair, he leaned forward and kissed me, long and slow, until I shivered too.

When we stepped apart, I cleared my throat. *Focus. You can do it.* "Um. So. Now I need to do the hard part." I remembered the pain of healing my two tiny blisters. "This is really going to hurt, isn't it?"

"Yes."

"Way to reassure a girl."

"Would you prefer I lied?"

"There's not a lot of point. I already know the answer." I brushed his cheek with my fingers and whispered, "I don't want to hurt you."

"I know."

"And I'm going to. What if—"

"It will be fine." His voice sounded calm until he added, "Just make it quick." Nervousness—not quite fear—shimmered in his aura like a heat wave. Trust pulsed there too, in time with the heartbeat I could see beating against the skin of his throat.

If he could be strong about this, I could too.

Gills. Webbed fingers. I pictured them in my mind as best I could, sending a silent plea to the *sidhe* to fill in the blanks.

Sweat beaded on Jack's brow as energy flowed from me. His eyes glassed over and his jaw clenched as he took long, slow breaths through flaring nostrils. I stared down at his hands, my vision blurring; flaps of smooth, pale skin grew between his long, slender fingers like tiny sails. The wetsuit's sides rippled and split with a sound that resembled tearing paper as gills ruptured from the skin under his arms.

I dropped to my knees, suddenly weak, and looked up at him. His aura swam before me, shot through with white lightning bolts of pain. I shook my head, slowly. Had I ever been able to see pain before? I couldn't recall, but if I could see it...

I reached out, drawing his agony into myself. A brief flash of fire through all of my nerve endings made me gasp. Then the feeling was gone.

So was the dizziness. I stood, staring at Jack. The frills of his gills were still growing, changing, along the length of his ribs. But his eyes were clear. I watched in fascination until the change stopped before studying his face. He was breathing normally, at least as far as I could tell without wetting my finger and holding it under his nose. "How do you feel?"

"Fine," he replied, his tone ringing with disbelief. "What did you *do*?"

"Gills and—"

He cut me off. "I mean it hurt and then it did not. That was you?"

"I took the pain."

"The same way you would an emotion?" I nodded, and he tried to run a hand through his hair before stopping to stare at the webbing. "I have never heard of an *aosidhe* being able to do that before. Isla, that is incredible."

I shrugged, faintly embarrassed. "It looked like a win-win situation. Because I felt like crap for a moment there. My body seems to have converted the pain to energy, same as if it was fear or any other emotion." My eyes widened as I realised the implications. Aunt Elizabeth had a friend who suffered chronic back pain. I could take it away, give him a normal life. Or I could make physical changes to any *duinesidhe* that wanted them, and it wouldn't cost me anything or hurt them. "Wow,"

I breathed.

"Wow indeed." Jack's eyes were wide, awestruck. I could see the whites around those sea-blue pupils.

Uncomfortable, I looked down at my still-normal hands. My watch bulged around my wrist, under the wetsuit; I took it off and tucked it into my backpack. "Unfortunately if it's anything like emotions, I won't be able to take my own pain," I said, thinking aloud. "Ah, screw it." And I willed the change on my body.

To say the pain was similar to what I'd experienced when I healed my feet was like saying a candle flame is similar to a bonfire. My fingers cramped with agony. My ribs screamed as though someone had slashed them with a knife: one, two, three, four times on each side. A long, low moan came from my lips. I didn't seem able to stop it. My hands wavered before my eyes, flaps of skin stretching from the side of each digit to meet in the middle. It hurt to breathe; I struggled for air, and it whistled in my throat...

The pain stopped as if someone had blown that candle out, doused that fire. I slumped in Jack's arms. He held me gingerly, tears glittering in his eyes.

"That," I wheezed, "was awful."

"I am so sorry. There was nothing I could do."

"I know. I didn't expect you to." Easing myself out of his arms, I stood up straight. I didn't feel as full of energy as I had moments before, but I wasn't falling over with weakness either. In fact, I felt like I'd walked for hours—which I had, so I guessed all was back to normal.

Normal. Yeah, right.

I examined my changes with a critical eye. The webbing between my fingers resembled Jack's. When I pinched it lightly, I discovered the nerves weren't quite as sensitive as those in the rest of my hand—it was more like touching the cartilage of my ear, although the webbing was more flexible than that.

The feeling of cool air where there had been none before drew my hands, tentative, to my sides. I ran my fingertips down my ribs, brushing the flaps where smooth skin used to be. "Ick."

"You will get used to it."

"Are *you*?"

He grinned a reply.

Picking up my waterproof backpack, I hooked it over my shoulders and turned towards the entrance. "Shall we?" I took a step forward. The tip of the flipper scraped on the tunnel floor; I caught myself before I tripped, reaching down to slip the awkward thing off over the boot. "Okay, maybe we should put these on once we're in the water."

"It is not that far to the ocean. I will be fine."

I glanced at him as I unhooked the back of the second flipper. "I thought we were going to walk along the beach to Barlings Island."

He shook his head, untying his bandana and shaking his hair free. It fell to his shoulders, the same length it had been since I met him. Did his hair even grow? Or did Evie cut it for him? "I would suggest not. Those fishermen are probably still there. We would attract too much attention in these outfits."

"Oh. That makes sense. I guess." My stomach quivered with nerves. I wanted to tuck my hands in my pockets to hide that they were shaking, but I didn't have pockets anymore. Instead, I put them behind my back.

Jack looked at the bandana for a moment as though wondering what to do with it. Then he folded it neatly and, drawing one of my arms back towards him, wrapped it around my wrist. He tied it securely. "There. For good luck. Not that we will need it," he added hastily.

I looked at the bandana, affection for him a warm spot in my chest. "Now I want to give you something."

"You have already given me gills." His eyes twinkled. "Is that not enough for one day?"

"Not really." I took the jar of stargems from his hand and studied it with a frown. Unscrewing the lid, I tipped the glowing specks of stone into my palm. *This is what stardust must look like.* Taking a breath, I curled my fingers around the little pile, willing it to change.

The light grew brighter, seeping between my fingers. I opened them to reveal a single gem in the shape of a star, no wider from point to point than the length of my thumb. A small hole at one tip allowed me to thread a chain through it—a chain I conjured from the glass jar, forcing it to shrink and change into silver, translucent links that looked like they were spun from glass. Which I guess they were.

"I hope you like it." I fastened the chain around his neck. The star sat in the centre of his chest, level with his heart.

"It is perfect," Jack breathed, taking my hand.

Together we walked through the portal and back into the real world.

The sun had set while we were inside the tunnel. The sky to the west was stained faintly with a blue several shades lighter than the sky above. Stars winked into life as I craned my neck to look up. The moon hadn't risen yet, and the headland blocked the lights from town. If it weren't for Jack's pendant, we would have been in trouble.

Water rushed across my feet, cool against the wetsuit. I glanced down, surprised—I'd forgotten the tide was coming in. The water looked black, only the lacy foam on top visible.

Feeling someone watching me, I turned to see Jack examining my face.

"What."

"You are beautiful."

"Uh, I... Thanks." I squeezed his hand. "You're not too bad yourself." Feeling awkward, I soldiered on. "Jack, I was just thinking. Should I have changed our eyes so we could see in the dark? It's going to be black as tar down there, and I don't glow in the real world." I swallowed acid in the back of my throat. The idea of experiencing that searing pain *in my eyes* made me want to flee screaming across the dunes.

Jack seemed to understand my hesitation. "We still have the stargems. Stargem, I mean." He brushed the pendant with his fingers, a soft smile tugging his lips. "We should be fine." He looked to our right, towards the smaller beach. It was empty—perhaps it was no good for fishing. "We should enter there rather than off the rocks. It will give us a chance to get used to our new condition before we fully immerse ourselves."

And make sure I did it right, I thought with a grimace. My self-doubt loomed as large in my mind as the headland did behind us; I pressed my lips together to keep it from spilling out in panicked words.

We turned towards the shore. Jack walked beside me, graceful despite still wearing the awkward flippers that had nearly landed me on my face. Maybe preternatural grace should be next on my list of physical upgrades.

Assuming I could face another bout of personal modification.

We stepped together across the last of the rocks and onto the beach. The ocean tugged at a few strands of seaweed left on the sand at the previous high tide, each wave sighing up the beach. The surface of the water farther out glittered in the light from Jack's pendant. I strained to see something—anything—deeper in. I couldn't. "You can tell I can't change the real world," I muttered, pausing near a limp strand of kelp. It looked black in the dimness. "If I could, a beautiful full moon the size of half the sky would rise right now. What phase of the moon is it, anyway?"

"Half." Jack led me forward when my steps faltered. Soon the water was up to my knees, then my waist. He trailed his hand through the swell of an oncoming wave, and then looked at his dripping fingertips with a puzzled expression. "Did you do something to our ability to sense the cold through our skin too?"

"No. Just the wetsuits."

"I would have expected the water to feel much colder than it does. When we were down here in mid-summer, it was colder than this at night." I nodded, remembering how frozen my feet would be by the end of one of my lessons with Mako, the siren who had taught me. "At first I assumed it was the suit, but it only feels cool to my fingers too."

"Maybe there's a warm current or something." I dipped my hand into the water. Jack was right. It was lukewarm, the same temperature as cooling bathwater when I stayed in the tub reading a book until my toes went wrinkly.

"Maybe it is an example of the *sidhe* doing what needs to be done to fulfil your desire," he said, turning towards me and squeezing my hand a final time before letting it go. His voice was soft when he added, "You should put your flippers on now. It is time to go deeper."

Shivering—and not with the cold—I dunked the flippers under the water to fill them, and then bent over to wiggle the toes of my boots into the holes. I fastidiously adjusted the strap on each one, not wanting to admit I was stalling, even to myself.

Think of Dad, I reminded myself, gritting my teeth. *This is for him.*

When the next wave rolled through, raising the water to chest height, I dived under it.

I'm not someone who jumps straight into a swimming pool. I like to ease myself in, growing slowly used to the change in temperature. The sudden onrush of cool water over my head and torso made me gasp.

Only my mouth was closed.

The gasp was the gills under my arms flaring as they tasted water, drinking it in and filtering the oxygen from it. I'd expected seawater to burn or sting. Instead, it felt … refreshing. A tall glass of icy water after being outside on a scorching-hot day.

I burst from the water on the other side of the wave, brushing my hair back from my eyes, and turned to face Jack. He stared, open-mouthed. A giggle bubbled from my lips. The relief was almost dizzying. "The gills work," I gasped, trying to swallow my mirth.

"Of course they do." His aura blazed with trust. "Were you able to see much down there, after all?"

I realised I'd forgotten to open my eyes, and burst out

laughing again.

A figure on the sand dune caught my attention. It was a silhouette, black against the ambient glow of distant streetlights, but I could tell it was a hob. He'd pushed his hood back and the shape of his ears was visible even at this distance. Perrin.

As I stared at him, he lifted a hand and waved. I waved back, trying not to notice how he shook his head as he turned away.

My laughter vanished like a popped soap bubble.

CHAPTER ELEVEN

We swam through the darkness, a couple of metres below the ocean's surface. Jack was in the lead, star pendant a beacon around his neck, its light drawing me after it. I swam after him, trying to find a stroke that worked underwater—at first I'd tried freestyle out of habit, but all that windmilling hadn't helped. The voice of my swimming instructor yelling at me echoed in my mind, making me grimace.

I looked down. Jack's light barely reached the ocean floor. As we swum over sand banks, I caught glimpses of furtive movement—fish scurrying for cover—but for the most part I could see only darkness.

Jack caught my attention by waving a hand in front of my face, pointing up to the surface, which shimmered and danced above us. I nodded and followed him up. One thing we hadn't considered was that we'd be unable to talk underwater. Once we got to the *sidhe* entrance—if we did—I could fix that. For now, there was nothing to be done but to surface periodically.

"What is it?" I said, wiping the water from my eyes with one hand.

"I just want to get my bearings." Jack narrowed his eyes, scanning the shoreline. We'd swum halfway along the beach—only we'd cut across where it curved around, the string to its bow. The water's surface seemed brighter to my eyes than it had earlier. At first, I thought it was just that I'd grown used to the dimmer world below, but when I spun in a slow circle, I spied the moon, peeking above the horizon.

That would make things easier.

I followed Jack's gaze to the looming shape of Barlings Island, dark against the stars. "Do you think Perrin's right?" I murmured. It seemed somehow rude to speak loudly, as though the night was holding its breath. I also wasn't sure how far the sound of our voices would carry over the water. The last thing we needed was an overzealous fisherman coming to our rescue. "Are there any sirens around?"

"I am not sure," he admitted. "If there are not, we can just as easily send that signal I mentioned from there as from the first headland. At least we have had a chance to grow acclimatised to the water."

"True."

"And why would you land faeries be looking for sirens?" a voice hissed from the black expanse of featureless ocean to our backs.

The hair stood up on the nape of my neck as we turned in a flurry of bubbles to look. Although we craned our necks, we couldn't see the voice's owner; he or she was lost among the bobbing waves.

"We want to make a deal," I said, trying to sound

confident—although my thoughts strayed to the great bulk of water looming below us, another way someone or something could approach, attack. I hoped my nervousness didn't show.

"What sort of deal?" There was amusement in the voice, reminding me that sirens—if it was a siren—could smell emotion as easily as I could see it. That was why Mako had taught me in the first place. So much for pretending to keep my cool.

With tiny movements, Jack drifted forward, easing himself between me and the voice. I was acutely aware of how futile the gesture was—he couldn't be everywhere at once—but appreciated it anyway. "We wish to find an entrance to the underwater *sidhe*," Jack said, "and were hoping a siren might take us to one."

"And why do you want to find such an entrance, hob?" The voice was suspicious. "Does your master plan an invasion?"

I couldn't help it; I laughed.

"Is something funny?"

"I'm sorry," I said, swallowing my mirth. "It's just that I wouldn't have thought the two of us were a particularly effective invasion force."

Jack glanced back, his eyes meeting mine. They were eerily lit from below by the pendant, which hung below the waterline; as Jack's movements made ripples, their shadows wavered over his face. "You would be surprised what a single, unopposed *aosidhe* can do," he whispered.

"I've been told not to underestimate the *aosidhe*," the siren said, echoing Jack's words. The sound of faint splashing accompanied a hint of movement as a low, round shape drifted forward through the water.

"You've been told?" I asked.

"I've never met one. There aren't *aosidhe* in the oceans anymore," the creature said, its voice heavy with satisfaction.

"Lucky you," I said fervently.

"You don't like your own kind?"

"Not so far. Look, we don't plan to invade anything. We just want to bargain with the merfolk for passage."

There was a pause in which the voice muttered, "Good luck with that." Then it addressed me again. "How do I know you're telling the truth?"

I tried to keep the impatience out of my voice. "I swear I'm not planning an invasion. Neither is he."

"Good enough." The creature's tone was bored. Maybe it didn't care that much what happened to the merfolk. "And what would you offer me to take you to an entrance?"

"We brought sausages." The offering was a little embarrassing. I'd been hoping for steak, not thin, cheap sausages. They didn't even have herbs in them. Unfortunately, they were all the store had.

"Oooh. Sausages." The shape drew closer. I could see its liquid black eyes now, wide and dark. The siren's head was hairless, covered with silvery-blue skin, and it had small, round ears. "Show me."

"First, do you swear to take us to the tunnel entrance, as agreed? With no attempts to trick or mislead us?" Jack scowled at the creature.

"Do you swear not to try and hurt me or my pod?" the siren countered.

"We will if you do," I said.

"Agreed."

Once the oaths had been exchanged, we closed the

gap between us and the siren. It regarded us with avid eyes as Jack moved behind me and removed the sausages, still in their foam packet, from a side pocket on the backpack. He handed the packet to the creature with a solemn nod.

"Excellent." It pierced the film with the tip of a finger, drawing the string of sausages out and releasing the packaging to drift away on the tide. I grabbed it before it moved out of reach and handed it to Jack, gesturing for him to put it back in the bag. Who knew when we'd next encounter a garbage bin? "Kids! Kids!" the siren called. "Mama has a treat."

Oh, she was female? Her face was similar, physically, to Mako, the male siren who'd taught me: small nose, tiny round ears and huge eyes. I couldn't see any obvious differences between her facial structure and his to indicate her sex.

There might be more obvious signs below the water, but I'd never seen Mako from the waist down. Mercifully.

Water splashed up around us as one, two, three heads popped up from the waves. Small hands waved as she broke the string of sausages into segments and tossed one to each child. They giggled and squealed, excited, as they snatched up the treats. They were kind of cute—until they opened mouths full of shark teeth and swallowed the raw sausages whole, gnashing enthusiastically.

"Land meat tastes so *good*, Mama," one child piped, its eyes drifting towards us with a glint I didn't like.

"I know, sweetheart." Her long fingers stroked the child's head, reminding me of the way Aunt Elizabeth used to ruffle Ryan's hair before he'd cut it short.

"If they drown," the child whispered, loud enough that

we could hear it, "are we allowed to eat them?"

"You swore to lead us to the entrance," Jack said, his voice hard.

"So I did." The siren looked at the child. "You know the rules. We can't harm anything not born in the sea."

"But if they *happened* to die..." the child said wistfully. I couldn't believe I'd ever thought it was cute, even for a second.

"If they did, their bodies would be fair game. But if they do, it won't be because of anything we did. Mama swore."

"Okay," the little siren sighed, long-suffering, before diving under the waves. The other children followed.

The silence was awkward. "I'm Isla, by the way, and this is Jack."

"I'm Angel," the adult siren replied, gazing after her children. Surprise widened my eyes at her name. Her nose quivered, obviously scenting my reaction at her words. Her laugh was a hiss. "Named after the shark."

"Oh."

"Let's go." Angel dived below the waves with elegant grace. Jack and I splashed after her, him again taking the lead. There was no sign of the juvenile sirens, for which I was grateful.

Now I was able to see the full length of Angel's body, I could tell she was female. Although she was lean with slender hips, small breasts curved across her chest. She was naked, but her physique was so alien it didn't occur to me for several seconds that I should be embarrassed at the frank way I was studying her. She swam lazily, kicking her legs in slow, powerful strokes. Her hands extended before her like the prow of a ship, cutting through the water with much less splashing than Jack or me. She glanced back at us, meeting my gaze with a contemptuous expression. I swallowed my irritation and, concentrating, tried to emulate her style.

Busy focusing on my strokes, I was surprised when we reached the ocean floor, almost propelling myself into the loose sand. As it was, my flippers grazed the surface, raising a cloud of loose silt to fill the water around us. It glowed white in the pendant's light. I narrowed my eyes to slits, unable to make out any details, and looked around for Jack.

Something grabbed my arm, hard. I squeaked as I was yanked upward, out of the cloud. Angel glared, letting me go.

I tried to look apologetic, rubbing my arm. Embarrassment made me cringe. I hadn't realised it would be so easy to stir up the sand at the bottom—I'd have to be more careful.

With a faint sound that on land I would've described as *humph*, the siren led us along the ocean floor, staying a couple of metres above it, where we couldn't get into too much trouble. As the ground dropped away, she followed it down. Soon the sand became scarcer, replaced by loose stones. Larger, shell-encrusted rocks stood out proudly, and a seaweed forest swayed back and forth in a hypnotic pattern, moving with the currents. I stared, fascinated, as a crab watched us pass with upturned, threatening claws, like a boxer anticipating a blow. What would it do if we came down there, I wondered? Maybe it was just drawn to the passing light. I glanced up; we'd descended so far the weak moonlight didn't penetrate. Or maybe the moon had gone behind a cloud.

I didn't own a diving watch so I had no way to judge

the passage of time. I guessed we'd been swimming for maybe a half-hour when the pendant's light revealed a greater darkness before us, a ravine that opened up in the ocean floor. Jagged rocks along its edges reminded me of the siren's razor-sharp teeth. Angel paused, pointing downward. Jack's gaze met mine and I shrugged faintly. We'd come this far. What choice did we have?

Squaring his shoulders, the hob nodded, and we set off again.

As we approached the top of the ravine, it loomed larger before my eyes. An enclosed space, underwater? My mind went blank. I froze, slowly drifting forward under my own momentum as my claustrophobia clawed through my chest and up into my throat, sitting there in a burning lump. I knew from bitter experience the feeling would normally make me choke, stop me from breathing—except my gills kept working as normal.

Realising I was no longer beside him, Jack returned to my side, taking my hand and stopping my drift with the current. His aura was full of concern, speckled with frustration. At me? Or that he couldn't speak?

Angel's face appeared before mine, liquid black eyes glittering in her alien face. There was no concern in her aura. Instead, amusement and greed warred there.

Greed?

Movements slow and graceful, she pointed from me to herself and back again. My mind struggled as though wading through mud, but I forced myself to focus on what she was trying to convey.

Rolling her eyes, she put her hand to her chest and opened her mouth. A single note came out, high-pitched as a whale's song. Then she dropped her hand and looked at me again. Questioning.

Did I want her to sing away my panic?

I nodded vigorously, my hair drifting around my face. Jack looked between us, a frown forming between his eyes.

Angel began to sing again.

Before they were bound with an oath not to harm anything living that was born on land, sirens had terrorised sailors across the world, drawing their ships to wreck on rocky coves and then picking over the smashed remains for tasty morsels. The poets had taken some creative license, describing them as beautiful women rather than shark-toothed monsters.

But they'd nailed it when it came to their song.

Angel's voice, wordless and beautiful, filled the water around us as though every particle absorbed and amplified the sound. It was as sweet as birdsong, as melancholy as a violin playing an elegy. The sound seeped into my body, filling it with a strange lethargy. Beside me, Jack's gaze fixed on Angel, a small smile curving his lips.

When the music finished, I looked around as though waking from a dream. The water was crowded with an assortment of small fish and a long, sinuous eel, summoned forward by the strange magic. Angel's children were scattered among the crowd. Even as I noticed them, they burst into action, snatching up fish from the water around them and shoving them into their hungry mouths. One sucked up the eel like it was a long piece of spaghetti, smacking its lips together with glee. Blood and ... other things ... clouded the water.

Gagging, Jack and I dived to escape the gore, down towards the chasm. After regarding her offspring with amused tolerance, Angel followed.

MELPOMENE'S DAUGHTER

In clearer water, I regarded the close darkness of the entrance with a wary eye. The panic didn't return. Angel had drained it from me. Jack's eyes were wide with concern; I gave him a close-mouthed smile and a thumb's up, before turning to the siren and mouthing *thank you.* Could she lip read? It seemed unlikely, but she'd be able to smell my gratitude.

Intellectually, I knew I should have been worried about what Angel had just done—except worry would require me to be able to fear. Instead, I shrugged and swam down into the ravine, the others trailing after.

Behind me, Jack's light threw my shadow onto the rocks opening up before us like ragged stone petals. Did that make us bees? How did plants under the water pollinate anyway? Did they even have pollen? A hint of movement caught my eye, drawing my wandering mind back to the task. I peered into the blackness. What fish or crab was staring back at us, paralysed with fear and hoping we wouldn't eat it? Maybe it could sense Angel coming. After the display with the fish minutes before, I wouldn't blame it.

I glanced back and noticed the siren had changed her swimming style. Instead of holding her arms before her, she'd folded them across her chest. My eyes darted forward again, just in time for me to jerk my outstretched arms back before I sliced myself open on a blade of rock.

Arms close to the body in confined spaces. Right.

The rock closed in over our heads, barely a foot above my hair. We now swam down a dim, sharp-edged tunnel, an undersea cave. If I wasn't careful I'd cut myself to ribbons.

The light from the portal grew around us so subtly I

didn't realise we were approaching it until it appeared before us. It shimmered like the surface of a pool—in fact, it appeared identical in every way to the portals I'd seen on land. Interesting.

Jack crowded in beside me. We turned to face Angel. Her eyes were unreadable as she gestured to the portal and nodded her head. I could guess what she meant: *I've done as we agreed.*

I nodded back, smiling, and mouthed my thanks again. Even if she couldn't understand me, Dad had always taught me to use my manners. And it was the thought that counted, right?

Angel spun in place and then swam away from us, kicking her feet in little movements to avoid stirring up the water too much. Still, it swished around me like a caress. Jack looked at me, eyes wide. Impulsively, I leaned forward and kissed him on the cheek.

Then I swam through the portal.

CHAPTER TWELVE

I paused on the other side of the portal, waiting for Jack to swim in after me. The tunnel was huge, the biggest I'd seen that wasn't an actual *sidhe*, the pocket realms where the *duinesidhe* lived. The dim, wavering light cast by the portal barely illuminated the tunnel's edges. Curious, I drifted downward about six feet, running a finger along the bottom. The particles making up the floor were less grainy than the soil-like tunnels on land. Instead, they were crushed shale and fragments of broken seashell, reminding me of the grit Dad used to give my childhood budgerigar. I nicked the tip of a finger on a sharp piece of rock. Blood unfurled in a dark tendril, slow as incense smoke.

The light level increased abruptly. Jack floated above me, head whipping from side to side as he looked around. Sudden anxiety flooded his aura. I made a sound in the back of my throat, swimming up to poke him in the ribs. Relieved, he grabbed my shoulders and hugged me tight, then held me at arm's length and gave me a stern look.

This is silly.

I brushed my fingers against his throat, willing the *sidhe* to grant him the ability to speak underwater. As soon as I saw the flashes of pain in his aura, I siphoned them away, using them to power a similar transformation in my own vocal chords. For several heartbeats, it felt worse than having my tonsils out without anaesthetic.

Then the pain was gone.

When I opened my mouth and inhaled to speak, water flooded into my lungs. Bubbles, the last burst of air I'd brought with me from the surface, scattered around my face and were gone. The saltiness of the water burned as it rushed in. I didn't panic. I knew, looking at Jack clutching his throat, that I should be terrified. This was what drowning felt like. But my vision didn't darken; my lungs didn't burn from lack of air.

"It's okay," I said to Jack, pulling his hands away from his throat and hugging him to me as he struggled. "You're breathing the water. We're not drowning. Calm down." I siphoned the edge off his panic, reduced it so he could hear my words.

His movements slowed, stopped. A faint tickle of water moved against my ear as he took a deep breath, then another.

"That was ... unpleasant," he said finally.

"Sorry." Although the sound of my voice was curiously directionless and muted, the words were understandable.

"You were not afraid?" Jack asked, studying my expression at arm's length.

"Why would I be?" I said slowly, experimenting with projecting my voice. I could make the sound louder, but

I still couldn't pinpoint the direction it was coming from. *So weird.* "I guess we must be breathing water fully now. I wonder if that means we can't breathe air anymore. Remind me to fix that before we try and leave at the other end, okay?"

"Isla, focus." His voice was tight with concern.

"On what?"

"On what Angel did to you. You are not worried?"

"No." I laughed softly. "I guess that's to be expected, right? She took my fear away, so I can't be afraid that she took my fear away."

"Isla—"

"I didn't have a choice, Jack." I threw my hands up in exasperation, and the sudden movement made me drift away from him. "There's no way I'd have been able to swim down into the ravine otherwise. I'm not sure I'd have been able to swim in here either. And there's no other alternative."

"You could have flown over on a plane, like we discussed."

"As if I'm going to turn back at this stage, and leave you on your own."

"I know," Jack said with a sigh that didn't quite work underwater. "I am just concerned her change may be permanent."

"I know," I echoed him, drifting back to his side and patting his hand. He watched my gesture, looking bemused as I curled my fingers around his and tugged him into motion. Hand in hand, we swam down the tunnel. "We've got a long way to go, and I just think that if I *was* going to worry, it would be about the merfolk, not about myself. What do you know about them?"

"Not much," he admitted. "They are reclusive, avoiding contact with the land *duinesidhe*. I have never even heard of one coming out into the oceans of your world. Sirens I have met, but never a merman or mermaid."

"They must have at some point though, right? Or humans wouldn't have myths about them."

"I suppose so, yes."

We swam in silence for a while. My mind whirled. What would the merfolk be like? Somehow I doubted they'd be adorable redheads with sweet singing voices. If they had retreated to the underwater *sidhe*, they'd probably regard me with about the same amount of enthusiasm as the Australian *duinesidhe* did. Many of those had fled to Australia to get as far away from the *aosidhe* as possible.

I pulled a face. It'd be nice, just once, to meet a new group of *duinesidhe* who were happy to see me. Or at least neutral, rather than assuming I was up to no good.

Beside me, Jack stopped swimming, pulling me to a halt. He'd tipped his head to the side.

"What is it?" I murmured.

"I hear voices." He looked around, eyes wide. "We should take cover."

"Why? If they're merfolk, that's why we're here. Right?"

"But..."

"There's nowhere to hide anyway. We haven't passed any side passages or anything, and we kind of stand out." I grinned at him. "We'll just have to win them over."

Jack raised his eyebrows. Then he nodded, his shoulders drooping with resignation.

When the merfolk swam into the light from Jack's stargem necklace, they found us waiting in the middle of the passage, our hands hanging empty and loose at our sides as we tried to look harmless.

They looked anything but. Each of the two mermen—I was pretty sure they were male—held a short spear, maybe as long as my arm, and wore rough grey breast-plates made of some kind of leather strapped across their chests. Bracers encircled each muscular forearm and lit the water around each of them, the leather painted with a glowing substance. Their heads were hairless, covered with fine scales that shimmered like blue-green skullcaps in the light—the same colour as the scales on their long, muscular tails. Angular faces with flat noses and thin-lipped mouths regarded us with identical expressions of wide-eyed alarm.

Both mermen raised their spears. "Who are you? What are you doing here?" one of the mermen demanded, the sound of his voice reminiscent of rushing water.

I tried to smile, but couldn't tear my eyes off the pointed tips of the spears, sharp-edged pieces of black rock strapped to metal poles. "My name is Isla, and this is Jack."

"I think he's a hob," one merman muttered to the other, "although I've never heard of a hob with gills before."

The other glared at Jack. "You. Are you a hob?"

He nodded, a single, sharp gesture.

"And you?" The creature's gaze was hard as it slid across to me. "You aren't a hob."

"No." I nibbled the inside of my lip for a moment, trying to think of an answer that wouldn't result in us being skewered. "I'm a half-human. For the other half, I have the misfortune of having an *aosidhe* mother."

The merfolk stiffened, their auras shot through with

anger and fear. One jabbed the empty water before him with the spear. "What do you want, half-human?"

Huh. That's new.

"We wish to barter with the merfolk for passage through the underwater *sidhe*. We're travelling to England to..." I regarded their military demeanour and chose my words carefully. "To bring a challenge to an *aosidhe* there. She has something of mine and I want it back."

"And how do you have gills?" the same merman said, eyes glancing down at my exposed ribs as he brushed a fingertip along the side of his neck, where his own gills opened and closed rhythmically. He drifted closer, holding that spear before him; however, now the gesture seemed more defensive than threatening.

Still, a weapon wielded in fear was no less dangerous than one wielded in anger.

"I did that." I tried to keep my gaze on his face. It was difficult—the spear tip loomed larger the closer he came. "A perk of being half-*aosidhe* is I can adapt my own body to circumstances."

"And others' bodies?" His tone was heavy with meaning.

"Yes. But don't worry," I added quickly, "I don't do it unless asked."

The merman glanced back at his companion before turning to regard me again. The spear dropped a little, and his shoulders relaxed. His aura was no longer frightened; instead, a tiny violet flower of excitement unfurled amidst the flickering yellow uncertainty. "My name is Marin. Follow me."

"Where are we going?" Jack said, speaking for the first time.

"We are taking you to our leader."

I put my hand over my mouth to suppress a laugh.

The second merman, who hadn't introduced himself, muttered something to his companion. Marin's shoulders rose and fell, resigned, but he turned back to us. "First, I want you to swear you will not use your *aosidhe* powers in our realm unless given leave by our king or queen."

I narrowed my eyes. "I won't agree not to use them at all. How do I know I won't be attacked?"

"You may use them in self-defence only, then."

I sighed. "I swear not to use my powers on the merfolk while I'm in their realm unless I'm given permission by the king or queen or I'm attacked first. Good enough?"

The first merman nodded, although the second still looked unhappy. Jack frowned. "Will you swear not to attack *us*?" he demanded, folding his arms.

Marin narrowed his eyes, calculating. Then he smiled. "I swear not to harm either of you unless the king or queen orders me to or I'm attacked first," he said. The other merfolk repeated Marin's words, voice sullen.

Jack looked mutinous but I shook my head before he could protest. "It's fair enough," I said.

The second merman fell in behind Jack and me, while Marin turned in a smooth motion I envied, shooting off down the tunnel. We followed hastily. Fascinated, I stared at his tail as it pumped up and down in the water. It was longer than I'd expected, almost twice the length of his head and torso combined. If he'd been a person with those proportions, he'd look like he was walking on stilts.

"I should've given us tails," I said to Jack, eyes wide with admiration. "Look at how much better they are!" Before me, the merman stiffened at my words.

"It would have made it difficult to walk down the

shore," Jack replied.

I poked my tongue at him.

Other than the shale-like substance the tunnel was made of, another difference between the underwater tunnels and those on land was the number of intersections. Most of my land-bound journeys had involved slogging through monotonous passages so straight they would have made an architect proud. Not the ocean tunnels. They were still round, as though burrowed by something huge, but branched regularly, honeycombing the earth in a more natural way. I was glad for our merfolk guides—or guards. Without them, we'd have quickly become lost.

Maybe that was the idea? Had the sea *duinesidhe* encouraged this chaos somehow, to deter intruders or defeat an invading army?

I murmured my theory to Jack, who shrugged. "It would be an effective strategy," he observed. "The Old World tunnels are the same as those on land in Australia—straight lines with orderly intersections, when they occur at all. Strategy does not play an enormous part in *aosidhe* conflicts. The path is rarely unclear."

"Let me guess," I said, "they throw large numbers of *duinesidhe* slaves at one another."

"For the most part. The more powerful *aosidhe* have oath-sworn, weaker *aosidhe* in their service as well. Those battles are always the bloodiest."

"I can imagine." Conscious of the mermen's listening ears, I didn't say what I was thinking—the damage I could do with my still-new power to change the *sidhe* was awful. Breathtakingly so. Shaking the earth until it crushed anyone walking on it. Raining flaming debris from the sky. Even snatching the air from others' lungs. The only limitation was my imagination.

For the first time since we'd entered the sea, I shivered with cold.

"That is probably one of the reasons Everest was so keen to trap you with an oath," Jack added. "To build his powerbase."

"And here I thought it was my sparkling personality."

"That too." He smiled and squeezed my hand.

"You're wrong about our tunnels," Marin said, glancing back. He paused, hanging in the water before a side tunnel. When we reached his side, he led us down the new passage, which was as mammoth as the first. "We've made some changes, but haven't added detours. It's always been like this."

"Then why would the land tunnels be so different?" I wondered.

"Our stories say it's because of the humans." Dislike bled into Marin's aura as though from a slow wound. "The crawling, expanding cities they build are slowly reshaping the insides of the *sidhe*."

"And polluting our water," the other merman growled from behind us. The merfolk clearly cared more about pollution than Angel, with her casual disposal of the sausage packaging.

Marin ignored the interruption. "If you found a *sidhe* in the heart of your country, away from the humans, the tunnels around it might be much like this. Organic. Natural."

I wonder what would live there? I'd never stopped to consider whether there had been native *duinesidhe*—or some Aboriginal Dreamtime equivalent—before the European ones arrived, refugees from violent overseas courts. Even the wild *karkadann* had come from overseas. After I met them I'd looked them up online, guessing at the spelling till I got it right, and discovered they were originally from Persia.

"After all this is done," I declared on an impulse, "I might just do that. I've always wanted to see Uluru anyway."

Raising his eyebrows, Jack opened his mouth to speak. Movement from beyond our guide silenced him.

Something dark extracted itself from a crack in the wall no wider than my forearm was long. I stared as it freed itself, shooting in front of Marin, who regarded it with narrowed eyes.

The creature was small, with a humanoid body the size of a child's—but from the waist down, instead of legs or a mermaid's tail, it had eight tentacles that undulated gently in the water. Both halves of the creature were the same colour, a magnificent midnight blue that would conceal it perfectly in the ocean depths.

I hadn't realised half-octopi were a thing.

As we stared, the creature opened its mouth and hissed. Then it uttered a series of clicks and hisses at Marin that sounded like a malfunctioning kettle. The merman shook his head once, sharply, and the creature turned to glare at us.

"This is a *cecaelias*," Marin said, glancing at us. He pronounced it se-*kay*-lee-ah. I noticed he kept one hand on the shaft of his spear.

"It doesn't like me much, does it?" I said. Scarlet rage that would do a *powrie* proud shot through the creature's aura. I tensed, expecting it to charge at us, but it hung in the water, snarling and spitting.

"Not much, no. She requested I slay you immediately."

Beside me, Jack stiffened. I tried to sound calm when I replied. "I hope you said no?"

Marin nodded, the hint of a smile twitching the corner of his lip. "Her kind universally hate humans."

"Seems reasonable," the other merman muttered from behind us.

The hair stood up on the nape of my neck as I imagined his eyes drilling into the back of my head. "I assumed it was because of my *aosidhe* parentage," I said. Jack scowled, his hand clenching around mine until my fingers ached. I wriggled them and his grip eased.

"The *cecaelias* are a simple people," our guide said. "They don't have the long memories merfolk do—I'd be surprised if they even knew what an *aosidhe* was. Humans, though? Humans they know." His tone was grim.

Being blamed for the actions of an entire species felt a little unfair. But trying to explain to this *cecaelias* creature or the merman glowering behind me that I hadn't littered a beach in my life wasn't likely to get me far. Besides, I was getting used to the *duinesidhe* blaming me for *aosidhe* actions; the only difference this time was the angle the blame took now.

Also, I haven't done anything to save *the beaches, have I? Other than picking up the occasional plastic bag?* Somehow I didn't think that would be enough for any of them.

"Please tell her I'm sorry. For everything the humans have done."

Marin stared at me for a long moment before hissing a brief phrase at the creature.

The *cecaelias* spun, tentacles swirling in a way that would've been beautiful if the creature wasn't so furious, and spat at me. Black ink shot into the water. Jack and I scooted backwards, flippers and hands flailing, before the cloud reached us.

When it cleared, the creature was gone, squeezing back into the crack in the tunnel wall.

The other merman regarded us with disdain. Marin's expression was contrite. "She said—"

"I can guess. It wasn't complimentary."

"No." He squared his shoulders.

"Don't worry about it." My smile fell flat. "Shall we?"

We followed him for another ten minutes before my skin began to glow: the telltale sign we were approaching a *sidhe*, a magical centre of the faerie realm. My heart beat faster as I tried to imagine what sort of home the merfolk might have, and wondered what sort of reception we'd receive from Marin's leaders. Jack still clung to my hand—although not as tightly as before. *He's scared they'll harm us. I should be scared too. Angel really did a number on me.* The thought didn't bother me.

Two mermen emerged from the distant murk before us, standing—well, floating—sentinel on either side of a bright patch of water. They were a male and a female, dressed in the same grey armour as our guides. The female was as flat chested as the male beside her, with narrow hips. The scales on her head, tail and outer arms had less of the blue-green shimmer; in fact, compared to the males, her colours were drab. Her build was more slender, but her arms, when she crossed them, were corded with wiry muscles. I was confident she could tear me apart with her bare hands if she wanted to.

I hoped she didn't want to.

Both merfolk regarded us with a mix of curiosity and

hostility. Marin spoke to them briefly in a language more musical than the *cecaelias's* hissing, but still one I didn't understand. Jack and I exchanged a glance. Were we being sold up the river, as Dad would say?

The pair nodded. The female gestured to the entrance with her spear.

Marin led us through.

CHAPTER THIRTEEN

The tunnel fell away behind us as we swam into the cavernous *sidhe*. Below us, shining softly in a multitude of pastels that would have sent Ryan scurrying for his sketchbook, coral encrusted the ground—a sharp-edged, beautiful forest that would cut the unwary to pieces. Paths of sand wound through the coral, detouring around shell-speckled rocks. Tiny fish hugged the ocean floor—although the way they stopped to stare at us as we entered the *sidhe* made me wonder if they were fish-like, rather than being actual fish.

I'd never met a regular animal inside the land *sidhe*, although some *duinesidhe* resembled animals. At least sometimes. Why would the residents of the underwater *sidhe* be any different?

Above us, the cavern's ceiling was lost in darkness. Because it was night-time, or because, like the Canberra *sidhe* before I'd first gone there, they had no source of light beyond the glowing coral? I crossed the fingers of my free hand awkwardly, hoping I didn't accidentally create a moon here as I'd done at home.

Before us, in the centre of the huge space, a spire of twisted rock in the shape of a conch shell loomed. The sand paths spiralled in towards it. As we approached, swimming out and down, the spire seemed to grow taller and taller, until it towered over us, at least ten storeys tall. A giant tortoise—easily twelve feet from nose to tail—finned slowly past the structure. The creature regarded us with a disc-like eye, as unfathomable as the ocean itself, before disappearing from view.

"Wow," I murmured to Jack.

"Quite," he replied, subdued.

"Oh, come on, you must be at least a little bit impressed."

"I am," he said. "But I am also concerned about the type of reception we are about to receive."

"I suspect you'll be fine." Marin turned to face us. He kept swimming backwards, reminding me of a dolphin finning back through the water. "Isla can do something they want. Very badly."

"Quiet, Marin," the other merman barked. "Don't reveal all our secrets."

Marin glared at him. "They are about to find out anyway, Kai. You know they are. Don't be foolish."

Kai scowled. Marin rolled back onto his stomach. The silence settled uncomfortably.

"Your English is very good, Marin," I said tentatively.

"Thank you." Marin didn't look back. "Our people are taught the dominant language of the nearest humans when we are hatchlings."

I stared at Jack, mouthing, *Hatchlings?*

He shrugged, not looking as amazed as I thought he

should be.

Marin led us down to a tall entrance at the mouth of the conch shell, a huge open arch teeming with activity—activity that stopped as we entered. Adult and juvenile merfolk turned to stare. A creature that looked like someone had crossed a dog with a seal bared its teeth in a silent snarl as we moved past, while a tiny water sprite no bigger than Welkin pulled a face that would've done a prepubescent boy proud. His tongue was silvery blue. Still, no one moved to interfere. Feeling uncomfortable, I tried to ignore the stares; Jack was doing enough looking for the both of us, tensed for an attack.

Inside, the spire was lit by clumps of glowing coral, growing in small pots fixed to the floor at regular intervals. Their placement struck me as odd—the floor couldn't be convenient—until I realised that most *duinesidhe* using the passage were swimming through its centre, not going near the floor at all.

The passage spiralled upward, following the contours of the tower. The walls were as iridescent as the inside surface of an abalone shell, changing between silvery white, pink, red, green and deep blue as we moved along. I reached out and ran a finger along the smooth, undulating surface, smiling as I remembered collecting seashells with Dad and Sarah on the beach as a child. Something spherical and spikey rolled towards me from between the coral pots, grumbling. I withdrew my hand hastily. Was it worried I'd get my human germs on the surface? Certainly it didn't seem to care that one of the merfolk children was pressing her face up against the wall to study her distorted reflection.

Many passages and rooms branched off the central

hallway. Still, I had no doubt of when we'd reached our destination. Two mermaids, again dressed in armour, floated at attention on either side of the first door I'd seen since we entered the spire. Marin spoke to them in a soft voice—not that we would have understood his merfolk tongue anyway. The door itself looked to be made of crushed coral, arranged in intricate patterns that reminded me of drawings of the wind blowing through the sky. "Oh, it's sea currents," I said aloud when it dawned on me. Jack gave me a nervous look. I kissed him on the cheek, murmuring in his ear, "Would you like me to reduce your fear a little? Just to take the edge off?"

He shook his head; his golden hair tickled my nose and I brushed it away. "Fear helps me stay wary of danger. One of us has to be."

"Are you cross at me?" I studied his face—and aura—closely, seeing only exasperation and anxiety.

"You know I am not," he replied. "But I am worried for you. And, right now, for us."

"The king and queen will see you now," one of the mermaids said loudly, drawing our attention back to the gathering at the doorway.

The door swung outwards in a swirl of current, revealing a cavernous chamber that peaked in a pointed roof: the top of the shell. The floor curved up towards the centre, corrugated like an open clamshell. A bare white path in the centre provided a way for land-bound supplicants to approach the throne. Anemones in red and purple swayed on either side. Although we didn't walk on the path, Marin swam close to it rather than rising to the centre of the room. We followed cautiously, craning our necks to see the rulers of the merfolk, sitting on top of a glossy pillar of milk-white stone.

The queen had a similar shape to the other mermaids we'd seen: wiry, slender, built for speed and grace. But instead of plain armour over her flat chest, she wore an ornate breastplate crusted with coloured shells. The dull scales on her tail were set with cream and pink pearls. The mermaid equivalent of a ball gown? A coral crown sat on her scaled head, over glowering eyes in a suspicious face.

When I looked at the king, my mouth fell open.

He had the same blue-green scales on his tail as the other mermen. But his arms were bare skin, and his head was covered in fine, dark blond hair that flowed around his bare torso, almost to his waist. His crown was larger than his mate's, set with a huge black pearl as big as my fist.

He looked like a human with a fish's tail, a stereotypical merman from all the books I'd read as a child. Although they didn't usually have neatly trimmed beards...

"King Moana, Queen Nerida, may I introduce Isla, a half-human half-*aosidhe*, and Jack, her hob." Marin bowed low, a curious gesture that involved dipping his head lower than his tail. We awkwardly copied, wavering in the water as our flippered feet struggled for balance.

Nerida spat something at Marin, making the merfolk tongue seem harsh as crashing waves rather than musical as water over stone. Our guard replied quickly, his tone—and aura—apologetic. She fired back, indignant. Peering up through my hair, I studied her aura for signs of an imminent execution order. Dark blue distrust pulsed. Not scarlet fury. Not yet.

Movement from beside her on the throne caught my

eye. Moana had leaned forward, resting his elbows on his tail, planting them where his knees would be if he were human. He studied me with bright curiosity.

"Is it true?" he said in English, cutting across the rapid exchange between his mate and Marin. "Can you change others' bodies?"

"Yes, your majesty," I said with another bow. I took Jack's hand and splayed his fingers to show the webbing. He met my gaze, expression troubled, but turned obligingly and parted the side of his wetsuit to show the gills.

"Please, call me Moana," the merman said. Beside him, Nerida stiffened with outrage. He patted her hand. "Hush. Isla is half-*aosidhe*. She's as royal as I am."

Nerida replied in the merfolk tongue, her eyes wide.

"So does human blood," Moana replied. "Please, my pearl, speak in English for the sake of our guests."

I leaned in close to Marin and murmured, "So does human blood what?"

"Run in his veins." He studied the shell floor as though it held some great mystery. The quarrel between his rulers had his aura blushing a salmon pink.

Moana nodded, hearing us despite our soft voices. "Indeed it does, as I'm sure you can tell." He brushed a lock of hair back behind one rounded ear.

"How?" I blurted.

Fortunately, Moana didn't seem offended. "Over a century ago, a younger daughter of the king sought an *aosidhe's* aid to become human so she could be with her lover. Her son, when he was born, had a merman's features, including a tail and gills. His mother returned him to the sea rather than let her husband kill him. His uncles took the hatchling in."

"He was your ancestor?" I asked.

Moana nodded. "The last war between the merfolk and the *cecaelias* resulted in a great loss of life. That boy came to inherit the throne."

"What happened to his mother?" I breathed, eyes wide.

"She drowned." Moana hung his head. His hair drifted before his face, despite his efforts to brush it back. I should introduce him to hairclips. "She was my grandmother."

"How awful. I'm sorry."

Surprise flashed across Nerida's face, quickly concealed. It was her turn to pat her mate's hand; he smiled at her weakly. "Marin thinks you can help us," he said.

"If I can, I will." Jack gave me a warning look, and I added, "In return, I'm hoping you can help me with a problem of my own."

"You wish to purchase travel to England via our realm."

"Swift travel," I amended. "Time's kind of a factor. I need to be there in a few days, at most."

"What is it the *aosidhe* have taken from you?" Moana asked.

"My father." The words came out in a rasp. Angel hadn't affected my ability to feel grief.

The king slapped a hand on his tail; the sharp retort startled me. I spread my hands to steady myself in the water. "Then you shall have our aid."

"In exchange for your help with our situation," Nerida added hastily.

I bit the inside of my lip to stop myself from smiling. Her insistence on a fair trade reminded me of Jack's, both of them so determined to make sure their partners didn't give everything away too generously. "And what's that, your majesty?" I asked.

Moana gave the queen a reproachful look. "Please call me Nerida," she said grudgingly. Then she looked past us to one of the waiting mermaid guards, who hung back by the door with Kai. The queen started to speak in her natural tongue but caught herself and, glancing at her husband, said instead, "Fetch the princess." The mermaid shot away through the water, vanishing between one breath and the next.

As we waited for the mermaid to return, I became aware of how exhausted I was. It had to be approaching dawn on the surface, at least in my world. Biting back a yawn, I glanced at Jack. His shoulders slumped and, although his expression was resolute, shadows gathered under his eyes.

"Are you okay?" I said, taking his hand and kissing the back of it.

"Are you?" he replied.

"Just peachy."

"Then so am I."

"Jack—"

The sound of a high-pitched voice caught my attention. I turned to see the mermaid guard entering the chamber, her hand fixed around the upper arm of what could only be the princess.

The girl looked to be eight or nine years old. She had her father's golden, free-flowing hair and absence of scales. However, unlike him, instead of a tail she had normal, human legs ending in normal, human feet. I tried not to stare as she struggled to keep up with the swift-moving mermaid beside her.

Other than the gills fluttering at her throat, the girl looked entirely human.

"Princess Pania, this is Isla. She is half-*aosidhe*."

Pania regarded me with wide, sea-grey eyes. "You're part-human, like me."

I nodded. "My dad is human."

"Pania was first-hatched from her clutch, and the only one to survive." Sadness crept into Nerida's voice, as deep as the ocean itself.

"My clutch mates had tails but not gills," the girl added.

"Oh no." My hand flew to my mouth. Compassion for her parents made tears well in my eyes. They were drawn away into the ocean around me, one drop of salt among billions.

"I'm lucky," Pania replied. "Although I can't be queen without a tail, at least I'm not drowned."

"Would you like me to give you a tail, Pania?" I wasn't sure whether that was the favour Nerida was going to ask. Right then I didn't care.

Awe flooded Pania's face, as lovely as dawn gilding the ocean. She was beautiful. "Oh, yes! Can you?"

"I can." Her smile was contagious. "With your parents' permission, that is."

"Is it safe?" Moana asked, his voice knotted with anxiety. "She is the crown princess and my only heir."

"I'm not an heir with no tail." Pania frowned at her father, folding her arms across her bright leather tunic.

"Well, then, you are still my only child," he said with a bemused smile that reminded me with a pang of my own father. "That is more important than being my heir." His gaze flickered back to mine. "So is it?"

"It is safe."

"Then you have our permission," Moana said with a nod.

MELPOMENE'S DAUGHTER

"You had better be right," Nerida added, clenching her jaw. Her hands curled into fists on her lap. The subtext was clear: if I screwed up, we wouldn't be leaving in one piece.

"I'm ready." Pania lifted her chin. She shared none of her parents' anxiety.

"Okay." I looked between the girl and her mother, trying to study Nerida's tail with a critical eye. It was hard, though—my gaze kept being caught by her intense stare and its silent promise of a slow death if I hurt her child.

A tiny bubble of nervousness stirred in my stomach. Was my fear returning? I grimaced. Now wasn't the best time.

"Remember, Isla," Jack murmured in my ear. When had he swum so close? "The *sidhe* will fill in the blanks."

"I know." I took his hand and then reached for the princess. "Your highness, please come here."

She paddled over to me and slid her slender fingers into my free hand. They were cool, gripping me confidently. Poor, sweet child, crossbreed of two species whose natural environments were hostile to one another. It wasn't that she was deformed; she was beautiful, but so ill-suited to her home. My heart ached for her and her baby siblings who hadn't survived. For the poor children she might have one day.

Closing my eyes, I spent a few moments insinuating myself into her aura, where a beacon of hope glowed. I spread my power in a net around her, so I could siphon off the pain of transformation instantly, before it even came close to her nerve endings. Even a second of the agony of transformation would be unacceptable—to me and Pania, but, perhaps more importantly, to her vigilant parents.

Holding the vision of Nerida's powerful tail firmly in my

mind, I held my breath and pushed my will onto the *sidhe*.

Pain would have torn through her legs and feet as though they'd been sliced with knives. It would have seared her flesh and left her screaming.

Instead, it flooded into me as though someone had opened up a funnel in the bottom of the ocean and I was standing at the base of it, the full force of thousands of tonnes of water thundering into me. Every nerve in my body caught fire with the strength of the power. Some of it then flowed back from me into Pania, into her legs and belly, driving the force of her transformation. I still felt full to overflowing, jittery with adrenaline, fatigue banished.

Jack's hand gripped my own, and I heard his voice, although I couldn't understand the words over the roar of the magic.

"Jack," I gasped, eyes flying open. I thrust some of that power into him, driving his own exhaustion away like shadows vanishing when the light is switched on. He gazed at me, mouth open in shock. I could see the reflection of my brightly glowing skin in his wide eyes.

"The opal." His words finally penetrated over the power's roar. I nodded my understanding, shoving the remaining excess power into Gall's gemstone, which sat tucked in an inner pocket of the backpack.

Finally, the tsunami of pain-to-power slowed, stopped.

"Oh!" Pania's hand slipped from mine.

I turned, heart in my throat. What had I done?

The princess danced through the water, twirling, hands out from her sides. Her long hair spun around her, tangling her in its golden threads. Her graceful tail swayed from side to side, propelling her through the water.

She looked down and laughed.

MELPOMENE'S DAUGHTER

The tail was like and yet unlike her mother's: long, slender and powerful, with wide, translucent fins spreading from the end. But the scales, instead of being drab like the other mermaids' or even blue-green like her father's, were a thousand shades of white and pink.

They were the same colours as the pearls Nerida wore as decoration.

"Oops," I said.

"I love it," Pania trilled, swimming over and grabbing my hands. She spun us around in a circle till I grew dizzy. Laughter bubbled from my lips at the wide-eyed delight on her face. "It's wonderful. Much prettier than anything the *boys* have!"

She released me. Jack caught me in one arm, embracing me against his chest. "Good job." He grinned.

"Indeed," Moana said. I looked over to see him swimming down from the pillar throne, sweeping his daughter into a powerful hug. "You have done well, Isla."

"The colour is a little … unusual," Nerida said in a neutral voice. Approval and irritation warred in her aura, along with a tiny sliver of envy. Uh oh. "She will stand out from the rest of her people."

"She would stand out anyway. She *should* stand out," Moana boomed, holding his daughter at arm's length and studying her with a fond smile. His hair drifted in the water around him, mingling with Pania's. "She will be queen one day!"

"Yes." Nerida smiled slowly. Tension I hadn't realised I was carrying ebbed from my limbs. We weren't going to be decapitated after all.

Jack held me against him as I studied the princess and her changed physique, recalling the sensation of power flowing back into her. Into her belly. I gnawed a fingernail. Had the *sidhe* interpreted my sadness at her future children's probable difficulties as a request to interfere with her reproductive system? To change her DNA so no child of hers would be born without gills or tail?

The thought felt right, somehow. However, I kept my speculation to myself, not wanting to raise anyone's hopes in case I was wrong.

Finally, the king and his daughter turned to us, hand in hand. "You have done well by us. Now let us repay the favour. Let us help you save your father."

CHAPTER FOURTEEN

I stared. A pair of giant eyes, each as big as my closed fist, stared back.

"It's like a griffon," I finally said, unable to tear my gaze away from the creature. "Only with the head of a horse and the hindquarters of a fish. And scales."

Jack nodded. "Although anyone trying to harness a griffon would find themselves minus their internal organs."

"Griffons are real too?" My mouth fell open. This trip had certainly been educational.

"Of course they are." He lifted a hand to his mouth, probably to hide a smile. His aura sparkled deep pink with amusement. I poked my tongue at him.

Marin moved around the waterhorse, tack hanging from his hands. Slate-grey scales covered the creature's tail, shimmering in the light of a wall-mounted coral cluster, while the rest of its hide resembled dolphin skin, a shade paler on the belly. He fastened the grey harness on either side of the forelimbs—large, seal-like flippers instead of hooves—and over the back behind the withers. A simple looped handle attached to the top of the harness. The creature arched its hairless neck and quivered all over, as though looking forward to the excursion.

When Marin led a second waterhorse from the cavern-like stable, I stopped him. "Is that the only tack they get? That loop thing?"

"What else were you expecting?"

"I don't know, a saddle or bridle? How do you steer?"

"Waterhorses understand basic merfolk commands. We don't need to physically steer them." He pursed his lips and then shook his head. "Sorry, I'm not sure what a saddle is."

"I suppose you wouldn't be, not having legs." My cheeks burned at the silliness of the question. But the idea of riding the horse both bareback and side-saddle made me grimace. "How do you sit on the waterhorse?"

"You don't. It pulls you along through the water. You align your body parallel to its back and hang on here." He pointed to the loop.

"I was afraid you were going to say that." I sighed, a watery exhalation.

Jack held his hand in front of the first waterhorse's face. It sniffed his skin, nostrils opening and closing like gills with each inhalation. "We do not speak merfolk."

"Then it's just as well we're coming with you," Marin said, turning to harness the next creature.

It didn't take him long to finish preparing four water-horses, attaching modified saddlebags to the front of each harness. The bags sat between the front fins—a curious location, although the creatures didn't seem bothered by it. They were all similar in build, with slight variations in size and colour. I wasn't sure which were male and which were female.

"Isla, Tiddas will be your waterhorse," Marin said to me, beckoning. I approached cautiously. "She and Jack's mount are the most cooperative of the four. They will be easiest for you to manage." Tiddas had the palest scales, the grey of fog. She twitched her tail and blue light shimmered across them.

"Good to know." I offered my hand to the waterhorse the way Jack and done. A faint current swirled around my fingers as she sniffed me, before lipping my palm as though looking for a treat. "Sorry, girl, I don't have anything," I murmured.

"Are we ready?" Kai grunted, swimming into the cavern. His aura seethed with resentment.

"Almost," Marin replied, double-checking each harness. Kai shouldered past him, snatching up the loop on one of the two unclaimed waterhorses. Marin's lip curled, revealing neat white teeth, but instead of arguing he turned away, heading to the fourth creature.

"I'm sorry you've been asked to babysit us," I said, speaking to Marin but hoping to soothe Kai's ruffled feathers. Ruffled scales?

"You restored Pania to the line of succession." Marin made a shallow bow in my direction. "It is an honour."

Kai snorted, keeping his back to us. Tension knotted his shoulders. Jack and Marin gave him identical glares.

"Still, you're going to be away from home for at least a week or two," I said. Moana had assured me we could get to England in three or four days, as improbable as it sounded. Apparently, the underwater tunnels allowed for even swifter travel than those on land. "I still think you should head back as soon as we get there, rather than waiting."

"The king has ordered us to wait for you, so we shall wait." The merman dismissed my objections with a shrug. "Now, position yourself above and behind the waterhorse's neck, and grip the loop here with both hands." The leather was rough and sandpapery under my fingertips. What was it made of? Shark hide? "The waterhorses will move swiftly, so hang on firmly or you will fall off."

"At least we wouldn't have to worry about landing hard, I guess. The water would soften our fall."

"Yes," Marin said, drawing out the word. "Although there's a risk of being buffeted by the waterhorse's tail. They pack quite a punch, and have been known to knock a mer into a wall."

"Or a cluster of coral." Kai bared his teeth at me. If the expression was meant to look like a smile, it wasn't very convincing. "It will shred you if you're not careful."

"We'll be careful," I said quickly before Jack could speak. My boyfriend's aura boiled with anger.

"Well, if you need to stop and rest, call out and we will do so. Travelling by waterhorse can be tiring on the upper body when you're not used to it."

When Jack and I were in position, Marin studied us both for several heartbeats. Satisfied, he nodded to himself and issued a short command in the merfolk tongue.

The waterhorses swam slowly out of the stable cavern and into the main *sidhe*. A crowd mingled, waiting to see us off. Most were there out of curiosity, judging by the emotional palette on display, although I did see one enthusiastic figure: Pania waved frantically and cheered in her high, clear voice between swimming loops with her new tail. The crowd was just as awestruck by that as they were by us. I settled for nodding and grinning back, too nervous about letting go of the loop to wave.

Marin's waterhorse led the way across the *sidhe* to one of a dozen identical tunnels on the opposite wall from where we had entered. I ducked my head reflexively as my mount followed his in, even though my head didn't protrude any higher than the waterhorse's pricked, leathery ears.

Glancing back, I grinned at Jack. He smiled, his eyes bright with excitement.

Kai travelled in the rear. The idea of having someone I didn't trust where I couldn't keep an eye on him made me clench my jaw, but what else could we do? Marin and Kai seemed to be partners; at least, the king hadn't separated them, despite Kai's lack of enthusiasm about the trip.

The passage twisted like a corkscrew. My waterhorse, Tiddas, spiralled along until dizziness churned my head and stomach. I gasped with relief when it straightened out into a more typical *sidhe* tunnel. *It's kind of like riding the* karkadann, I realised. *And then I didn't even have a bridle to hang onto.*

"Ready to run?" Marin called back.

"Yes...?"

Another command I couldn't understand, and the waterhorses surged forward.

I'd thought the mermaid I'd seen moving at full speed was fast—so fast, in fact, that I'd wondered why the merfolk bothered with mounts at all.

Now I knew why.

My heart leapt into my throat as Tiddas surged forward, so close behind Marin's waterhorse that, if I reached out, I could almost touch that strongly pumping tail. Instead,

I hung on for grim life, pulse thundering in my ears. I'd never ridden a motorbike, but the speed with which the water rushed past me made me think I never should. My hair streamed back from my head, and the wake from Marin's mount stirred the water into a fierce current that ached against my eyes. I slitted them, peering out from between my eyelashes, and glanced back to see how Jack was doing. He looked pale and his aura was surprised, but I couldn't tell much more. "Are you okay?" I yelled over the churning water.

"Fine. Are you?" he called back.

"Yup!"

And I realised it was true. Once the first shock passed, my heart returned to its normal place in my chest and I relaxed my white-knuckled grip on the harness loop to a more comfortable, steady hold. I was going to have little divots from the rough leather's texture on the insides of my fingers for a while, though, if the ache there was anything to go by.

We rode—swam?—for what seemed like years but was probably only hours. The tunnels didn't change much, and after I got used to the view in front of me, it wasn't that interesting either. I yawned, and my grip started to loosen... I jerked myself awake, and took several deep breaths of the briny water. "Uh, Marin?" I called. "I could use a break."

At first I thought he couldn't hear me over the rushing water. Then our horses slowed. The merfolk must have keen hearing.

"Is everything well, Isla?" Marin said when we'd come to a complete stop. The waterhorses clustered close together in the tunnel, nuzzling and brushing each other with their noses and flippers.

"I could use a sleep, to be honest. We've been going for more than a full day, now." I stifled a yawn behind one hand and then glanced down at my palm. Yep, divots. "We had, um, a bit of a burst of energy when we met the king and queen, but it seems to have worn off."

Kai grumbled something under his breath, and Marin glared at him. "You're tired too, Kai."

"No, I'm not," the other merman bit back.

Although I wasn't familiar enough with merfolk physiology to spot the signs I'd look for on a human—or a hob—Kai's aura was faded with exhaustion. I rolled my eyes. "Shall we stop for a few hours for a sleep? Um, do merfolk sleep?"

"We do." Marin's displeasure with Kai faded into a smile. "I suppose we should have rested before leaving the court."

"I wasn't tired then," I said.

"Neither was I," Jack said, glancing at me. The corner of his lip tugged upward. "I am hungry, though. I do not suppose you packed food?"

"Of course," Marin said. "First, let's find a cavern."

We travelled at a slower pace along the tunnel. After a couple of left turns, Marin led us into an underwater cave no bigger than my old high school gymnasium. It seemed small compared to the enormous *sidhe* where the merfolk court resided, but was still large enough for all of us, with room to spare.

"Kai," Marin ordered, "tend to the waterhorses. I will prepare the food."

Scowling, the other merman clicked a command at the creatures, which followed him placidly to the other side of the cave.

"Is it necessary for them to be so far away?" Jack said, looking across at the creatures. I wondered what he was thinking. That they were inconveniently far away for us to make a quick getaway if we had to?

"Yes." Marin glanced at the hob. "In case the water-horses, ah, relieve themselves. It takes a while for their waste to settle, and it's easily stirred up."

"Oh," I said. "Ew." I hadn't thought about that side of things—although now I was, I had an uncomfortable urge to pee. When was the last time I'd been?

"It's not toxic and it's practically odourless," the merman hastened to reassure me, "but it's better not to breathe it in."

I grimaced. "On that note, I'm going to go find some-where for a little private time."

"I should come with you," Jack said, turning to follow me.

My eyes widened. "No, you really shouldn't. I'll be fine. Half-*aosidhe*, remember?"

"Oh. Right. Call if you need me. I will stay right here." He patted a smooth rock, sitting down on it. I took the backpack off and left it beside him before swimming from the cave.

Taking care of necessities, as Nana would have called it, was a complicated process in a wetsuit. After strug-gling with the garment for thirty seconds, I swore, willing its bottom half away entirely. The act made me feel even wearier, but the alternative was worse.

When I wished the wetsuit back into being, I made sure to add Velcro panels.

Jack was swimming towards the cave entrance when

I came back in, a frown marring his smooth forehead. It vanished when he saw me. "I was getting worried."

"Wetsuit," I said by way of explanation. "Let me take care of that for you." I modified his wetsuit with a thought. A little more energy trickled from me, and I drooped. Jack slipped his arm around my waist and I leaned against him gratefully, curling a finger in a lock of his hair. "Thanks. I'm pretty sleepy all of a sudden."

"It is hardly surprising." He kicked his legs, pulling me alongside him as we returned to Marin.

"Don't you ever get tired?" I grumbled.

"Of course I do." He kissed me on the top of the head, a quick peck that warmed me to my toes. "You might feel better after you eat something."

When I looked at the range of delicacies Marin had to offer, I wasn't so sure. There was pale meat I was sure was raw fish, as well as seaweed-like strips of greenery and caviar in several different colours. Other things I didn't recognise at all. But the merman watched us expectantly, so I took a small piece of fish and nibbled it, hoping it didn't make me sick. I'd never been one for sashimi.

The fish was delicious and faintly sweet. It was raw, as I'd expected, but not chewy. "Oh, yum!"

Marin showed us how to wrap our choices in seaweed so we didn't drop them. Plates weren't a thing here, which made sense when I thought about it. "I wonder if the Japanese learned to make sushi from the merfolk?" I speculated before taking a bite of some seaweed-wrapped caviar. The little orange balls popped under my tongue, not as salty as I'd been expecting. Breathing briny water seemed to have changed my palate. "Although they added the rice themselves, obviously. Unless there's underwater rice?"

"I don't know what that is," Marin said, shaking his head. He sat beside us on the flat rock.

"A type of grain. You boil it in water to cook it."

"Cook?"

"Never mind." I laughed.

Once the waterhorses were unharnessed and grazing on some water weeds sprouting from a crack in the cave floor, Kai swam over to us, sitting on Marin's other side. He took the proffered food before facing the other way.

An awkward silence fell. Marin looked furious, biting into a piece of seaweed with more force than was necessary.

"Did you know this cave was here?" I asked him, curling my free hand around Jack's. I did have more energy now I'd eaten, but my arms and legs ached from unfamiliar exercise. Sleep sounded good. Or coffee. I missed coffee.

"I did," Marin said, nodding. "Kai and I know this area pretty well. We patrol through here."

"What about further out from the *sidhe*?" Jack leaned his head against mine.

"Those tunnels I haven't been to. But don't worry. The neutral thoroughfares between each territory are clearly marked." With a fingertip, he drew a sketch in the sand: a vertical line with a U shape at its top end. The bottom of the U intersected the line partway down, like a bent cross or a curved pitchfork.

"Territory?"

"The merfolk have different courts. Moana is the king of Oceania. We will pass through, or near, other courts. So long as we stay in the main tunnel, we are entitled to safe passage. No one will interfere with us."

"I assumed he was the king of all the merfolk," I

murmured sleepily.

Kai turned, glaring at me with dark eyes brimming with contempt. "And how do you explain the way you found the king of all the merfolk as quickly as you did? The *sidhe* oceans are more closely woven together than they are in your world, but the odds of lucking across one court in all the world's waters must be astronomical."

Jack stiffened beside me, his hand balling into a fist under my fingers. "There is no need for that tone."

"I agree." Marin wrapped strong fingers around Kai's arm and turned him to face us. "Apologise to the lady. Now. Remember, our king declared her to be his royal equal."

Kai hesitated, staring at Marin for a long moment. The other merman didn't relent. "I'm sorry," he grated from between clenched teeth.

"That's okay," I replied, although my stomach tightened with anxiety. I was relieved when, without another word, Kai swam across to the other side of the cave.

Marin cleared his throat and shifted beside me, rubbing his long tailfin across the rough ground like a child scuffing his shoe. "I'm sorry too." His voice was quiet. "It's no excuse, but Kai's younger brother died in a fish net, out in your world. He has never forgiven the humans for it."

I gazed after the other merman. He'd settled near the waterhorses—not too near—curling on his side in a patch of sand. From this distance, he looked small. "That's so sad. I don't blame him."

"Also, the topic of a single ruler of the merfolk is controversial," Marin admitted, packing away the remains of our meal. "We used to have a single ruler. He was cruel."

"Let me guess," I said. "He was an *aosidhe*."

He nodded. "As well as having the gift you do to change

things, he had a powerful item. Magic, they say. A trident that gave him the power to control all *duinesidhe* of the sea: us, sirens, *cecaelias*, everyone. It was a black time in our history."

I glanced down at the symbol Marin had drawn in the dirt. *A trident. Of course.* "What happened to him?"

"He grew too powerful. The other *aosidhe* declared war on him, and he was destroyed. Afterwards, the merfolk and *cecaelias* worked together to collapse the connections between the land and water tunnels. Before another *aosidhe* could move into Neptune's palace *sidhe*."

I wrinkled my nose. "Neptune? Like the sea god?"

"That's what he called himself."

"The *aosidhe* just love to big-note themselves, don't they?" I threw my hands in the air. "Gods, mountains, muses, demons. They must have an inferiority complex, naming themselves after such powerful things."

Jack laughed quietly. Marin looked bemused. Then he excused himself and swam across the cavern to have a conversation with Kai. We could hear their voices, but they spoke in the merfolk tongue and I couldn't understand them. The tone was clear, though, as were the emotions: Marin was scolding the other merman, who was sullen in reply.

Not wanting to listen anymore, I scooped up my backpack and looked around until I found a patch of relatively clear sand against the opposite wall, picking a few rocks out and tossing them to one side. They sank to the floor some distance away. I sat on the sand, curling my hands around my knees. The cave loomed above us, huge and darker now Marin and Kai had taken their glowing armour away. I looked back at Jack and, although my cheeks reddened, patted the sand beside me. "Want to cuddle before bed? If you can call this a bed."

"I would be delighted." He swam over and wrapped his arms around me, curling against my back. The light from the stargem pendant dimmed, pressed between us. I pillowed my head on the backpack. It was somewhat lumpy under my ear, but if I opened it to rearrange the contents, everything would get soaked. "It's been a crazy day," I murmured. "Sarah would never believe it."

"No," he replied, brushing my hair down and tucking it under my shoulder.

"Was it tickling you?"

"A little."

"I'm sure all this salt water is very bad for my hair." My eyelids slid closed. Jack was a warm and reassuring presence behind me and, now I was letting myself relax, the fatigue washed in, inexorable as a wave smashing a sandcastle. "I'll need to do moisturising treatments for months when we get home…"

Jack's laughter chased me down into sleep.

CHAPTER FIFTEEN

We had a quick breakfast before helping Marin harness the waterhorses. Tiddas regarded me with what I suspected was amusement as I gingerly eased each loop over one of her powerful flippers.

"Stop laughing at me." I brushed the soft skin of her nose with a fingertip. She nudged me back, seeking more scratches.

"Where is Kai?" Jack said, looking around with narrowed eyes. The other merman had been gone when we rose. I was quietly hoping he'd abandoned us, heading home in disgust. At least we'd have a more peaceful journey.

"He was on second watch," Marin said, waving a hand towards the entrance. "He's out there. I took him food already."

"Is he still mad at me?" I looked down at my hands, absently stroking the waterhorse's muzzle. Her eyes were slitted and her throat rumbled like a cat's. Was she purring?

"Kai is mad at everyone these days." Marin sighed, picking up the other harness and turning to Kai's waterhorse, preparing it with practised efficiency.

"You were posting a watch?" Jack tipped his head to the side. "You should have told me. I would have helped."

"But you are our guests. Besides," Marin gave Jack an appraising look, "I assumed you wouldn't be willing to leave Isla with the two of us to take up a post outside the cavern."

My cheeks burned with embarrassment, but Jack nodded. "True. You seem trustworthy, but your friend is holding a grudge."

Lips pressed tight together, Marin nodded back and swum to mount his waterhorse. When we were ready, he ordered the beasts forward. Kai's waterhorse fell in at the rear of the group, following us from the cavern.

We found Kai a short distance outside. At first I didn't spot him, because his blue-grey scales blended into the shale-like outer surface of the tunnel. It was only when he swam out in front of us as we approached that I saw him, my eyes widening with surprise. He noticed my reaction, sneering faintly before glancing at Marin and schooling his expression. His emotions were a mixture of intense dislike and smug satisfaction.

At least once we set out I didn't have to see them, or him, anymore.

That day's travel proceeded much as the previous one had. We stopped every couple of hours for a break, to stretch out cramped muscles and give the waterhorses a rest. Unable to take my watch from my bag, I judged the passage of time based on when I got hungry, wondering as I ate my lunch whether it was actually lunchtime in the real world. By the end of the meal, I'd decided it didn't matter. Besides, calculating the time zone difference between New South Wales, where we'd entered the water, and England was enough to confuse me without worrying about what time it was in the *sidhe*—where there was no sun anyway.

After lunch, we raced along another trident-marked corridor. Now I knew what to look for, I caught occasional glimpses of the protective symbol, always in the same spot on the curved wall, halfway up on either side, and at each intersection to mark which of the paths was the safe, neutral territory.

What would happen if we took one of those side paths? I glanced down each untaken tunnel as we passed, but all I ever saw was darkness.

Until I caught a hint of movement as we shot past yet another passage.

We passed it so fast I thought I might have imagined it. I craned my neck, peering back past Jack and Kai at the already receding tunnel entrance. Tentacled creatures boiled out of the black hole, bodies stretching and contracting as they shot out into our tunnel. The light from Kai's armour glinted off a sharpened spear tip.

"Look out!" I yelled. "*Cecaelias*!"

I whipped my head around as Tiddas rose up underneath me, flippers churning the water as she sought to avoid colliding with the waterhorse in front of her. The back of her head smacked into the bottom of my chin. Pain seared through my mouth as I bit my tongue, tasting blood, but I managed to keep hold of the harness.

My heart sank into my flippers when I realised *cecaelias* also filled the tunnel in front of Marin. They clustered together, spears bristling between them like the spines of a strange, marine echidna. If we tried to swim past them, we'd be skewered.

Leaving his mount, Jack swam to my side, hands curled into fists as he looked forward and back with narrowed, furious eyes. We were surrounded.

"What do you want?" Marin snapped at the creatures, unhooking his spear from its fastener on his back. I winced at his tone. They were small, but they outnumbered us four to one. "You breach the terms of the treaty, accosting us on the Trident Road."

"That one human," a *cecaelias* hissed, speaking in broken English as it inched forward from the rest of the pack. It looked similar to the one we'd encountered previously. Perhaps it was the same creature, although I couldn't be sure. They all looked very much alike.

"So?"

"Treaty between merfolk and *cecaelias*. Humans and that—" the spokesman glanced at Jack "—not protected."

Marin's back was to me; I could see his indignation in the straightness of his spine, the set of his shoulders. "That is a lie."

"Not lie."

"You've never accosted sirens or other *duinesidhe* using the Trident Road before."

The creature's lip curled and its gaze slid across to me, burning with a rage so hot I expected the water to boil around it, cooking it in its own fury. "She not *duinesidhe*."

Nerves fizzing in my stomach like champagne, I met the *cecaelias's* gaze. "Yes, I am. At least, fifty percent of me is. How else could I be here?"

The creature stared blankly. Then it looked back at Marin,

ignoring me. "Give human, and rest of you leave safe."

"Like hell," Jack growled.

Kai, right behind me, said, "She's yours." He wrapped a strong arm around my waist, yanking me from Tiddas's back. The harness loop tore from my fingers, stinging.

"Hey!" Heart racing, I rammed my elbow into Kai's midriff. It scraped across the front of his rough armour. He grunted but didn't let me go.

"Release her!" Marin demanded, rushing towards us.

Jack was faster. Weaponless, he launched himself at Kai, fingers jabbing at the merman's eyes. Kai pushed himself backwards with a powerful sweep of his tail, dragging me with him. I struggled like a rabbit in a trap.

The press of a sharp-edged knife against my throat stilled me. "Stop it, human," Kai said in my ear, his lips so close I could feel them brush against my skin. I shuddered. "You *should* be afraid," he murmured. "I would gladly cut you from one ear to the other. But I'll have to let the *cecaelias* do it for me."

I met Jack's gaze. He was frozen, just out of reach, his aura rigid with rage and fear. Beside him, Marin gaped, horrified.

"I'm not afraid," I told Kai, lifting my chin. It was true. I felt nervous, but the siren's fear-deadening gift was still largely in effect. "I'm pretty pissed off, though. You set this up, didn't you?"

Kai didn't answer. Marin's eyes widened as he stared past me at the other merman. "Tell me it's not true!"

"If it was, who could blame me?"

Marin's aura shot through with plasma-purple shock. His fingers convulsed on the haft of his spear, as though he wanted to leap forward and attack. "You betrayed the king!"

"The king is part human." Kai's tone was dismissive.

Realisation dawned. "That's what this is about, isn't it?" I said. "It's not that I'm a half-human, not exactly. It's that I changed Pania so she can inherit Oceania. You wanted the crown to go to some else. Someone not part-human."

"Someone pure," Kai hissed, his hand tightening on the knife. A sharp line of pain drew across my throat as it bit into my skin. "Yes, why shouldn't I want that?" he said, an odd note in his voice.

"Because she is the crown princess!" Marin shouted.

Jack's eyes were fixed on the blade and the trickle of blood unfurling into the water. He grabbed Marin's arm. "Careful."

"Interesting," the *cecaelias* said in a bored tone that gave lie to its words. "Give girl, or kill you all."

"You said you'd let me and Marin live," Kai protested.

"Give girl. Now."

This has gone far enough. I visualised the dagger at my throat appearing in Jack's hand. He stared down in shock at the stone blade as it materialised, swift as thought.

Snarling in the merfolk tongue, Kai snagged my hair in his now-empty fist. He yanked my head backward. Before I could scream, his other hand curled around my throat, fingers digging into my windpipe. I clawed at them, tearing his skin with my nails. Jack and Marin darted forward.

A *cecaelias* rushed up behind Jack, spear raised to drive through his unprotected back.

Fury coursed through me. I ripped Kai's rage from him, adding it to the furnace of my own, and jabbed a blade of terror at the *cecaelias*. "Leave us alone!"

The *cecaelias* dropped its spear. Tentacles writhing, it fled past its fellows, vanishing in a cloud of black ink.

Kai's grip loosened around my throat as Jack and Marin tore at him, freeing me. I pitched forward, stopping between them and the *cecaelias*. Seeing me within reach, one of them cried something in its own tongue. The creatures surged from the shadows, mouths screeching with outrage. They resembled something out of a Cthulhu-esque nightmare.

And I struck at them all, laying about like a soldier with a sword—only terror was my weapon. As my gaze flicked from one creature to the next, they reacted. Most turned and fled. A couple went limp, sinking to the floor of the tunnel. Unconscious or dead? I didn't know. With each attack I grew less full, Kai's rage draining from me until my fingers no longer trembled with too much power.

When the tunnel before me was clear, I turned back to the others.

Jack and Marin had Kai backed up against one wall of the tunnel with knife and spear. The trapped merman was making a peculiar sound in his throat, a keening wail. His aura was the silver-black of despair. His dark eyes flicked down to the blade Jack held close to his throat—

I opened my mouth to cry out a warning—

Kai grabbed Jack's hand, the one holding the knife—

And jerked it forward, towards himself. The sharp stone slid through Kai's flesh. Slitting his throat. Staining the water red around them. Marin screeched. Kai's skin blanched with pain.

Gentle as a goodnight kiss, I took the pain away. Kai's eyes found mine, acknowledging what I'd done.

And, with a flutter of gills in a final gasp, he died.

I turned to the *cecaelias* at our rear. My skin blazed bright with power, so bright they shielded their eyes with an arm or a tentacle. "If you don't go, I'll kill you all."

They fled.

Jack swam over, wrapping me in his arms. The combined light from the stargem pendant and my power made his eyes glow as blue as the heavens. "Are you okay?"

I nodded, wordless.

"The energy cost...?"

I glanced at Kai. Marin had closed the dead merman's eyes and lifted him up from where he'd slumped; Kai's tail draped, lifeless, over one of Marin's muscled arms. A knot formed in my throat—I could almost taste Marin's grief. "Replenished." I didn't elaborate, in case Marin blamed me for the other merman's death. I'd taken his dying pain, not his life. And I hadn't made him kill himself; his own shame had driven him to that.

Although if I hadn't taken the rage sustaining him, or had been quicker to take the despair... I shook my head, shaking the thought away. The wound on my throat tugged open, stinging in the salty water.

Seeing me wince, Jack looked down at the cut. "He very nearly did to you what he ended up doing to himself. Here, let me." Before I could protest, he tipped my head back and leaned in, running his tongue along the wound. The sensation was slow and somehow sensual. My lips parted in a silent gasp.

When he looked back at me, I kissed him fiercely, giddy with relief that we'd survived, that he was okay. The memory of that spear almost driving through his back gave my arms strength as I clutched him to me. His lips parted, surprised at first, but after a heartbeat he kissed me in return, curling his fingers in my hair. His lips tasted of the ocean, like my blood and Marin's tears.

Marin's tears. I drew away and met the merman's gaze, shame heating my cheeks. He watched us with an unreadable expression. Finally he spoke. "I need to bury my cousin."

I let go of Jack. A red line marred the hob's throat, fading to pink even as I watched, his preternatural healing beginning to work.

I cleared my throat. "Of course. Lead the way."

CHAPTER SIXTEEN

*M*arin insisted on carrying Kai's body rather than strapping it to a waterhorse. Not that I blamed him. Even though I'd had mixed feelings about Kai, I could see how Marin wouldn't want to tie him to a waterhorse like old baggage. My abraded fingers throbbed in time with my heartbeat as I swam through the water, the ache a constant reminder of Kai's betrayal. I was glad he hadn't been successful, grateful to be alive—and yet couldn't dislodge the guilt churning my stomach like the water behind the waterhorses' tails. The combat replayed in my head on a continuous loop, as my mind searched for ways I could have prevented Kai's suicide. If I'd acted more quickly to siphon off his despair. Or realised sooner the significance of his smug satisfaction that morning. Or even manipulated him to like me when we'd first met, taken his loathing away before he'd done something irrevocable.

Of course, if I had changed Kai's feelings when we first met, without the benefit of hindsight to spur me on,

I would have been doing it simply to make things easier for myself. I'd promised myself I wouldn't do that. I wouldn't become my mother.

I could have told Jack about my throbbing fingers, but the pain was my penance, a counterpoint to Marin's grief. So I swam beside him with a heavy heart, hands curled into loose fists against my chest. The waterhorses trailed after us in an obedient line.

We were a sombre procession.

When we reached a small tunnel branching off the Trident Road, Marin paused, biting his lip.

"Are you worried about causing a diplomatic incident?"

He nodded. "We've passed into the territory of the Indiania Court. There's a rock-filled cavern not far down here. Kai and I found it once, exploring when we were younger. Being daredevils. It would be p—" he swallowed and tried again "—perfect."

I tamped down my anxiety at the delay. "Then let's do it."

Without saying anything else, Marin set off down the side tunnel. Jack gave me a troubled look.

"I didn't realise Kai was your cousin as well as your patrol partner," I said after a while. "I'm sorry."

"His betrayal brought him to this end." Marin's dull voice carried back to us, although he didn't turn to look. "I'm just glad he wasn't successful. It would have brought shame to his parents."

Was ritual suicide a custom among the merfolk, like the Japanese samurai I'd read about in high school? Looking at Marin's slumped shoulders, I decided not to ask.

This tunnel twisted more than the main road had, but still had the basic cylindrical shape of a burrowed passage as it headed gradually downward. The water seemed warmer, although maybe it was just the sudden exertion after I'd been towed along for so long by waterhorse.

Our destination was a small cavern—about the size of Aunt Elizabeth's bedroom at home—connected to the tunnel by a jagged crack in the wall. We left the water-horses outside, swimming through the gap in single file. Marin manoeuvred Kai's body through the narrow passage, a feat I could never have achieved. He'd had a lifetime of practice at swimming while holding things, I supposed. Though hopefully, for his sake, not bodies.

Inside, the cave was dark, its floor littered with loose stones. Marin lay Kai down among them and swam as though in a daze to the far wall. He moved several rocks aside to show a place where two symbols had been scratched into the wall.

"Your names?" I murmured.

"The first letter of each of them. We thought we were so brave, marking the wall inside Indiania territory." He smiled faintly. "Not brave enough to leave our full names, though. Or to put them in plain sight. I doubt anyone has been to this spot since the last time we were here."

Gazing down at Kai's face, I could imagine him egging the more sensible Marin on, and Marin's laughing protests. The wound at Kai's throat drew my eye no matter how much I tried to focus on his face. I looked up to find Marin studying me. "Can we help?" I said.

"The merfolk build a cairn for their dead."

I frowned, not sure what he meant. Seeing my expression, Jack murmured, "A cairn is a mound of rocks, to protect the body from predators."

Marin nodded sharply. "Quite. We need to move these stones to one side, to make a space in the centre. Then we can place them on top..." He folded his arms across his chest, biceps tightening as he hugged himself.

My throat tightened. "Marin, will you let me do this for you?" I rasped.

"What do you mean?"

"We're happy to help move rocks. Please don't think we're not. But if your people's rites don't require you to do this yourself, I can do it for you."

"With your magic?"

I nodded.

He gazed down at Kai's body for several long minutes, his jaw clenched as he considered my offer. Had I offended him? Or was he saying goodbye? I couldn't tell. The whirlpool of grief in his aura was so overwhelming it smothered any other feelings.

Not for the first time, I wished my gift had brought me a little bit of telepathy. I opened my mouth to apologise, but before I could find the right words, he looked back up at me and spoke softly. "I would appreciate that, thank you."

"Does the cairn need to look a certain way?"

He shook his head.

"Okay." I looked around the cave, forming an image in my mind. "Can you give me a bit of space?"

The two men swam behind me, Jack giving my hand a brief squeeze as he passed.

Conscious of Marin's sorrowful gaze on my back, I pressed my will onto the *sidhe*. The loose rocks scattered around the room rose in the water, drifting towards Kai's body. One, then another, settled on him, covering his arms, his chest. Marin's choked sob brought tears to my eyes as rocks covered Kai's face. I may not have liked Kai, but my cousin was my best friend. The idea of Sarah, lying there with her throat cut, tore my breath away, replacing it with nothing but pain.

The pile of rocks grew into a tall cone that almost reached the ceiling, each rock clicking as it settled onto the pile. Smaller pebbles and sand wedged into the gaps, each finding a home and making the tower more stable. The shape was reminiscent of a merman's tail.

Smiling with a sudden thought, I ran a hand over the rough surface. It transformed in the wake of my touch from a cluster of stones—some ragged, others smooth and round—to one solid piece, marked with a scale pattern. A fin sprouted from the top, growing outward with a grinding of stone like a great fan opening.

"Thank you," Marin breathed.

"You're welcome."

"If the Indiania merfolk see this, there will be no mistaking it for something natural," Jack said.

"I know." I looked at Marin, who was smiling through his tears. "But it was worth it. I can seal up the cave entrance when we leave, though, if you think it's necessary."

"Don't." Marin ran a hand over the blue-green scales on his head. They rasped faintly under his touch. "They won't know who or what caused it. There's no way they could attribute it to Oceania." He lowered his voice. "And I hate the idea of him being shut away entirely."

"Okay."

Conscious of Jack's observant gaze, I forced myself to move normally as we swam back to the waiting water-horses, ignoring the tired ache that stiffened my muscles. Although building the cairn had drained me more than I wanted to admit, the ever-present anxiety about Dad wouldn't let me stop and rest. I supposed I could feed on my companions' emotions like some sort of vampire, but the idea made me feel ill. No, I could push myself a little further. And, although my hand protested when I wrapped it around Tiddas's harness, at least I didn't have to actually swim.

As the waterhorses surged into motion—Kai's trailing an empty harness—my head spun as though the earth was shaking. Maybe I was more tired than I thought? Marin glanced back at us, eyes wide.

"Was that an earthquake?" Jack called from behind me.

"I don't know," Marin shouted back. "Let's get back to the main road." I didn't hear what he said to the waterhorses, but the jolt through my shoulders as Tiddas lunged forward nearly threw me from her back. The tunnel spun until I scrunched my eyes shut, willing myself not to be sick.

The tunnel lurched with another tremor. Tiddas careened into a wall. The backpack smashed against the side. Shale tore along my thigh, tearing the wetsuit like tissue paper and grazing my skin. I clung to my harness as the waterhorse pushed herself off from the wall and shot after Marin's mount. Jack's waterhorse, which had almost collided with us, followed after. "Marin! Is it the Indiania merfolk?"

"I don't know." Not very reassuring.

We burst from the narrower tunnel onto the Trident Road, and I smiled with relief. Then something lunged at us. My scream was lost amidst terrified waterhorse shrieks.

The creature's eyeless head was huge, its gaping mouth full of rounded teeth like heavy rocks, each one the size of my fist. I glimpsed a snubbed nose darting forward, striking the shale floor of the tunnel. Silt exploded upward, clouding the water. I couldn't see Tiddas's head in front of my face. Eyes burning with grit, I peered around blindly. "*Jack*!"

Tiddas bolted, and I clutched the harness, heart in my throat. Jack's name was on my tongue, my lips. I bit them to stop from crying out again, fear of the creature's gaping maw silencing me. The ground shook; the monster still pursued us.

A barely seen glimpse of a churning tail in front of me made me realise we were moving clear of the silt cloud. It was seconds more before I could see Marin, still on his waterhorse. I craned my head, staring backwards through my streaming hair. *Please be there, Jack. Oh, please.* The silt cloud glowed, a light that moved with me. His stargem pendant? When I saw his horse's wild-eyed face and caught a glimpse of golden hair I gasped, relief flooding me. He was still alive.

The tunnel shook. Silt rained down but didn't cause a complete whiteout this time. I peered around wildly. Were we still on the Trident Road? There could be a mark on the wall right beside me and I wouldn't be able to see it, given the poor visibility and the speed with which we moved. From the trembling, I guessed the creature was still behind us, though we couldn't see it.

A black shadow coming up on the left caught my eye. "Marin, take that tunnel!" I yelled.

He didn't hesitate, urging his waterhorse down the darkened passage. It shied back. Tiddas rose up in the water, fins working frantically to avoid a collision. Her rearing head narrowly missed smashing my nose to pulp.

Marin growled something and his horse moved forward.

As soon as we were all inside the side passage, I said, "Stop here." Quick as thought, I pushed my will onto the *sidhe*, urging it to make us invisible to the blind monster's other senses: scentless, soundless, giving off no vibration or other hint of our presence.

Its head thundered across the tunnel entrance, as loud and fast as a freight train. We rattled around like dice in a cup. Suddenly weak, I lost my grip on Tiddas's harness. My head slammed into the wall—or was it the floor? Dazed, I watched the serpent's body slither past. Its skin resembled a fistful of precious stones, from ruby near the head to amber, emerald, sapphire, and amethyst at the tail.

"It looks like a rainbow." My voice sounded funny. Why did my voice sound funny?

The creature vanished from sight. Then everything else did too.

Yellow light pressed against my closed eyelids, insistent as dawn at the edges of my bedroom curtains. I yawned, rubbing my eyes—and froze as the sensation of water all around recalled me to where I was.

The water was warm.

"Isla, thank goodness." Jack's face appeared above me, blue eyes wide with concern. When I met his gaze, relief flooded his face. He leaned down and kissed me tenderly, as though afraid he might break me.

The glowing star on the chain around his neck swung

forward, cool against my cheek. The gem's light seemed dim in the greater glow surrounding us.

Sitting up with Jack's help, I stared.

The chamber's walls were made of smooth stone, sparkling with flecks of quartz. At first, I thought they were stargems, but they reflected the yellowy light from elsewhere, capturing it like tiny mirrors and bouncing it back in a glittering display. The ground underneath me was fine golden sand that trickled through my fingertips. Seaweed swayed in small patches near the edges of the room. To one side of the chamber, near a dark entrance, three waterhorses clustered, heads hanging wearily, eyes closed as they slept. We'd lost Kai's mount along the way. Had the serpent eaten it? I bit my lip, recalling the size of that mouth. It would have barely needed to chew. Maybe that's why it had let us escape. It was full.

"Where are we? Where's Marin?"

"Over there." Jack nodded towards the far side of the chamber, where the light was the strongest. Squinting, I could see a merman's silhouette. "After we left the side passage where you hid us, we discovered the tremors had opened up a new chamber off the Trident Road, on the opposite side. We came in here so I could heal you."

My fingers brushed against my temple, where I'd hit the wall. I should have had a huge bruise, but the skin wasn't even tender. Gently moving Jack's hair to one side, I revealed the fading yellow and green injury that should have been mine. "You shouldn't do that to yourself."

"Why not?" he replied, curling his fingers through mine. The rose red love in his aura warmed me to my toes. "I cannot bear to see you hurt."

"What makes you think I want to see *you* hurt?"

"I know you do not. Still, I heal faster."

"Yeah, yeah," I grumbled. "One of these days I'll change myself so I heal as quickly as you do. Then you'll have no excuse."

"What if I like licking you?" He raised an eyebrow.

I blushed so hotly I expected the water to start boiling around me—especially when I realised the graze was gone from my thigh, the skin clean and whole under the torn wetsuit. Jack grinned, mischievous, and I searched around for a way to change the subject. "Uh. Do you think that creature was one of those that dug the *sidhe* tunnels in the first place? Your prehistoric serpents?"

His grin turned wicked but he answered my question. "I do not know. It was smaller than the main road, but it may have dug some of the lesser tunnels. Perhaps it was a juvenile."

Marin swam over to us, saving me from having to contemplate what an adult serpent might look like. The merman's expression was neutral, his aura troubled. "What's wrong?" I asked. "What's over there?"

"Nothing." He sat in the sand beside us. "Just another cave beyond this one. It's a dead end. We should move on as soon as you're ready. We have a long way to go. At least another two days' travel."

"What's the glowing light coming from?"

"It's just a light," he said, looking down at his knotted hands. "Let's go, okay?" He was lying. Why? Panic flared in his aura as I pushed myself up from the sand, swimming towards the back of the cavern. "No, wait!" He chased after us.

Jack at my side, I approached the glow, my eyes adjusting

to the brightness. It flooded from a jagged cave entrance in the shape of a mouth, slitting the back of the chamber as though someone had slashed a hole in the wall.

I stiffened. "I recognise this place."

The shape perfectly matched the grotto entrance from Ryan's drawing. Dazed, I swam forward, passing through lichen-covered rock incisors without a thought.

The trident glowed many times brighter than the stargem around Jack's neck. It was the source of the golden light spilling into the outer room to make the quartz gleam. Its shaft, grey beneath the illumination, had been plunged into a heavy black boulder sunk deep into the surrounding rock. The three prongs, each shaped to resemble a piece of coral, were as long as my forearm.

As I approached, my own skin began to radiate light. Chiming sounded in my ears, as though someone was ringing delicate bells.

"Isla, please don't," Marin begged, swimming in the entrance behind Jack. He reached for my shoulder.

Jack shoved him back, glaring. "Do not touch her."

"Do you know what that is?"

"Neptune's trident," I said, looking back at the merman.

"Yes!" Voice filled with desperation, Marin reached for me imploringly. "With that, Neptune was able to enslave all the people of the sea. My people, the *cecaelias*, sirens— all of us."

I frowned. "I'm not going to enslave anyone."

"So you say, but no one is meant to wield that kind of power. It corrupts even the purest of hearts. Neptune could bend the underwater *sidhe*—all the courts—to his will. His power was nearly limitless."

I stared back at the trident. It sang to me, bells chiming

together in a delicate chord. My voice when I spoke was flat by comparison. "Not that limitless. The other *aosidhe* beat him."

"Only after a terrible war. So many deaths. Please, Isla, let's just go."

"We can't just leave it here. Anyone could find it now. Do you want the *cecaelias* to take it?"

He bit his lip. "We can seal it up."

My hands itched to take up the weapon; it drew me as though I was a leaf caught in a current. Was I meant to have it, or was Ryan's painting a warning? "Jack?"

His expression was troubled, his answer reluctant. "You are powerful, Isla, but full-blooded *aosidhe* in their own domains are more powerful. If you wish to compel Melpomene to give up your father..." His meaning was clear. I needed the trident.

Marin cried out with despair when I reached for the weapon. Its glow and my own overlapped, merging and brightening until I had to narrow my eyes to slits or be blinded. The bells rang triumphantly. My fingers closed around the shaft and I pulled. The trident slid free of the rock as easily as a knife from its sheath.

The glow faded to a bearable level. I turned, the trident in my hand, unable to suppress a smile at the joy surging through me. My fatigue was gone, brushed away like cobwebs. Energy thrummed through my veins.

The smile faded when I saw Jack, shoulders straining as he held Marin up against the wall. Marin's spear lay, fallen, at his feet. "Let me go," the merman cried, eyes full of terror as he regarded me and the spear. "She'll enslave us all!"

"I will only use it to get my father back."

"If you use it, the underwater *duinesidhe* will declare war on you," Marin replied. A threat or a promise? "Isla, please—" His words were cut off as I willed him back to his home *sidhe*.

Jack fell forward, stopping himself before he collided with the wall. "Where did he go?"

"I sent him home. The waterhorses too."

His eyes widened. "You can do that? Teleport them?"

"And us too." I smiled, feeling like I could do anything. "We could be in England today. Right now."

"And do you feel okay?"

"I feel freaking amazing." I laughed. "Let's go save Dad!"

CHAPTER SEVENTEEN

"You cannot teleport us straight into another *aosidhe*'s domain."

"Why not? Because it's rude?" I regarded the trident with wonder. Since I'd drawn it from the rock, the shaft was no longer a dull grey. Instead, it shimmered as iridescent as the inside of a mother-of-pearl shell tinged gold, as though the rock had been bleaching its true colour even as it couldn't stop the glow. The bells still chimed, playing a delicate tune as though talking to me in a language I couldn't understand.

"Because they will not let you." The coral-shaped prongs glittered as I turned the handle, regarding them with wide eyes. I bit back a protest when Jack caught my arm, lowering my hand so the trident moved from view. "Isla, please, you must listen to me."

"What?" I frowned at him, irritation surging.

"Do not let the weapon enchant you."

"I'm not!" I protested, glancing down at the trident

where it hung from my hand. I realised my knuckles were white from clutching the shaft. "Okay, it is really pretty. But I'm fine, I swear. It was just a bit of a surprise. I've never seen anything so … so magical before."

Jack regarded me for a long moment before releasing my forearm. "I have. Marin was right about one thing, at least; the power can bewitch you. You must remain on your guard and only use the trident when necessary."

"Teleporting us to Dad seems pretty necessary to me."

"It will not work. That is what I have been trying to tell you."

"How do you know?" My gaze drifted down towards the shimmering trident but, feeling Jack's disapproval, I forced myself to give him my full attention.

He sighed, sitting on the rock that had so recently imprisoned the weapon. "Because I know. Isla, you have been able to do wondrous things within the *sidhe*. It has responded to your requests. However, that was in Australia and here under the sea, where no *aosidhe* holds dominion. No other will competes with yours to shape the *sidhe*. In the Old World, there is not a single *sidhe* that is unoccupied by the *aosidhe*. And most of them have dominated their homes for hundreds of years."

I sat beside him, feeling deflated. "You're saying I won't be able to change the Old World *sidhe*."

"Not exactly. But it will be a contest of wills, and one where they have had centuries to prepare the ground in their favour. It is why conflict between the *aosidhe* is rare—and when it does occur, it is either on neutral ground such as in the human world or done through a structured challenge, with rules that control how power can be used."

"I've got the trident..."

"Yes, and it will give you an edge. But you must be on your guard. Avoid going head to head with the *aosidhe*."

I stared at his solemn expression for several heart-beats, a feeling of helplessness growing in my chest. How was I going to save Dad? It seemed impossible.

Jack read my expression, taking my free hand in his. "We can still do this," he said, his tone reassuring. "Your innate power to manipulate emotions will stay with you no matter what. And you proved when you defeated Everest that you are an *aosidhe* to be reckoned with. They will be as wary of you as you need to be of them, and you can work within the rules of their society to bargain for what you want."

"Thank you." I kissed his cheek, a gentle peck. "I'm glad you're with me."

"Because I know the rules?"

"That too." We stared at each other for several long heartbeats; his sapphire eyes filled my vision and suddenly my heart was fluttering like a butterfly in my throat. "I love you, Jack." The words slipped out without conscious thought. I'd known it since the day I thought I would lose him, sending him away to keep him safe from Everest. But now, my heart was so full of emotion it hurt not to tell him.

"You know how I feel," Jack replied.

I tried to scowl. It came out as a soft laugh. "It'd be nice to hear you say it, though."

"Okay." He inched closer to me, so close I could feel the faint movement of the water with every word he spoke. "I have loved you since the day I first saw you."

My heart leapt, but he looked so serious I couldn't

help teasing him. "The day you sniffed me, you mean?"

He chuckled, deep and throaty. The tips of his long ears flushed with embarrassment. "Are you ever going to let that go?"

"That doesn't seem likely, does it?"

Another silence. The water felt charged, heated between us. I don't know which of us moved first. Maybe we both moved at the same time. Jack's hands curled in my hair, and mine were in his, running through his golden locks and curving around the back of his neck. Our lips locked in a saltwater kiss; his tongue was gentle at first, but my kiss grew demanding and he responded in kind. One of his hands trailed down the side of my wetsuit, hesitating as it crossed the unnatural shape of my gills before settling on my hip, close to the tear in the fabric on my thigh. I groaned, shifting so I sat on his lap.

Suddenly he stopped, staring at me from an inch away. His hands were around my waist, still when I wanted them to be moving. "What?" I touched his face, tried to pull him back to me. "What is it?"

"Are you...? Is this...?"

"What?"

"Is this because of the trident?" He said the words in a rush. "Items like that can intoxicate you with their power. I do not want to take advantage of you."

I stared at him, incredulous. "Jack, where is the trident right now?" He looked around, his eyes widening when he realised I'd left it on the rock beside us. It still glowed, although the chiming was less insistent, as though it was giving us some privacy. "This isn't about some magical doohickey. I'm kissing you because I love you." I lowered my voice to a whisper. "Because I want you."

"Want me for what?" It took me a second to realise he was teasing. I growled, biting his lip gently. "Ow," he laughed, disentangling himself. "Seriously, Isla. Are we talking about...?"

"Making love? Yes." My cheeks burned with embarrassment, so hot I was surprised I couldn't see their glow reflected in his eyes.

"You are ready?" His words reminded me sharply of the last time we'd had this conversation; we'd been walking from the beach back to the bungalow where I was staying. My answer had been no—only then, we were talking about Dominic.

"Jack, I share everything with you. I love you and I want you, and yes I'm ready and if you don't start taking advantage of me, I will take advantage of you." I paused. "Assuming you're ready, too."

His answer was to kiss me again, drawing me against the hard lines of his chest as though wanting to press us together until we were one person.

I wanted that too.

When the wetsuits got in the way, I willed them to vanish.

And when we joined together under the sea, bathed in the trident's warm glow, we lost ourselves in each other.

"So what do we do now?" I ran my hands down the sides of my newly conjured wetsuit. It looked much the same as the previous one—minus the tear—except the wetsuit highlights were now the same sapphire blue as Jack's eyes. There were also no longer slits in the side for our gills to breathe through; instead, the material there was thinner. It felt like exhaling through wet cheesecloth but I could still breathe, and now the wetsuits looked normal. "If we can't just teleport to Dad, I mean?"

Jack shouldered my backpack. "The same thing we planned to do from the start. Rejoin your cousins in the human world, find an entrance to the *sidhe* and locate Melpomene's domain. Then bargain with her or force her to give him back."

"Right." The idea of finally meeting my mother stirred a tumult of emotions in me. Anger at what she'd done to my father so many years ago, curiosity at what she'd be like, sadness she hadn't been the sort of mother I'd wanted, determination to make her give Dad back.

Jack watched me with a knowing look. "I will be with you the whole time."

I smiled, picking up the trident. It rang silently, grateful to be held again. "I know. It's the only thing that makes me think this could work."

"You should have more faith in yourself."

I shrugged, pushing the statement aside. "We can port to the underwater *sidhe's* exit, though, right?"

"Theoretically." He ran a hand through his hair, smoothing out the tangles. "Only without Marin, how will we know which one it is?"

"You always tell me to trust the *sidhe* to fill in the blanks." I held my free hand out to him. "Let's do that."

Teleporting felt like stepping through the portal between my world and the *sidhe*, only amplified. We were flying. We were falling. Everything spun around us, blurring into an indistinct mass. I clung to Jack's hand, determined not to lose him, and focused on what I wanted: the underwater *sidhe* exit closest to Sarah and Ryan.

When the spinning settled, we found ourselves floating before a shimmering portal. Peering through, I could see murky water on the other side, and a profusion of rocks and sand. Visibility wasn't as good out there as it was in here, where the water was pure. Still, it wasn't pitch-black, which was a plus. "It must be daytime."

He nodded. "We will need to organise dry clothes before we go. And a hat." He ran a hand along the top of one of his ears and grimaced.

"Oh." I'd been thinking we'd do the same thing we had in Australia: find a land *sidhe* where I could conjure what we needed. I guess it wasn't that straightforward. "Um. If I call up a second waterproof bag with dry clothes, we could take it out with us."

"Right."

I nibbled my lip. "I'll need to change our breathing too. I think when I made it so we could speak, it changed our bodies so we couldn't breathe air anymore. But we won't be able to get rid of the gills or we may not make it to the surface." I couldn't tell from inside the tunnel how far underwater the entrance was; I didn't have the diving experience to know how far down sunlight would filter. Given how crowded London was, the portal would have to be well hidden, and probably quite deep.

At least, I hoped we were near London.

"That should not be a problem, since the gills are on our sides. It just means we cannot let anyone who does not know what we are see us without a shirt on." His eyes twinkled, coaxing a smile to my lips.

MELPOMENE'S DAUGHTER

"I'm not sure England's weather is conducive to skinny dipping. It's spring here, but…" The enormity of what we'd done, crossing several oceans and travelling so far around the world that the seasons were reversed, struck me with force. "Wow."

"What are you going to do about the trident?" Jack eyed the shimmering weapon with distrust. "It stands out even more than my ears do."

I looked at the weapon, feeling overwhelmed—like I imagined a mountain climber must when, already tired, they confront yet another towering slope. Not because I was tired, but because the task ahead seemed so great. *One thing at a time,* I told myself, holding the trident up so it was before me. *I need you to be hidden,* I explained to it silently, feeling as though I was speaking to a wilful toddler. *I need to have you with me, so I can protect you, but I can't hold you.*

The weapon chimed once, joyous. There was a flare of light so bright that I closed my eyes.

When I opened them, the trident was gone.

"Where is it?" Jack looked around wildly.

My forearm tingled, giving me the clue I needed. Shoving up the sleeve of my wetsuit, I discovered what looked like a new tattoo on my inner arm, running from my elbow down to my wrist. It shimmered, pearlescent as the trident was in real life. Unlike other tattoos I'd seen, it didn't have a black outline; in places, the flecks of light on the golden shaft were the same pale shade as my skin.

"So you will need long-sleeved shirts then," Jack said blandly.

"Apparently," I replied, bemused. I'd been imagining the weapon might shrink to pocket size. It seemed it had other ideas.

Organising a waterproof bag stuffed with suitable clothes and shoes for Jack and me didn't take long. I braced myself for the consequent drain of energy, but it didn't come. The trident was still feeding me its power even though I wasn't holding it anymore. The new bag was bulky; Jack handed me the smaller backpack with my passports and other documents and shouldered the larger one.

"And my ears?"

I took the bandana from my wrist, smoothing the crumples from it and handing it back to him. He tied it around his hair. "There's a hat in the bag. This will have to do for underwater." My eyes drifted to the stargem pendant. "You'll have to take that off too."

He nodded, slipping the chain over his head and putting it in the outside pocket of my backpack, next to the waterlogged packaging from the sausages we'd given Angel. The seams glowed faintly; I reinforced them with a thought until no light seeped through.

I'd left the hardest part for last. "Ready?" I asked Jack, bracing my shoulders. He nodded, and I placed my hand on his chest. The touch was unnecessary, but I couldn't resist. The warm feel of his skin under my fingers lit a fire in my belly, reminding me of earlier. His pupils dilated as he looked at me. Was he thinking the same thing?

The flare of pain Jack felt when I willed his lungs to process both air and water was sharp, but I drained it away before it reached his nerve endings. I held my breath for a second, waiting to see whether he was okay. He gave me a thumb's up, and I sagged with relief. I noticed the webbing between his fingers and willed that away too.

MELPOMENE'S DAUGHTER

"Can you speak?" I asked. A flurry of bubbles rushed from his mouth, muffling any sound he might have made. Ruefully, he shook his head, and I grinned back. "This has potential. I could say whatever I like and you couldn't do anything to—"

His kiss made me forget what I was going to say next.

"Okay, you could," I gasped when he released me, fanning the blush heating my cheeks. "Fair point, well made. Anyway, my turn."

Nerves fizzed in my stomach. To deliberately do something, knowing the pain it was going to cause me, made my fists curl with anxiety. More anxiety than I'd felt last time. My fear had returned, something I had mixed feelings about. Where was a siren when you needed one?

The trident chimed a question.

"No, no," I said hastily, ignoring Jack's strange look, "that's fine." What would it have done if I said yes? Would a siren have popped into being right beside us? The hairs on the back of my neck stood on end. I willed my body to change before the weapon decided to take matters into its own hands, clenching my jaw against the pain that exploded in my lungs and throat like a bomb, shooting burning tendrils down my arms and legs. My fingers burned as though I'd dipped them in acid as the webbing retreated into my skin.

When I came back to myself, Jack was holding me against his chest, stroking my hair. When I stirred, he released me. Together, we turned to the portal. And England.

CHAPTER EIGHTEEN

The portal emerged beneath a rocky outcrop near the mouth of a river. I hoped it was the Thames, but couldn't be sure. After a brief, whispered conversation under a deserted pier, we decided to swim up the river as far as we could before emerging onto the shore once we found somewhere we wouldn't be noticed. It was hard to judge the angle of the sun given the heavy rainclouds hanging across the sky in a drab sheet, but the light where we swam, just above the silt clouds choking the riverbed, had thinned out, growing dimmer. Late afternoon?

However, we hadn't been swimming for long when Jack brushed my hand to get my attention, nodding towards the shore with a grimace. I raised my eyebrows before indicating my agreement. After being in—and breathing—the pure water of the underwater *sidhe* for two days, the heavily trafficked seawater here left a metallic taste in my mouth that grew increasingly unpleasant as we made our way upstream. Boats grumbled over our heads, filling the water with engine reverberations and setting my teeth on edge. The closer we got to the shore, the closer we came to the muddy bottom, our eyes straining harder to see through the silt. Still, there was beauty here too. Rain speckled the water's surface. As we drew closer to it, I stared from beneath, fascinated, as each drop pockmarked the water, turning it into a shimmering, dancing sheet.

Waiting until there was no nearby engine noise, we popped our heads above the waterline, craning our necks to see beyond the churning water to the shore. Fat drops struck my head, my face, cleaner than the water in which we were submerged. Squinting through the haze of rain, I made out an empty beach, and apartments beyond a row of trees. A single jogger, visible between the trees, ignored the weather.

After checking for oncoming boats, we swam towards the shore. Conscious of the possibility of watching eyes behind apartment windows, I tried to breathe normally, reminding myself that it would look weird if my freestyle stroke didn't include lifting my face out of the water now and then. The air felt strange in my lungs after so long breathing water, warm and sharp at the same time, like fresh lemon pie when the baker has forgotten to add sugar.

When we reached the sucking mud at the shoreline we paused to take off the flippers and so Jack could readjust his bandana before trudging in our dive boots up the beach. I was glad to be wearing them; the mud wasn't something I'd want squelching beneath my toes. *I was just breathing that.* I shuddered.

We paused on the bank, looking around for somewhere to change. From here, I could see the other shore of the wide river. The buildings on that side were taller than the ones closest to us. Everything looked familiar and yet different; the grass was a vivid green, as though drawn with kids crayons, and the gardens were dotted with flowers, a striking reminder of the fact it was spring here, not autumn. The street sign marking the one-way street beyond the concrete retaining wall was in English, but was blue and white rather than the black and white ones I was used to.

"Oh my god, Jack, we're in England!" I clutched his hands, grinning like a loon.

"I knew you could do it." He smiled back. "Have you ever been overseas before?"

"No. Well, yes, I was born here. Dad brought me to Australia when I was still a baby." I shook as the cool air cut through my wetsuit. "How is it I can swim around in the ocean with no worries but a cold breeze gives me goosebumps?"

He shrugged. "A peculiarity of the change the *sidhe* made, I suppose. We should get you somewhere dry so you can get dressed."

"Where?" There wasn't a public toilet or shopping mall in sight, just rows of houses and apartments. We'd popped up in the middle of suburbia. Wealthy suburbia, I guessed, given the nicely maintained gardens and lack of graffiti. Who else could afford a riverside view?

"That building has parking underneath." He nodded towards one of the buildings.

"I'm sure it will be locked."

We crossed the beach and its hem of grass, hopping over the concrete retaining wall. An older gentleman walking a small dog regarded us with surprise. "You've been swimming?" he blurted, then looked away, embarrassment flushing his aura pink.

I folded my arms across my chest, conscious of how tightly it clung to my curves. "Yeah, we're tourists."

"Barmy tourists," he muttered, walking around us. The rain pattered on his umbrella. "Good afternoon."

"Excuse me," I called after him, "is there somewhere around here we could dry off?"

He hesitated as though not wanting to engage with the crazy people. I couldn't say I blamed him. Then he nodded to a paved alley running between two buildings. "Go down there, turn right at the end of the street, and follow it along. There's shops down there. Although," he added, "this time on a Sunday they'll be closing soon."

"It is Sunday?" Jack murmured with surprise as the man hurried away, dog trotting behind him. "I thought we left on Saturday morning?"

"We did," I replied, equally surprised. "Although if it's Sunday evening here it's some time on Monday in Australia. I think." Still, two days was impressive—that was only twice what it would've taken to fly. A surge of gratitude towards the trident made it hum softly in response.

The underground car park was locked. I glared at it, and the lock refused to comply when I willed it to open, a sobering reminder that I was back in my world now. No more superpowers. Or fewer, at any rate. I'd been downgraded from Supergirl to a lame sidekick.

We followed the dog walker's directions, trying to ignore the strange looks from passers-by as we squelched along the street in our wetsuits. At least our gills were hidden, I thought ruefully, or they'd have a lot more to stare at. A horrified teenager behind the counter at a pizza place directed us to a dim little toilet block on the edge of an adjacent park, which gave us somewhere to change. I tried not to touch anything in the cubicle as I shucked my wetsuit and dried myself with a spare shirt and some wadded toilet paper before pulling jeans, T-shirt and jumper over damp skin. The sneakers fit comfortably, although as I regarded them I realised ruefully that they weren't quite a perfect match for the pair I'd turned into flippers before we left Australia. The logo on the side was all wrong: how I'd remembered it rather than how it actually was.

Oh well, people would assume I was wearing knock offs, I supposed.

Holding the dripping wetsuit out so it wouldn't soak me all over again, I regarded myself in the mirror, looking for anything out of place, anything to reveal I'd just arrived in the country by emerging from the water like a character from a bad spy novel. Although a journey by midget submarine would have probably been less eventful. A smile tugged my lips, turning to a grimace as I regarded my bedraggled hair. Raking my fingers through it did little to help untangle the knots, although I did find a tiny piece of seaweed. How long had that been there? I tossed it in the bin with a grumble. No wonder the dog walker had been so wary of us. I opened my now well-travelled backpack, breathing a sigh of relief that it was only slightly damp inside; my purse and passport documents, in their cling wrap, were dry.

The sausage packaging I'd saved followed the seaweed into the bin, and I ran my hairbrush under hot—well, lukewarm—water for thirty seconds to get rid of the ocean tang before running it through my hair until the tangles were gone. I'd been right, though. I was going to need some intensive moisturising.

When I finally emerged, dry and craving a hot shower, Jack was waiting for me outside the toilets. The rain rattled against the awning above his head. He held the big waterproof bag open and I dropped my wetsuit, flippers and boots into it gratefully.

"So what now?" I said.

He slung the bag over his shoulder, showing no sign of discomfort even though it had to be heavy with all that water. "I was going to ask you the same thing."

I sighed, regarding the wet street with distaste. I hadn't thought to conjure us an umbrella or rain coats, and now I wanted to it was too late. "I know London has trains and buses..." At least, I'd seen red, double-decker busses on plenty of television shows. The idea of navigating my way across a huge, unfamiliar city made my stomach roil. "First, let's see if we can find a phone so I can call Nana's house. Aunt Elizabeth was staying there, so I guess Sarah and Ryan will be there too. Maybe they can help." If we couldn't find a phone booth I could always make the teenager at the pizza place like me enough he'd let us use the store phone, I supposed.

I wasn't totally superpower-free, after all.

"Is that a telephone over there?"

I followed the line of Jack's pointing finger and my mouth fell open. "Yes."

"You are surprised?" he said.

"I am. Not complaining, though. Let's just hope it works."

I got some change for the phone from the pizza shop. Then Jack waited under the dubious shelter of a leafy tree rather than squeezing into the glass-and-steel booth with me. I pulled a scrap of paper out of my purse and punched in the number. It was significantly shorter without having to dial out of Australia or enter the country code.

"Please be home." The phone rang. And rang. And rang.

"Hello?" My aunt's familiar voice sounded breathless, anxious.

"It's me. Isla."

"Isla! Thank goodness." A voice in the background spoke and, for a moment, the sound on the other end grew muffled as my aunt covered the receiver. Then she came back on the line. "Sorry about that. Where are you?"

"At the airport. Heathrow. But, um…" My ears burned as I realised how poorly I'd thought this through. "Our baggage got lost."

"If you'd told us when your flight arrived, we could have arranged to pick you up," she said, tone sharp. Then it softened. "That's no good about your bags. Just part of this family's luck lately, I suppose."

"And news about Dad?"

There was a brief pause. "No, I'm afraid not. I thought when the phone rang it might be the police with news. I'm sorry."

"It's okay." Disappointment sat on my chest like a stone, even though I hadn't expected anything else—I was sure Melpomene had my father, and she wouldn't just let him go. Not after she'd waited so long to find him.

"You said 'our'."

"What?" Her change of subject startled me.

"You said 'our' bags got lost. Who came with you?"

"Jack." I met the hob's gaze through the scratched glass. He studied me intently; with his keen hearing, he could no doubt hear me, and probably my aunt too.

"That was sweet of him," Aunt Elizabeth said after

another telling pause. I could hear the doubt in her voice, though—it was an expensive flight to take on a whim.

"Is Sarah there?"

"Yes. She's bouncing up and down, waiting for me to hand her the phone. Here."

After a few seconds, my cousin's voice came on the line. "Isla! You're here…?"

"Yes. After a fashion. We're at a shopping strip in—" I craned my neck, peering back towards the shops "—I think somewhere called Thamesmead? Is that far from Nana's house?"

"Only, like, the other side of the city." I didn't have to strain myself to imagine her rolling her eyes at me. "We're in Putney."

"I just walked out of a river, Sarah," I muttered. "Give me five minutes to get my bearings, yeah?"

"You can have ten. So why are you calling?"

"Do you have a car? Could you come and get us?" I hated the desperate tone creeping into my voice. But it would be nice to have someone else take charge for a bit.

"Not a chance Mum will let me or Ry drive Nana's car after dark." The sun hadn't set yet, although it was getting close to the horizon. I bit my lip, wondering what I should do. Maybe I could buy a map of the subway from the newsagent. My aunt's voice murmured something in the background. "Aunt Elizabeth said catch a taxi. You got some money out, didn't you?"

I eyed my remaining pound notes with a frown. After buying my cousins' plane tickets, I hadn't had much money left to exchange. "Yeah, but if we're catching a taxi all the way across London I don't know if it will be enough."

"We can meet you out the front and pay for the rest

if you need us to."

"Good idea." Relief made me giddy. "Tell her thank you."

"I will." She lowered her voice. "She's pretty mad at us, Isla. I told her how I accidentally deleted your email with the flight times, but she says you should've sent it to her too. Or called once you had a booking time."

"Damn straight," my usually well-mannered aunt said in the background.

"I'll prepare myself for some serious grovelling then."

"You do that," Sarah said brightly. "We'll see you soon!"

CHAPTER NINETEEN

Nana's house was at the end of a small cul-de-sac. Our black cab pulled up under the streetlight; before I could suggest the driver honk the horn to let them know we were here, the front door swung open and two figures emerged. Aunt Elizabeth and Sarah. My aunt paid the driver, waving off my paltry contribution, and we got out of the car. My efforts to be discreet about unbuckling Jack's seatbelt for him failed; Sarah noticed, eyes widening.

"I'm so glad you got here safely." My cousin wrapped me in a hug and kissed my cheek as the cab pulled away. Then she wrinkled her nose. "You smell a bit."

"Sarah!" my aunt protested, horrified.

"It's okay. Long haul flights don't have showers," I said quickly, linking an arm through Jack's so my aunt didn't try to give me a hug too. Normally I wouldn't mind, but the *Eau de Thames* perfume I was wearing might raise questions. "I'm looking forward to a long shower with lots of soap."

Jack nodded.

"I'm surprised to see you here, Jack," Aunt Elizabeth said as she led us down the short gravel driveway to the front door. A wisteria vine grew up the wall next to the awning, purple flowers cascading down and filling the air with their sweet aroma.

"When Isla told me what happened to her father, I had to come," he replied simply. My aunt headed in first and I caught the screen door, holding it open for the hob.

"That's very kind." My aunt looked Jack up and down. Wondering how he could afford the flight, no doubt, and too polite to ask. "This place only has the three bedrooms, so you'll be sharing with Ryan. I hope that's okay."

"Of course," Jack replied. "Thank you for your kindness." His manners smoothed her ruffled feathers, although not so much she'd let him share a room with me—I was sure of that. A tiny surge of disappointment made me sigh; after cuddling with Jack last night, and ... everything ... that had happened since, I would miss not having him at my side.

From the outside, I'd thought Nana's place was huge. Now I realised it was half of a duplex, the larger outer building divided into two, smaller homes. The three bedrooms and the bathroom were upstairs, and the kitchen, lounge and laundry downstairs. My nose tickled with the scent of lavender. My room had smelled like that for a week after Nana's visit. The thought made me queasy.

"Would you like a cup of tea?" Aunt Elizabeth asked.

"I'd love one!" I said, my enthusiasm earning me a curious look. Oops. Hard to explain it would be my first hot drink in two days.

"Jack?"

"Yes, please."

"Right. Sarah, did you want to show them where they can put their things? Such as they are?" She glanced at the large bag Jack was holding. "I'm surprised you were able to get such a large bag on as carryon luggage."

Jack smiled and shrugged, but, before he could answer, Sarah dragged us down the hall to the stairs. "Can I borrow a pair of pyjamas?" I asked her meekly as we climbed upwards.

"You should've brought more clothes," she murmured. "And what happened to your sneakers?"

"We weren't really in a position to drag a couple of suitcases around after us." I ignored the second question. Admitting I'd forgotten the details of the logo was a bit embarrassing. Although trust her to notice.

"Anyway, Jack, this is the room you'll be sharing with Ryan." She rapped on a closed door at the top of the stairs. Ryan opened it, smiling with relief when he saw me. Behind him, I caught a glimpse of an old-fashioned room with heavy timber furniture and blue-and-cream wallpaper. On the floor lay a pallet, bedding hastily thrown together. "Sorry, it's not going to be comfortable."

"I have had worse accommodations," Jack replied. He glanced at me. "Isla, the iron...?"

"What?" I blinked. Was that why I was feeling queasy? Of course it was.

"There's iron?" Ryan looked around as though expecting it to be obvious. "Where?"

"I do not know, but I can sense it."

I swallowed. "If we help you guys track it down, can you remove it? At least from the bedrooms?"

"Of course." Sarah nodded.

A quick search uncovered a piece of iron in every bedroom—and one hidden under the vanity in the small bathroom. Ryan took the odd assortment of sculptures and iron bars downstairs to put in the back yard until our visit was over.

"This feels ghoulish," I said to Jack as we stood in Nana's bedroom doorway, his arms around my waist. A heavy floral bedspread covered the bed; my aunt's suitcase sat against the wardrobe door, stuffed with clothes and blocking one side of the room. Despite the inconvenience, she hadn't unpacked.

"She was sleeping in her old bedroom," Sarah confided from behind me. "When Ryan and I arrived, she moved in here. I don't think she was comfortable with it, though." She looked down at her hands. "I know she hasn't gone in the garden."

"That's where..."

"Yeah."

"God." My stomach churned, and not from the presence of iron. It must have been hard enough for Dad and Aunt Elizabeth to come back to their family home when their mother was no longer living in it. Worse that she'd died here. I tried to imagine sleeping at the farm under those circumstances. Tears burned the backs of my eyes.

Seeing my expression, Jack kissed my cheek softly. "We will get him back."

"I know." My voice cracked.

Sarah watched the casual intimacy with a glint in her eye that meant I'd get the third degree later. "Did you want those pyjamas now, and a shower?"

"Yes," I sighed wistfully. "Although the tea...?"

"I'll tell Mum you'll be down soon." She glanced at

Jack. "Don't be in there too long if Jack wants a shower too, though. The water runs out pretty fast."

"I do not mind waiting."

"Yeah, but Ryan might." She wrinkled her nose. "You guys really smell like fish."

I poked my tongue at her.

The hot water drumming on my scalp was pure bliss. Helping myself to Nana's toiletries with a twinge of guilt, I washed my hair twice before I was satisfied the river stink was gone. Then I scrubbed my skin—although I was more timid when cleaning the sides of my ribs, where my gills were. Even closed, the faint lines felt strange under my fingertips, like evenly spaced scars from some huge, clawed animal.

Sarah was going to freak right out when she saw them. I'd had them for two days, and I was still a little freaked out, staring at myself in the mirror. They were a reminder that, even though things seemed a bit more normal after a hot shower, nothing was normal about my life.

Once I was dry and in Sarah's pyjamas, I could detect the stink Sarah was referring to on my clothes. It was subtle, given the clothes hadn't been directly in the river, but noticeable. I sighed. Tomorrow I'd have to either wear them again or borrow some of Nana's clothes; both Sarah and Aunt Elizabeth were too tall for their clothes to fit me. I'd had to roll the pyjama pants up so I didn't trip over the cuffs.

Maybe the laundry had a dryer? I could wash my clothes overnight.

The others were in the kitchen. Sarah talked fast, chattering about how cheap everything was here compared to back home. Jack looked relieved and Aunt

Elizabeth tired. She stood to make me some tea when I entered. Brushing damp hair back from my face, I waved her back to her seat. "I'll do it. It's fine."

She sat reluctantly. "So, I was just asking Jack how the flight went."

"The duty free was awesome, wasn't it, Jack?" Sarah said, giving him a significant look.

So that was why she'd been talking about shops: to stop Jack from saying something that would be a dead giveaway. He'd never been in an airport or on a plane in his life. Once again, I owed Sarah for covering my butt.

"It looked good." I plopped a teabag into an empty cup sitting on the bench. "But we didn't get anything. Just as well, given they lost our bags."

"The flight was good. Long though," Jack added, fiddling with the hem of his bandana. His hair, where it poked out underneath, had dried into bedraggled strands. I resisted the urge to run my fingers through them, smooth out the tangles.

"You both must be exhausted," Aunt Elizabeth said.

"Uh huh," I replied, drowning the teabag in boiling water. Steam filled my nostrils. "I want to get a good night's sleep so tomorrow I can go looking for Dad."

"Sweetheart, the police are already doing that," she replied, her voice soft with pity.

I thrust out my jaw. "I can't just sit here and do nothing. Besides, he's one missing person. I doubt he's got, like, a taskforce assigned to him or anything."

"Where would you look?"

"Like you always say when we lose stuff, we'll start in the place we last remember having him."

That brought a faint smile to her lips. But surprise

cut through the grief and anxiety in her aura. Was she expecting me to be less together about it than I was? I'd been psyching myself up for days to bring the battle to my mother. I was ready for it.

The trident chimed its agreement, bells only I could hear.

The floor was hard and cold under my bare feet. I looked down, surprised, and couldn't see my toes beneath the swishing black fabric of the ball gown's voluminous skirt.

Wait, ball gown?

Eyes wide, I stared around at a huge room that was strange and yet eerily familiar. I'd dreamed of this place once before, with its distant walls and stargem-flecked ceiling, with its strange mirror bearing my mother's shocked reflection.

My palms, sheathed inside long black gloves, began to sweat. My stomach fluttered with a sense of impending danger. *Wake up, wake up, wake up...* I tried to pinch myself, but the black satin around my thumb and forefinger slipped off my skin.

A hand resting on my shoulder made me startle so badly that, for a moment, my feet left the ground. I whirled, knowing who I was going to see even as I turned. Sure enough, the figure in the scarecrow mask stood before me, long hob ears protruding out from behind the woven straw. Golden-brown eyes blinked slowly at my reaction, and the hob spoke.

"Mistress? Are you well?" That was new: last time I hadn't been able to hear him.

"Ah…"

"Mistress?" Those eyes narrowed, regarded me intently. "Oh dear. It is you again. You should not be troubling my Lady Melpomene, wretched creature."

I lifted my chin. "Well, she should stay the hell away from me and mine."

"You will not tell her what to do, half-breed."

Fury boiled up in me like lava. Before I knew what I was doing, I swung my hand, fingers curled into a clumsy fist, at the jaw under that mask. The straw gave way under my knuckles and I struck his chin, knocking the hob flying.

I sat up, kicking the heavy fabric off my legs with a strangled cry.

It took me several seconds to realise the fabric was my blankets, not a cumbersome dress. I was awake. My heart thundered, trapped in my throat. The sound was so loud it was a wonder Sarah was able to sleep through it, sprawled across the bed as though she didn't have a care in the world. The bedroom was dim, the only light from the streetlamp outside, sneaking in through the gap in the curtains.

My hand ached.

I took several deep breaths, willing my pulse to slow as I rubbed my bruised knuckles. *It was just a dream.* Except I didn't believe it, not really. Last time I'd dreamed about that hall had been just before my powers awoke— then, Melpomene had thrown me from the dream amidst the shards of a shattered mirror. That was just before I'd made Ryan an *aislinge* and my father had been elf shot. Just before my life took a turn from the normal to the terrifying and strange.

But also just before I'd met Jack.

I fumbled for Sarah's watch on the bedside table, angling it so I could read the time. Four in the morning. Eyeing my pillow with distaste—there was no way I'd be able to sleep again—I rolled off the low pallet and crept from the room.

Jack found me downstairs fifteen minutes later, sipping on a steaming cup of instant coffee. A small smile crept onto my lips; he looked adorable in a borrowed pair of rumpled pyjamas that were too long for him, and his hair was a tangled mess—although at least it was clean. I was grateful I'd taken the time to brush mine before I came down to boil the kettle.

I patted the couch beside me and he sat; I scooted closer, so I could run my fingers through his soft hair, smoothing out the tangles one at a time. He sighed, leaning into my touch. "You should get your bandana before my aunt gets up," I murmured.

"Do I have to do it just yet?" He sounded wistful.

"Not yet, no." I turned so I could put my cup on the side table, pushing a doily to one side so I didn't ruin it. Then I wrapped my arms around Jack's chest; the pre-dawn air in the house was cool and he was as warm as always, like a giant hot water bottle. He smelled of fresh soap and a spicy smell that was all him. "Sorry I woke you. I was trying to be sneaky."

"It was not that."

"Were your Spidey senses tingling?" I laughed softly at his blank look. "Never mind."

"I felt something troubling you."

"So they *were* tingling."

"I am serious."

"Me too." I ran a fingertip along the smooth top of one of his long ears. He shivered. "Are you sure nothing is tingling?"

His lips met mine, silencing my teasing laugh. When we came up for air sometime later, his gaze was dark and intense. "Now, be serious and tell me what is bothering you."

"If being silly results in kisses as punishment, I'm going to swear off seriousness for good."

"There will be no more kisses until you tell me what the matter is."

"Damn." I sighed, staring down at my hand, which curled through his, our fingers interlaced. "I had another dream."

He sat up straighter. "Of your mother?"

"Yes. Well, no. Of her hob, I think. But it was in the same place as the first dream." I lowered my voice to a whisper. "I'm scared it's real. She knows I'm here now."

"We would not have been able to sneak into her realm without her knowing. Losing the element of surprise is not a great concern."

"What if she comes for us first? Or for the rest of my family?" A memory surfaced, of Sarah kneeling on the frigid ground as Ariel stood over her. He'd gloated about how he liked redheads, stroking her jaw as though thinking about crushing it. Ariel worked for Everest, not Melpomene, but I didn't have to stretch my imagination to think of the ways my mother could hurt my loved ones. Ways she might already be hurting my father. And because she could manipulate emotions, she could make them welcome it if she wanted to. In Dad's case, she wouldn't even have to do anything. He already loved her beyond reason.

MELPOMENE'S DAUGHTER

Jack's gentle kiss on the back of my hand brought me back to myself. I realised tears were prickling my eyes. I blinked and one escaped my lashes, running down my cheek. "We will find him. We are so much closer to him now, and we have the trident. Nothing will get in our way." His sapphire eyes were earnest, gazing at me over our intertwined fingers. His breath tickled my skin when he spoke.

"You can't know that." My voice was hoarse.

"I do. Because I believe in you." He drew me forward, slow and inexorable, until I was cradled in the circle of his arms. His kiss was hot and sure, and his fingers on my hip under the loose pyjama top stole my breath away, making me forget my troubles—for a time, at least. It was a special kind of magic, all Jack's own—and I gave him everything in return.

CHAPTER TWENTY

After breakfast, Jack and I dressed in clothes freshly washed and dried in the laundry overnight. They smelled of apple-scented fabric softener, a definite improvement over fish and polluted water.

"We're going to have to take both of you shopping," Sarah said, eyeing the pair of us as we joined the family in the dining room, walking hand-in-hand.

"Make sure you call the airline today to see if they have located your bags," Aunt Elizabeth said, bringing a plate of toast to the table as we all sat. It reminded me of Sunday breakfasts at home. "Hopefully you won't need to replace everything."

Sarah grimaced, knowing the lost bags wouldn't arrive. How would we convince her mother not to ring the airport and start yelling when we seemed to be having no luck retrieving our imaginary luggage? I glanced at Jack and he nodded slightly.

"Aunt Elizabeth, there's something we need to talk about."

My aunt caught the look between Jack and I, and raised her hand to cut off what we were about to say. Her eyes shone with amusement. "There are some things I really don't need to know, dear."

"Oh?" She assumed I was talking about me and Jack. The blush burned my ears. "Oh! No, not that. Something more important." I curled my fingers through the hob's and amended what I'd said. "Not more important. More serious."

The twinkle in her eye faded and she sat, ignoring the food on the plate before her. "What is it?"

"It's about Nana. And Dad. And my mother." I looked at my boyfriend. Before the others had woken, he and I had agreed to tell my aunt everything. Now he smiled encouragingly. "And Jack and I, only not the way you think."

Sarah rolled her eyes. "Just spit it out, Isla."

I opened my mouth, wondering where to begin. Closed it again.

Sighing, Jack took the bandana off his hair, revealing his long ears.

"Remember all those stories Nana told you about the *duinesidhe* as a girl?" I said as my aunt stared at Jack. "They weren't just stories. Jack is a hob. My mother is an *aosidhe*. And I think she kidnapped Dad."

My aunt's aura shifted from scepticism to disbelief to dawning shock as she realised I was serious. Hand trembling, she reached out a finger to touch Jack's ear, poking it as though she thought it might come loose and fall to the floor with a rubbery *thunk*.

I'd done much the same thing the first time he'd revealed himself to me.

"Aw, Isla," Ryan said, snagging the top slice of toast

on the pile, "don't you realise the more people who know the secret, the more it cheapens it for the rest of us?"

I glanced at him, realised he was joking. A faint smile tugged at the corner of my lips, fading as quickly as it had appeared. "Sorry, Ryan. Under the circumstances…"

"Yeah." His shoulders slumped for a moment. Then he reached for the marmalade.

"And Mum?" Aunt Elizabeth murmured, her gaze drifting to a black and white photo on the wall beside the fridge. It was of a much younger Nana, with a teenage boy and girl on either side of her. My aunt and father. "How does she tie into this?"

"I don't have proof, but there is a hob named Ariel who had a serious grudge against her. I think he might have…" I bit my lip, seeing the shadow of pain in her eyes.

"Why did he…? Why would he…?"

"Because she killed another hob, Moray, who was trying to kidnap Dad."

Aunt Elizabeth sat back in her chair, face as white as the milk in Jack's glass. Taking a deep breath, she said, "I think you'd better start from the beginning."

So I told my aunt what had really been behind the events of the last five months: Dad's coma, Ryan's strangely insightful paintings, Nana's hostility towards me. Sarah and Ryan interrupted to elaborate when I missed something, while Jack sat quietly, hands folded in his lap, conscious of my aunt's furtive glances at his ears.

"You didn't lose your bags at the airport, did you?" she said finally, when my nervous babble fell silent.

I shook my head.

"How did you really get here?"

"Honestly, I'm not sure you want to know. It was pretty

freaky. But Jack couldn't fly."

"And you've suddenly decided to be honest with me because...?" There was faint admonition in her tone, although far less than I—we—deserved. My reasons for not telling Dominic didn't apply to my aunt. I'd known her all my life, trusted her implicitly. I just hadn't wanted to worry her. *That's the same reason Dad kept it a secret from me for eighteen years.*

Shame made me hang my head when I replied. "Because if Melpomene—that's my mother's real name—if she knows I'm here she may come for me. If she does, you could be in danger. All of you."

"It sounds like we were already in danger, back in Australia."

I grimaced, acknowledging the truth of her statement. Jack spoke in my defence. "Not as great a danger as you are here. Forgive me, but the truly dangerous *duinesidhe* race is the *aosidhe*, and with the exception of Everest, there have not been any of those in Australia. Here there are dozens. Hundreds, maybe, throughout Europe. All powerful and narcissistic. Many evil. Most cruel."

Aunt Elizabeth gazed at Jack through narrowed eyes. "My mother always said no *duinesidhe* was to be trusted." She stumbled over the strange word; my Nana may have told her stories as a child, but that had been decades ago.

"That sounds familiar," Sarah muttered.

"Not like an *aosidhe*," Jack said, ignoring the aside. I nodded vehemently in agreement.

"And yet you think a hob killed my mother?"

The statement hung in the air, a silent accusation. Ryan came to our rescue. "Yeah, but Nana started it."

"Sort of," I said. "Moray was trying to abduct Dad for

Everest. So really, Everest started it."

My aunt stood abruptly. "I think I need to lie down. Please, don't leave the house until I... Just until."

After she shuffled up the stairs, I looked between my cousins. The guilt sat in my stomach like a stone, driving my hunger away. "Maybe I shouldn't have told her," I said, the question in my voice.

"There's no way we were going to get away with keeping Jack's nature a secret for long, given we're all under one roof," Sarah said pragmatically, reaching for her coffee. She sipped it and wrinkled her nose. "Cold."

"I should've told her sooner. When I told you guys. That way it wouldn't have been such a shock, on top of what happened to Nana."

"Yeah," Ryan said around a mouthful of toast. Sarah gave him a dark look and he swallowed before admitting, "It didn't occur to me to suggest it either. I guess as a teenager you sort of get into the habit of keeping some things from your parents."

The truth of that made me and Sarah nod. Jack took a small sip of his milk. "Either way, it is done now. Let your aunt have some time to think it over. We should decide what we are going to do next."

"I wish we had Talbot here," I said, thinking about the *puca's* keen sense of smell. "He might be able to track Dad. Or confirm whether Ariel was the one who killed Nana, since he knows his scent."

"Although it's rained a fair bit since then." Sarah stood, putting her coffee cup in the microwave.

"I take it there has been no sign of Welkin since you arrived?" Jack asked.

"No." She looked troubled. "Do you think he got lost

or something? Sucked into a jet engine?"

"One can only hope," Jack said dryly. She glared daggers at him and he ducked his head, abashed. "*Piskie*s have an excellent sense of direction and can ride air currents like a bird. I am sure he is fine."

"Besides, aeroplanes make a lot of noise. I'm sure he'd hear one coming." Ryan reached for another piece of toast. He dropped it on my plate and gave me a pale-eyed glare. "Eat."

"Yes, Mum," I murmured sarcastically, picking up the jam jar. Unfortunately—but unsurprisingly—my grandmother didn't have any Vegemite in the house.

Jack hid a grin behind his glass. "When Welkin arrives, he may be able to talk to the local *piskies*, find out the quickest way to get to Melpomene's *sidhe*."

"I don't suppose you know any *duinesidhe* here? Anyone who could help?"

He shook his head. "None that would help us. Remember, I am a wanted criminal here and, unlike in Australia, Old World *duinesidhe* are almost universally sworn into the service of one *aosidhe* or another. They would have to turn me in."

"Why are you a wanted criminal?" Ryan frowned.

"I killed my *aosidhe* master," Jack replied simply.

My cousin looked at me. Suspicion flared in his aura, the dark blue of a twilight sky. "You knew about this?"

I nodded around a mouthful of toast. It tasted like ashes as I swallowed. "His master was evil. He tortured Jack's sister, Evie, and god knows how many human girls. It was the only way they could escape."

"It is true," Jack said. "I am not proud of what I did, but I do not regret doing it."

Ryan considered this for a moment before nodding once, sharply. "Fair enough," he grunted.

The microwave beeped and Sarah retrieved her mug, blowing on it as she returned to the table. "Still, I wouldn't tell Mum that story right now if I were you. She's still reeling at the idea Nana killed someone. She'd seriously wig if she knew you had too."

"Good advice," Jack said.

"I've been trying to see whether I can do another vision drawing," Ryan admitted, running a hand through his short red hair. "I packed my sketchpad and pencils. But no joy." He looked at Jack. "Are all *aislinge* powers as fickle as mine?"

"Not usually," Jack replied, smiling to soften the words. "Take Everest's Shannon, for example. She was able to locate things whenever he wanted her to."

My heart fluttered in my chest. "How?"

"I do not know." Jack reached out and squeezed my fingers. Sarah tracked the gesture with her gaze, pursing her lips. I'd fallen asleep so quickly last night she hadn't had a chance to interrogate me about the past few days. I was sure she could sense the change in intimacy between Jack and me; relationships were her sixth sense.

"Do you think maybe he was able to activate her power?" Ryan said, glancing at me.

"Perhaps, but I do not know how," Jack admitted.

The trident chimed gently and I frowned, wondering why it had decided to make itself known—it had been silent since the evening before. I rolled my sleeve up to look at it, ignoring the startled gasps from my cousins. The weapon's golden shape looked the same as it had when it merged with my skin in the underwater *sidhe*.

"You got a tattoo?" Sarah breathed. "Your dad is going to kill you!"

"I *am* eighteen," I murmured, distracted, running my finger along the skin. A memory scrabbled at the edge of my brain. The trident chimed again, more insistent.

Gold. Child's glitter scattered across a page.

Eyes widening, I looked up at Ryan. "When you've had your visions, there's a colour in your aura. Golden flecks."

He leaned forward, hands gripping the edge of the table. "Do you think you can create it?"

"I can try."

"Isla, is this a good idea?" Sarah said. But I was already reaching for his hand.

I didn't add *much* gold. Just the tiniest dusting, as though from a single twist of a pepper grinder. But the result was instantaneous. Ryan sat back, his eyes growing distant as he seemed to look right through me, staring at the door at my back. "Excuse me. I need my sketchpad."

We watched him leave. "That was dramatic," Sarah said. "Are you sure he's okay?"

"Yes." I could always take the flecks away again if they harmed him. *Fingers crossed.*

"Let us just hope the vision he has is relevant to our current predicament," Jack said.

"Or that it's tonight's lotto numbers." Sarah grinned, looking between us. "So what now? Do we just wait?"

"Aunt Elizabeth asked us not to go anywhere," I said with a sigh.

"Since when do you always do what you're told?"

"Today it seems like a good idea. I want her to know she can trust me right now. She's probably up there wondering if she can."

Sarah downed her coffee with a pout. "I wanted to go shopping."

"We can do that tomorrow. London isn't going anywhere, and Jack and I have enough clothes for today." My gaze slid to the screen door leading into the garden. The sight of it weighed on my chest. "Have you been out there since you arrived?"

"Once," she said, her blue-green eyes darkening with grief. "There was still some police tape up. I took it down."

"I assume the police are okay with us staying here? Like, they've finished their investigations and everything?"

"I guess." She shrugged. "I know the funeral was delayed until after they'd done an autopsy."

After tidying up the kitchen—very little of the toast Aunt Elizabeth had made had been eaten—Sarah and I went out into the garden. Jack hung back, giving us some space.

A small fan-shaped awning covered the back stoop. An outdoor table and chairs were to my left—even from the doorway I could feel the wrought iron under the white paint. The grass was such a vivid green that—to my Australian eyes, used to a country with less rainfall—it looked artificial. The lawn was thick and several inches high; it hadn't been mown in weeks. Leafy trees lined the fence on all sides, screening the yard from the neighbours' view—even from the top-storey windows in the other half of the duplex.

That privacy had allowed someone to kill my grandmother here.

"You can see how Ariel could've done it," Sarah murmured, echoing my thoughts. "No one would've seen."

I nodded grimly. Staring at the long grass, wondering exactly where she'd died, my heart ached for Dad and Aunt

Elizabeth's loss. My own ambivalence about my grand-mother made me feel guilty I wasn't sadder in my own right. But my relationship with Nana had been fraught. She'd ignored me for most of my life—easy to do when we lived in different countries. After Dad's coma, though, she'd come to Australia, where her dislike had been blatant. She blamed me for Dad's condition, assuming because I was half *aosidhe* I was somehow responsible.

I bit my lip and frowned. "Did they ever find out whether the pole she defended herself with was iron?"

"I don't know. I'm sure Uncle David knew—" she glanced at me "—knows, I mean, but I don't know if he mentioned it to Mum. I couldn't figure out how to ask without look-ing crazy."

"That's one upside of telling her everything, I guess. Now we can."

"Does it matter?"

"It would give us a better idea of whether it really was Ariel. We're assuming it was him, but it could've been a mugger or something."

"Nothing was stolen. I know that much." Sarah sat on the concrete and curled her arms around her bent knees. She didn't want to go any further into the garden either. It felt like trespassing somehow.

"Oh."

We lingered in silence for a while, each lost in our own thoughts. When my cousin turned to me and said, "So, about you and Jack—" I shook my head at her.

"I'll tell you, but not here."

"So there is something to tell?"

I suppressed a smile. "Not here!"

"Where, then?"

"Our room?"

"Okay." She stood and turned to the door.

"Hang on a sec." I stepped down onto the damp grass, walking into the centre of the garden. Was Nana looking down at me from somewhere? If she was, no doubt she was scowling with disapproval, urging me to go rescue her beloved son rather than hanging about.

On that, I agreed with her.

"I'll find him, Nana," I whispered. "Just you watch me."

CHAPTER TWENTY-ONE

"You guys had *sex*?" Sarah whispered fiercely, rocking back against the wall. A huge smile split her face, revealing bright white teeth, and her aura shimmered with delight. "I *knew* it! I knew something had changed between you. I could smell it."

"Ew." Sitting beside her on the bed, I hugged a pillow to my stomach. A glance in the side mirror told me my face was bright red. "Gross, Sarah!"

"Well, not *smell* it smell it. But my instincts for relationships are keen."

"Uh huh."

She leaned forward, resting her chin on her hands. Her blue-green eyes were as intent as a police helicopter's searchlights on my face. "So what was it like?"

"Well, the first time—"

"The first time. Ooh!"

"—we were under water. So it was different. Wet. Not like that! Only, yes. Um." My cheeks were burning. If I blushed any harder, I might spontaneously combust. Like Everest had. The thought was sobering. "Maybe we should leave it there. Fade to black and stuff."

She muffled her laugh behind her hand, lest she attract uncomfortable questions from her mother or Ryan, holed up in the bedrooms on either side of ours. "It must've been pretty good, since you went back for more."

"Oh, it was!" I said with conviction. Then I had to laugh too.

"Did it hurt?"

"It was a bit uncomfortable at first. Not super-painful."

Her lips pressed together tightly as she regarded me. Many people assumed Sarah wasn't a virgin; she'd had several boyfriends and wasn't shy about rounding a few bases. But she said she hadn't found the right guy for her yet. The idea Dominic might be that guy didn't bother me anymore.

Her next question snapped me out of my thoughts as though she'd jabbed a soap bubble with a pin. "So, if you were under the ocean, I'm guessing you didn't use protection."

"Oh. Um." My stomach swooped. The thought hadn't occurred to me, either in the ocean or out of it.

"*Isla!*" Sarah's hand flew to her open mouth. She stared at me, eyes as wide as dinner plates.

"I didn't even..." I stared down at my hands, embarrassed to admit that, even after all the lectures at school and a terribly awkward conversation with my father, I hadn't thought about it at the time. Either time. "What if I get pregnant?" My thoughts spun, spiralling down into a whirlpool. I wanted kids, one day—but not yet. Not before I had a house of my own, and was hopefully married. Not while my father was missing, presumed abducted by my mother, and my Nana's murderer walked free with a grudge the size of Tasmania on his shoulder.

"Maybe you and Jack can't get pregnant," Sarah said dubiously. "What with him being a hob and all."

"Melpomene managed to with Dad," I squeaked, clenching at the pillow slip as though it were a lifeline. An onset of queasiness tightened my throat and made me even more anxious as I wondered when morning sickness started.

"Well, okay, that doesn't mean *aosidhe* and hobs can interbreed. Or humans and hobs." She took my hands in hers, prying my fingers from the fabric one at a time. "Breathe in. You're probably not pregnant. And out. And if you are, you and Jack will decide together what to do about it. And in. You were able to give yourself gills with a thought, so I expect you could give yourself the magical equivalent of the morning after pill if you needed it." She rolled her eyes and dropped my hands. "Just for the love of god buy some condoms before you have sex again, okay?"

The idea of having to explain to my otherworldly boyfriend what a condom was and how to use it made me want to crawl under the bed and hide. But Sarah was right.

A rattle at the window made us both jump. We turned together. A tiny winged figure stood on the timber frame outside the glass, grinning like the Cheshire Cat. "Welkin!" Sarah cheered, sliding the window open so the *piskie* could step across the sill. He slumped in the palm of her hand, melodramatically flinging an arm across his face. His wings drooped like a cartoon rabbit's ears. "You poor thing, you look exhausted!"

"I am." He sighed, but his aura was the deep pink of

amusement. "I flew all the way from Australia, you know. Around half the world, just to see your face again."

Her cheeks flushed at the compliment. "Is there anything we can get for you?"

Welkin's keen blue eyes shifted from my cousin's face to my own. "I am pretty thirsty. Hello, Isla."

"Nice of you to acknowledge me," I said, not in the mood for the *piskie's* theatrics or outrageous flirting. "So you want some blood then? Your next payment isn't due till tomorrow." I was pretty sure. Although it was hard to tell, with the time zone differences.

"It seems fair, given how far I've travelled. Halfway around the world? Remember?"

I sighed, holding my hand out. Welkin leapt up with an agility that belied his feigned exhaustion, stepping across onto my palm. He already had his copper needle out. At least it looked clean as he used it to prick the pad of my pinkie finger, curling an arm around the digit and hugging it to his tiny torso as he lapped the blood up. Last time he'd fed on my thumb; these days Welkin knew without asking to alternate which finger he stabbed.

Sarah wrinkled her nose and looked away, uncomfortable with the sight of blood. Or maybe she didn't want to see this side of the mosquito-like fairy, the side that made him toss his blond hair back and smile winsomely at me, revealing teeth stained pink. "You taste amazing, as always, Isla, but what are you worrying about?"

"What?" I gasped.

"I can taste anxiety in your blood."

"Nothing," I said, shooing him off my finger and onto the blanket. He stared up at me, radiating scepticism from every tiny limb. I wasn't about to discuss my pregnancy scare with the *piskie*.

"If you say so," he said, yawning so hugely I could see the tiny fangs in his mouth. Those fangs would be enough to pierce my skin, but Jack insisted I never let the *piskie* bite me directly, worried about germs. "Is there somewhere I can get some sleep? I really am tired."

"Over here," my cousin said, cradling him in one hand and cracking open the top drawer of the cupboard with the other. It was full of neatly folded pillowslips—Sarah was living out of her suitcase and, of course, I didn't have one. "Will this do?"

"A bed fit for a king." Welkin settled onto a square of floral fabric. My cousin smiled as he blinked slowly a few times and then fell asleep all at once, his hands curled around a belly distended with blood. We tiptoed downstairs to wait with Jack in the lounge room, exploring the English TV channels. My boyfriend ran his fingers along the back of my hand, a gesture that under other circumstances I might have found soothing. But the added anxiety of wondering whether he was going to be a daddy tipped me over the edge, until there was no chance I could relax. I glanced up every few minutes, hoping my aunt or Ryan would appear and give me something to do before I started screaming.

Finally, around lunchtime, they both did, my cousin following his mother down the stairs. He looked tired, and the golden flecks were fading from his aura like reflections from the setting sun. My heart leapt into my throat and I jumped to my feet; he was holding a piece of paper in one hand, which he gave me before I could snatch it away.

Sketched in lead pencil was a kneeling man, head

bowed and hands pressed together as though he was praying. A thick pair of shackles, marked with strange carvings, bound his wrists together, a short length of looping chain linking them and then running to a barely glimpsed band around his throat.

I couldn't see the figure's face. But I knew that fall of hair, the set of the shoulders. It was Dad.

"Is this one of your … vision drawings?" Aunt Elizabeth whispered, staring over my shoulder. I hadn't realised she was so close.

"Yeah." Ryan dragged his feet as he headed over to the seat I'd just vacated and slumped down beside Jack. Sarah hurried over to me.

"What does it mean?" Aunt Elizabeth said. Sadness had carved deep lines into her face and a frown marred her forehead. She looked older than her years; the past week had been hard on her. Hard on all of us.

"It means Uncle David is alive," Sarah declared, hands on her hips. I knew from her aura that the bright determination in her voice was forced, but I was grateful to her for trying. "This is great news, Ryan!"

My aunt studied the drawing as though hoping to divine Dad's location from the neat strokes of the pencil. GPS coordinates, maybe, or—more likely, knowing my aunt—a map reference. "So where is he?"

"I don't know." Ryan rubbed his closed eyes. He always seemed so flat and exhausted after a vision painting. Knowing this too was my fault, I crossed the carpet and brushed my hand along his arm, sending him a small jolt of energy. He stared up at me with widening eyes. The trident hummed, replacing the lost energy between one note and the next.

MELPOMENE'S DAUGHTER

I turned to face the rest of the room. "I've got a pretty good idea. Melpomene's got him. And I'm going to get him back."

Sarah clapped and my aunt clenched her jaw, reaching for her car keys. "Okay, let's go."

"Go where?" Ryan said, looking confused.

I looked at Jack helplessly, not wanting to admit to my aunt that I had no idea where my mother's *sidhe* was. But Aunt Elizabeth saw the look. Her shoulders drooped for a moment before she stood up straighter again. "They met in Edinburgh, so she's probably from around there, right?" She looked at her watch. "It's a seven-hour drive if the traffic is good. We could be there just after dinnertime if we left now."

"If I may make a suggestion?" Jack said, standing and bowing slightly to my aunt. Her eyebrows vanished into her hairline but she nodded for him to continue. "We can attempt to find out where she is via *duinesidhe* means before we undertake such a long drive. Let us explore that option beforehand. It should not be too time-consuming."

"What exactly is 'that option'?" she replied

Jack blinked his sapphire eyes, ran a hand through his hair. "Did your mother ever tell you about *piskie*s?"

Aunt Elizabeth frowned. "Weren't they fairies? Like Tinker Bell?" Jack nodded, and she pursed her lips. "Why?"

"Because there's a Tinker Bell asleep in Nana's linen drawer," Sarah said with a straight face. "Come on, Mum, I'll show you."

When they returned, Welkin was perched on Sarah's shoulder, his preferred seat when the two of them were together. One hand curled around a lock of her hair; the other rubbed his eyes. Behind my cousin, Aunt Elizabeth descended the stairs, her face pale and her eyes fixed on the *piskie*. Her aura was violet with shock.

"How was your nap?" I asked as they reached the landing.

"Good. Short." His look was reproachful. "Sarah tells me you want me to find out where your mama lives."

"Melpomene," I corrected him gently. "Can you do it?"

"Of course." He preened a little. "Now?"

"If you're not *too* tired," I said, my tone a dare. Beside me, Jack rolled his eyes, but my statement had the desired effect. Welkin puffed out his chest before launching himself into the air and whisking towards the door.

"Uh, Red, can you open this for me?"

"Sure thing," Sarah said, again keeping a straight face while I had to bite the inside of my cheek to stop the laughter bubbling out. My cousin deserved some sort of medal for acting. She swung the screen door open and the *piskie* shot through the gap, disappearing beyond the trees.

"He is so tiny," Aunt Elizabeth murmured, dropping onto the couch like a stone. "Will he be able to do it? Find David?"

"Probably not David," Jack said, his eyes sympathetic. "I doubt he would be courageous enough to go into Melpomene's *sidhe* on his own, if at all. However, the *piskies* are an incredibly well-informed part of *duinesidhe* society. The other races underestimate them," he added sheepishly. Jack didn't like Welkin much, but after the *piskie's* help with Everest, he could at least see his worth.

"Okay," my aunt said, nodding slowly. "Now, tell me again what a *sidhe* is?"

Sarah sighed and went to fetch a dining chair. I understood her frustration, but felt sorry for Aunt Elizabeth;

she had a lot of catching up to do and hadn't had months to do it like the rest of us.

Still, if Welkin didn't return soon it would be a long afternoon.

CHAPTER TWENTY-TWO

The sound of car tyres on tarmac lulled me into a doze, my head rolling sideways onto Jack's shoulder. Our thighs and arms pressed together, and the heat of his body made me sleepy in the stuffy cabin. The hob sat in the middle of the back seat, stiff as a board, with Ryan crammed in on his other side—when my aunt had rented the car it had only been for her and Dad, so she'd opted for a smaller model. Because we were sitting so close together, we'd swaddled the seatbelt buckles with hand towels to reduce the chance Jack might brush against them. But he still looked faintly green, and an itching sensation shivered along his nerve endings, on the edge of pain. I squeezed his hand and drained both queasiness and discomfort, giving him a brief respite; they soon bubbled up again, and I drained them again. And again. I recycled the power his emotions gave me by feeding it to Aunt Elizabeth in the form of slow-burning energy— since she wasn't willing to let any of the rest of us take a turn driving.

Long-haul car trips weren't something the hob would normally agree to, or be able to tolerate. But these weren't normal circumstances. And I guessed other *aosidhe* couldn't drain pain the way I could.

If I'd known I could do this before we left Australia, we could've flown, I realised with a sinking sensation as I drew the pain and nausea from Jack for the fourth time. Of course, then I wouldn't have found the trident, so maybe it had been for the best after all.

The weapon tinkled its agreement.

Sarah sat in the front seat, a map splayed open on her lap, while Aunt Elizabeth drove along the motorway. Somewhere outside the car, above the glow of headlights and streetlamps, Welkin kept pace with us. I was pretty sure Jack would've given a lot for a set of wings right then so he could join the *piskie*—of course, without going into a *sidhe*, that wasn't an option, and here in the Old World we couldn't just pop through a portal for ten minutes. Both Jack and Welkin agreed trying would be a terrible idea.

The *piskie* had returned at about two in the afternoon to confirm that Melpomene's *sidhe* was indeed in Edinburgh. Sighing at the delay but glad we'd checked, we'd piled into my aunt's hire car and set off for Scotland and its capital. It seemed strange to me, that people could drive from one country to another rather than having to fly or sail. Or swim via underwater tunnels. For a time I'd watched, fascinated, as the English countryside rolled by, with its hills like crumpled bed sheets covered in green. By comparison, Australia's hills were low and weary, worn down by time and weather, and its sky far vaster.

We'd stopped for dinner at a quiet and comfortable pub that made me appreciate what Dominic meant when he said the pubs here were better: not as crowded, not dedicated only to getting drunk. This one was closer to a tiny restaurant, with heavy timber furniture and several grizzled blokes drinking at the bar. While we were waiting for our meals, my aunt made a few calls, finding a hotel with vacancies.

We inhaled our dinner and set off again.

The slowing engine brought me out of my sleepy stupor; I looked around, blinking. Jack gave me a soft smile, brushing a strand of hair from my face. I smiled back, flicking a glance at his shoulder. I hadn't drooled all over his jumper. Phew.

"I think our hotel is up here on the right," my aunt said, leaning forward over the steering wheel. Sarah nodded, looking between the map and a wall of apartments and shops around us with such regularity it was as if she were watching a game of tennis. Here and there, between the tall buildings, I caught a glimpse of a looming blackness off to the right, beyond the lights. A hill, perhaps? If so, it was huge.

In the back seat, the three of us also peered out the window, gawking at the unfamiliar streets. In some ways it reminded me of home: the closed car dealership on our right was the same as any I'd ever seen in Australia, the traffic drove on the left side of the road, and the petrol stations were laid out in the same way. But, again, little notes of difference made it clear we were in a foreign country: the petrol station was an Esso, a brand I'd never seen before. And the houses looked old—far older than anything in Canberra, which was established only a hundred years ago—with tiny eaves that reminded me of a person wearing a swimming cap rather than a broad-brimmed sun hat.

The sigh of relief when Sarah spotted the hotel was universal. When Aunt Elizabeth parked the car, we all tumbled out, inhaling deeply of the fresh night air. I caught myself staring as Jack stretched, slow and graceful as a cat. He caught my look and winked, adjusting his bandana to make sure his ears were properly covered. I blushed at being caught but didn't look away.

As she slid the invoice across the counter, the older woman working at the reception desk asked whether we had more bags in the car—Sarah, Ryan and my aunt each carried a small overnight bag scavenged from Nana's closet, with two changes of their own clothes. Jack and I shared a canvas tote bag holding our borrowed pyjamas, and my purse and passport. Aunt Elizabeth shook her head, studying the invoice. She paled as she handed over her credit card, and guilt surged in my chest. She was footing the bill for the four of us dropping in, more or less without invitation. We had our reasons, but still. I'd find a way to pay her back, even if it meant doing *duine-sidhe* renovations for the next ten years.

"Here are your keys. Enjoy your stay," the woman said, her Scottish brogue making me smile. She smiled back, although her aura was uncertain.

Our rooms were adjacent. Each had a double bed and one had a single bed on wheels in the tiny living area, replacing the little table. "Girls in one room, and boys in the other?" Aunt Elizabeth's tone made it sound like a suggestion, but I knew her well enough to know it wasn't. Still, the disappointment in Jack's aura mirrored how I felt. The idea of falling into an exhausted sleep in the warm circle of his arms was so tempting.

"I can't wait to have a shower." Sarah yawned, stretching until her vertebrae popped.

"Me too, although I might stretch my legs first," I said. A thought had been bothering me and I wanted to discuss it with Jack—alone. "You and Aunt Elizabeth go first."

"Is that safe?" Aunt Elizabeth said, rubbing her forehead. "Aside from the fact you don't know your way around, it's the middle of the night. And if this is close to—" she glanced at the open door behind Ryan and Jack "—where your mother lives, you don't want to be wandering around. If she took your father..."

Jack stepped forward, hands in his pockets. "I will go with her."

"Still..." She pursed her lips, dubious.

"Jack's able to look after himself," Sarah said, coming to my aid. She took her mother's arm, shooing us with her free hand. "For that matter, so's Isla. Her, um, mixed heritage has its perks. And I'm sure they won't go far." She gave me a significant look that warned me of dire consequences if we did. I was sure she thought we were sneaking off to make out in the bushes. Or to buy condoms.

"We won't," I said.

Hand in hand, Jack and I wandered along the outside of the hotel. Most of the windows were dark, but we still kept our voices to a murmur.

"You wanted to talk about something?" Jack said.

I nodded. "Am I that transparent?"

His eyes were amused. "Since I swore my oath to you, I have become much more..." he hesitated "...attuned to how you are feeling."

"Oh." I frowned. "Is that normal?"

His shrug was eloquent. "I did not experience it with Cacodaemon. I would not have wished to."

"No." I shuddered. We turned a corner and found a small courtyard area edged with bushes whose blooms had closed up for the night. Our shoes slapped on the paving stones as we crossed to a park bench. "Let's sit. I don't really want to stretch my legs. It's funny how sitting still for so long makes you tired."

Jack nodded and examined the bench—looking for iron bolts, I assumed—before sitting gingerly beside me. "So what is bothering you?"

"Two things." Knotting my fingers together in my lap, I decided to broach the easiest subject first. "I've been wondering whether I'm being crazy, bringing my family this close to danger. To Melpomene. I know they're all gung-ho about helping get Dad back, but maybe we should find Welkin and sneak off tonight? Otherwise they'll want to come into the *sidhe* with us." My throat tightened. "I can't bear the thought of something happening to them too."

Jack's lips quirked in a tiny smile. "Sarah would kill us both if we left her behind."

"I know," I mumbled. "But better that than her getting killed by her own aunt."

Jack was silent for what seemed like an eon, but was probably only a couple of minutes. It was too dark where we sat for me to clearly see the face of my watch. I studied his aura and expression for clues to his thoughts; all I could read there was love and anxiety. Finally, when I was just about ready to shake an answer out of him, he sighed and kissed my cheek. "I know you want to protect them. But you should at least take Ryan. You have much greater odds of success if you present Melpomene with a show of force. You need to convince her you should be treated as a full *aosidhe*. To convince her she should fear you. Part of doing that includes proving you have a court. It is difficult, given most of them are back in Australia—"

"The Canberra *sidhe* counts as my court?" I blurted, surprised.

"To another *aosidhe* it does. She does not need to know your changes to the *sidhe* there have been with the residents' consent, or that you have not enslaved them. Given you are the only *aosidhe* in Australia, you should lay claim to the entire country."

I stared at him. "You know how ridiculous that is, right? The *aosidhe* here are packed in like people in a mosh pit, and you want me to get them to believe I have power over a huge continent like Australia?"

He shrugged. "If they believe you control the country, they are far less likely to risk a long ocean voyage to come over there. The fact you killed Everest when he tried it makes your claim more legitimate."

"I didn't kill him," I whispered, eyes wide. Everest had killed himself. Although a ruthlessly logical voice in the back of my mind added, *I just made him want to kill himself.*

Jack put a finger to my lips, his touch gentle. "I know. And what you did was in self-defence and to protect your loved ones. Except here, now, you need to say you did kill him. Without qualms. Remember, Melpomene needs to believe you are a true *aosidhe*."

"Vain, powerful and selfish." The words burned on my tongue.

He nodded. "And part of presenting that image means

arriving with a court. Remember, Everest brought two *duinesidhe* slaves and his *aislinge* when he came to you. You must take Ryan as your *aislinge*, as well as Welkin if he agrees to come."

I bit my lip, knowing how Sarah and Aunt Elizabeth would react to me leaving them behind, especially if I took Ryan with me. "Would taking two humans along actually prove anything? Wouldn't an *aosidhe* ignore them as inconsequential?"

Jack's expression turned grim, his eyes hardening as he stared away into the darkness. "They regard other *duinesidhe* that way already; you would not be looked down on for having humans in your retinue, so long as you could convince Melpomene that they are there to be of use to you. Some *aosidhe* do take humans into their court, particularly talented ones such as artists. Having a gifted artist in your possession is a mark of pride for an *aosidhe*." He turned back to me, hooking an arm around my shoulder. "I know you are reluctant, and I love you for caring about your family. But if you can think of a way to make them seem useful to an *aosidhe*, you should bring them."

I rested my head against his shoulder, drawing comfort from his warmth, his strength. I didn't want to endanger my family, but if having them with me would make it easier to get Dad back, I would do it. The realisation made me hate myself. Yet if I asked them if they wanted to come, they would be shocked I'd ever doubted their willingness.

"Sarah is a musician," I said with a sigh, accepting the inevitable.

Jack nodded. "We can dress her as your court entertainer. A minstrel, perhaps."

The idea of my cousin dressed in poufy pants and tights made me smile. "What about Aunt Elizabeth?"

"What does she do for a living?" Jack stroked my hair. I shivered, wanting to kiss him, but forced myself to concentrate on his question.

"She's a bank manager."

"She could be your major domo."

"My what-a-who now?"

Jack laughed softly. "The manager of your household. Your chief steward."

"Like a butler?"

"The person in charge of the butlers."

"She'll like that." I sat up straight, brow furrowed with thought. "Although we'd need to get her a bit of haematite jewellery or something before we went into the *sidhe*, to stop her from going crazy in there." Human minds were vulnerable if they entered the *sidhe* unprotected, but when Sarah had my haematite necklace—the one Nana had given me for my eighteenth birthday—she'd been okay when she entered the Canberra *sidhe*. I hoped my aunt would be similarly protected.

It hadn't helped Dominic but, in his case, the damage had been done before we gave him the necklace.

"We can do that before we leave tomorrow morning." Jack grimaced. "Usually a major domo is a hob, though, so we will have to think of another role for me to fill."

I stared at him. "Can't you just be my boyfriend?"

He paled slightly. "No. Definitely not. *Aosidhe* do not date other *duinesidhe*." He hesitated before adding, "They sometimes use them for, ah, carnal pleasure though."

"As sex slaves?" Nausea churned my stomach. "Did you...? Have you...?"

MELPOMENE'S DAUGHTER

"I was not to Cacodaemon's taste." Jack's free hand curled into a fist in the fabric of his pants. "He liked his victims young and female."

Evie's loathing of the *aosidhe* made even more sense to me now. Their master hadn't just tortured her and taken her eye. Bile rose in my throat. "I won't do that to you. You're not masquerading as my sex slave. You're my boyfriend, and that's that."

Jack's sapphire eyes widened as he regarded me. "It may cost you your reputation with Melpomene."

"I don't care!" I said with more vehemence than I'd intended. "She slept with a human and had a baby with him, so she's hardly in a position to judge." I took a breath and added more softly, "Besides, you're forgetting she can read emotions. She'll know I love you from the start, so why bother pretending I don't?"

His kiss was fierce on my lips, conveying gratitude and love in equal measures; his tongue flicked across mine, sending heat rushing through me. For several heartbeats, I lost myself in his embrace, curling my fingers through his silky golden hair and wishing we had somewhere private to go.

That reminded me of the other thing I needed to talk to him about. The thought sobered me as effectively as if someone had dumped a bucket of iced water over my head.

"What is wrong?" His eyes were inches from mine; I wanted to lose myself in their blue coolness. "Isla?"

"Jack, what if I … what if we…?"

"What?"

"We haven't taken any precautions. And I'm not on the pill. What if I'm pregnant?"

He sat back slightly, keeping his arms around me.

"What is the pill?"

"A type of human birth control. To stop unwanted pregnancy. There are other types as well, like condoms." My cheeks felt as though they were on fire. I whispered, "They go on over a guy's penis, to stop his sperm from getting to a girl's egg and making a baby."

"Oh." He looked baffled for a moment before shrugging and running a hand down the side of my face. For once his fingers didn't feel warm against my skin, confirming how hard I must be blushing. "If you are pregnant, you are pregnant. Although if you would prefer we use these condom things or the pill next time we make love, I am happy to do that."

"I won't be able to get the pill until we get home and I can go to the doctor," I mumbled.

"Then you can show me how to use a condom," he said simply. "Or we can refrain from making love until you have been to the doctor, if you prefer." I didn't want to wait. I wanted to throw myself at him right now, if I were honest. But before I could speak, he continued, "You should know, Isla, that I have never heard of an *aosidhe* getting pregnant accidentally. It is possible you cannot do so without willing it."

"We can't know for sure, though, since I'm half-human." I leaned my forehead against his and closed my eyes. "It's not that I don't want to have kids, ever. I'm just not sure now is the best time."

"I understand." He kissed me again, chastely. "Although you would make a wonderful mother."

"Thank you," I whispered. "I love you, Jack."

"I love you too, Isla."

The walk back to our hotel rooms was too short.

CHAPTER TWENTY-THREE

We set off at lunchtime the next day. Our group appeared to be tourists rather than a royal court, all dressed in jeans and shirts. You'd never have known, looking at me, that I had a trident tattoo on my forearm and a super-charged opal in my jeans pocket. Jack's ears were hidden, as always, and Welkin was tucked in the hood of Sarah's jumper, which hung down her back. She relayed his whispered directions with a faint smile that made me wonder what else he was telling her in his tiny, piping voice.

Ryan gazed around with wide eyes, drinking in the view as Holyrood Park and the adjacent lake—loch—came into view. In one hand, he clutched a tourist brochure the concierge had given him, which talked about the hill at Holyrood's heart: Arthur's Seat. "They say it might have been the site of Camelot." His tone was reverential as he stared at the hill. It dominated the landscape, seeming much taller than its half-kilometre height.

"That sounds like the sort of place an entrance to a

sidhe would be," I murmured. "The *aosidhe* are nothing if not pretentious."

Jack nodded in agreement.

"And we have to climb it?" Aunt Elizabeth said, pursing her lips. She ran her finger along the smooth haematite stone set into her new pendant. The stone was heart-shaped and a bit girly for her, but it was the best we'd been able to find at short notice.

"Not all the way," Sarah said. "The spot we want is around on the western side, set into some cliffs."

Ryan glanced at the brochure. "Salisbury Crags? That's the steepest side."

"Oh."

The walk wasn't as difficult as I was expecting; a tarmac track branched off from the street and climbed the slope, approaching the cliffs at an angle rather than directly. Looking at the shrub-covered, steeply sloping hill due west of the cliffs, I was grateful. I was even more grateful when we paused at the top of the foothill to catch our breath—I'd done a fair amount of swimming over the past few days but no walking, a point my sore calves made emphatically with every step. The cliffs loomed behind us, but didn't block our view north and west, where central Edinburgh sprawled. My gaze lingered on the tall spires of churches or cathedrals—I couldn't tell from here. When I took in the blocky bulk of Edinburgh Castle where it squatted atop another hill, I gasped.

Jack, who stood beside me, holding my hand, raised a curious eyebrow. I shrugged, although I couldn't keep the awestruck smile off my face. "I've never seen a castle before."

"Australia, not known for its castles," Sarah added. A breeze blew her red hair around her face; she brushed it back with an irritated flick of her wrist, blue-green eyes fixed on the castle.

"Hopefully, we'll have time to do a little sightseeing before we head home." Aunt Elizabeth shaded her eyes as she gazed at the city. "I've seen castles in England, but I never travelled this far north when I lived here."

"How could you not?" Sarah stared at her mother. "It's so close!"

"Have you been to all the tourist attractions within a day's drive of Canberra?"

"No. But … castle!" Sarah said, pointing towards the castle walls as though her mother may have missed them.

My nerves couldn't cope with an argument—even though I knew it was nerves that were making them argue in the first place. I turned my back on the view and ran my eyes along the cliff face, looking for the telltale signs of a portal. Jagged brown rock, worn smooth in places and crazed with cracks in others, greeted my eye. I hoped getting to the portal entrance didn't involve climbing. "Sarah, can you please ask Welkin where to next?"

"He can hear you, you know," she grumbled, but muttered something to the *piskie*. After a few heartbeats, she replied in a more even tone, "We need to follow this road around a little further. There's a spot where the cliff face kinks inward, and there's a little overhang. He said it's in there."

"I wonder how they stop tourists from blundering into it," my aunt said as we set off, the cliff to our right. "On a weekend, this place would be crawling with them."

"There are still a few even on a Tuesday." Ryan pointed to a pair of figures walking along a track at the bottom of the slope, camera in hand. "We're going to have to be pretty discreet not to get spotted heading through the door."

"The door conceals itself," Jack said, patting his bandana to make sure the wind hadn't dislodged it. "But yes, people could fall through by accident."

"There's also that," I added, pointing to a triangular sign fixed to a rock, warning of falling rocks if you left the trail.

"You think the *aosidhe* organised signage to discourage climbers?" Aunt Elizabeth peered at the sign.

"I wouldn't put it past them," I said with a shrug.

We walked in silence for several minutes, my tote bag swinging against my hips. To our left, bright yellow flowers the colour of wattle smothered a low wall of bushes. They were broken up by occasional taller shrubs, green and dense.

"Here," Sarah said as we drew alongside a thicket of those shrubs. She turned to face the cliff, and we all stopped, studying the point she indicated with a nod.

A grassy mound scattered with loose rocks rose on our right, one of those "no climbing" signs fixed to a nearby boulder. Sharp rocks poked out from the mound, uninviting, and above that a narrow cleft gouged the cliff face. Sure enough, a lip of rock overhung the cleft, casting it into shadow.

"In there?" my aunt gulped, clutching the pendant around her throat. She was paler than usual, strands of auburn hair standing against her forehead. Beside her, Ryan scanned all around, presumably to see whether anyone was watching us. But there was no one above us, looking down, and the tall shrubs blocked the view of anyone down the hill.

"That's what Welkin says." Sarah took a step forward,

off the path. Her eyes were bright, eager. Even after how her last journey into the *sidhe* had turned out, the new adventure excited her. Ryan's eyes gleamed too, although his lips pressed together in a thin line. Ambivalent.

Jack hurried past her. "Please, allow me to go first. To make sure it is safe."

"And I need to go second," I said with an apologetic look at my cousin. "We all need a makeover as soon as we're inside the tunnel, and I won't have long before that draws Melpomene's attention." The hob nodded. "Sarah, I need you and Welkin to go last." My cousin narrowed her eyes, preparing to argue, and I raised my hand before she could speak. "Please. You're the only one that's done this before. I need you to make sure Aunt Elizabeth and Ryan make it through okay."

Ryan's aura shot through with alarm as he regarded his sister. He looked from me to Jack with wide eyes. "Any tips before we go in?"

"When you get to the portal—the place we tell you the portal is—close your eyes and walk forward," Jack said. "You may experience a brief, dizzying sensation. On the other side, drinking water helps if you experience any nausea."

"That reminds me." I reached into the tote bag and pulled out three bottles of water, giving one each to my relatives. "I bought these."

Sarah took the water gratefully, glancing at her brother. "I find it helps to hold my hand in front of my face as I'm walking in. Otherwise, the idea I'm about to face-plant a wall of rock freaks me out too much."

"Right." Ryan took the bag off my shoulder. I frowned at him, and he gave me a fleeting smile. "From this point forward we're your servants, right? A lady doesn't carry her own bag."

"Oh. Right. Let's go then, I guess." I squared my shoulders and followed Jack up the scree and into the shadow of the cleft. Its sides were barely two feet wide; I had to turn my shoulders in places to avoid scraping them on the sharp rock. "I'm guessing the *powrie* must use another entrance," I muttered, recalling how huge they were. Jack laughed softly.

The portal wasn't very far into the cliff face—just far enough that we were hidden from the path. It shimmered, casting a blue-green light I usually found soothing. This time, it shot me through with nerves. On the other side of that door was my father. And my mother.

Just do it, I told myself. The trident chimed emphatically, urging me on. I held my breath and stepped forward, close on Jack's heels, my aunt's startled gasp in my ears as—to her eyes—I seemed to step through solid rock.

As my feet slapped onto smooth stone, my first thought was that the trident's chime had become audible, reaching my ears as well as my mind. After a second, I realised the sound was different, closer to the tinkling of a bell. A doorbell? I stared around, searching for the source; Jack took my arm and tugged me away from the portal. Looking back, I saw Aunt Elizabeth hesitating on the other side, running her hand over the doorway with a frown on her face. From what Sarah had told me previously, the shimmering surface felt like solid rock to a normal human.

"Isla, you need to get started." Urgency widened Jack's eyes. "That sound is an alarm. Melpomene's soldiers will be here soon. Do your clothes first."

MELPOMENE'S DAUGHTER

"Okay." I'd given some thought to our outfits already that morning; now I glanced down at my day-old jeans and T-shirt, willing them to change into something formal and glittery, inspired by the dress I'd worn to Sarah's and my birthday party last year. Pushing my will onto the *sidhe* felt strange. I was used to it changing as readily as if I were sculpting wet clay, accompanied by a steady energy drain—like I was a drink of water and the *sidhe* had jabbed a straw into my chest. This time it was more like carving stone. A frown creased my forehead as I pressed myself against the invisible barrier, insisting it let me do as I wished. Panic made sweat prickle my brow. *Come on, dammit!*

The trident clanged, a clarion call, and the obstruction abruptly lessened, although it didn't vanish entirely. My clothes shimmered and morphed into the dress I had imagined. It was cut above the knee at the front, and loose enough I could run if I had to, but with a back made of ruffles and lace running in stylised waves to my ankles. Gems studded the bodice, Gall's opal glowing faintly in the centre, and the shoes were flat and silver, like Dorothy's in the book version of *The Wizard of Oz*.

Except for the shoes, everything was sapphire blue with flecks of darker navy—the exact colour of Jack's eyes.

"Excellent," Jack said, and I looked up, startled. Was he referring to the colour? But his aura was the shade of a tropical ocean, flooded with relief. "I had not been sure her *sidhe* would respond to you."

"It was hard," I admitted, turning my attention to his clothes, conjuring a fancier version of the zoot suit he'd worn to that same party last year; instead of pinstripes it was lined with thread spun from actual silver. "The trident helped me."

He nodded understanding and held a finger to my lips. "Do not mention it again here. Best to keep that one a surprise if we can."

I looked down. The tattoo was visible on the inside of my lower forearm. "Gloves, maybe?"

"Good idea."

Behind me, someone gasped as silk rippled across my skin, appearing from nothing like a cartoon superhero's armour, wrapping around my forearms and hands as though the gloves were custom-made. Which I guessed they were. My aunt stood in the doorway, eyes as wide as saucers, her skin so pale it looked grey. Ryan stood beside her, holding her arm so she didn't fall.

"Aunt Elizabeth? Are you okay?" I started forward, but Jack shook his head, moving past me to take my place.

"The clothes, Isla," he reminded me. "Presentation is critical. I will take care of her."

As he moved the pair away from the entrance so Sarah could enter, I hastily imagined my aunt into a dove-grey business suit whose fabric was as fine and soft as feathers. Ryan's clothes transformed into slacks and a loose, bronze shirt that shifted between red-gold and green as he raised his arm to give his mother a drink of water. A leather-bound sketchbook poked out of the tote bag, which was now made of soft kidskin instead of rough canvas.

Behind me, tromping footsteps clattered, growing nearer with every heartbeat.

Sarah appeared through the portal, swallowing repeatedly. Even as she raised her own water to have a drink, I changed her clothes to something that wouldn't have been out of place at a renaissance faire: a poufy shirt with a black vest over the top, and a long skirt slashed up the middle to reveal tights underneath. Welkin squeaked and fluttered off her shoulder as I added an ornate golden guitar, slung from a strap that ran across her chest.

"What the—" she gasped, disoriented.

"Sorry. In a rush." I spun to look down the corridor. My gaze ran over the walls and floor, finally having a moment to take in the fact it wasn't made of compressed dirt and cobblestones like the ones at home, or shale like the ones under the sea. This tunnel was white marble, veined with black and red in a way that both drew and repulsed the eye.

Jack darted to stand beside me, adjusting his black felt hat more comfortably on his head so his ears weren't hidden. And not a moment too soon. A phalanx of *dui-nesidhe* marching in close formation came into view, silver armour clattering as they moved forward.

When they saw me, standing there with my hands on my hips, they stumbled to a halt, their auras violet with shock.

"I am Isla Blackman, Melpomene's daughter," I declared. "And I am here to see my mother."

CHAPTER TWENTY-FOUR

The half-dozen *duinesidhe* led us down the tunnel, leather boots stomping in a perfect unison that spoke of long practice—especially apparent given two of the six were *powrie*, who had to match their stride to the shorter hobs.

Occasionally, one of the *duinesidhe* glanced back at me, eyes wide as they took in my familiar features and glowing skin. I knew I resembled my mother, but seeing the way my appearance spooked them made me appreciate how much.

"Are you guys okay?" I murmured from the corner of my mouth, glancing back at the rest of my family. They walked together, Sarah and Ryan on either side of Aunt Elizabeth. My aunt had a bit more colour in her cheeks, although her eyes were still wide enough I could see white all around.

"I'm fine," Ryan whispered. "I didn't feel sick coming through."

MELPOMENE'S DAUGHTER

"Perk of being an *aislinge*, I guess," Sarah said, her tone light. Was she finally beginning to accept her brother's accidental favoured status? I wanted to look back at her aura, to see if she was hiding anything, but kept my gaze fixed on the soldiers' backs. I knew the hobs, with their long ears, would be able to hear every word we said. Would they report my unusual concern for my "minions" to Melpomene?

I realised I didn't care. "Aunt Elizabeth, how about you?"

"A bit shaken," she mumbled back. "We're inside Arthur's Seat!"

"Not exactly." A flutter of wings and a startled gasp made me peer back again. Welkin had landed on Aunt Elizabeth's shoulder; she craned her neck to peer down at his beaming face. Sarah looked miffed, crossing her arms across her chest. "Let me explain..."

I turned back to the front to hide the smile on my face as Welkin's low voice continued, explaining the physics—or lack thereof—of the *sidhe*. He had taken the same role, tour guide and giver of pep-talks, for Sarah the first time she'd come into the *sidhe* with us.

It was a relief, since I wasn't in a position to do it.

The tunnel opened up into a tall chamber with heavy maroon drapes obscuring the walls. On each side of the entrance was a white marble statue about twice my height; one was carved to resemble a long-limbed dragon, the other an ostentatiously feathered griffon with a sharp beak.

The statues' heads turned to watch as we passed. My hair stood up on the back of my neck.

A laugh, dripping with sarcasm, echoed across the chamber. I turned to see a familiar figure standing in the middle of the empty room, hands on sackcloth-covered hips. The scarecrow mask's expression didn't change, but I didn't need to see his expression to read the contempt in his aura. "So you have finally come slinking here to beg from my mistress," the hob said.

I narrowed my eyes and inhaled to launch a blistering rebuttal. However, before I could answer, Jack scowled. "You forget yourself. Is that how Melpomene has you treat visiting *aosidhe*?"

The hob sniffed. "She may be my lady's pale reflection, but this child is not a true *aosidhe*."

"Oh, really?" I raised my eyebrows, staring at the hob's aura. Dislike burned there, but the emotion was easily transformed to the greenish yellow of anxiety. "Are you so sure about that?"

"Uh. I, I," he stammered, taking a step back.

"Perhaps you could *do your job*—" I added a dash of salmon-pink shame, a swirl of syrup on top of a bilious ice cream sundae "—and let my mother know I'm here."

"Uh. Okay. Yes." He scurried towards one of the drapes, disappearing behind it. I glanced around; the soldiers had lined themselves along the wall behind us, standing almost as still as the alabaster statues—even the two *powrie*, whose auras surged with fury. I admired their control even as their red, beady eyes on my back made me wish for a weapon.

The dragon and griffon stared at us. They didn't blink or even seem to breathe, and they had no auras. Were they alive?

Sarah looked around, lips pursed. "It's big, sure, but it looks like a chamber you'd see in a fancy house in the real world, more or less." Disappointment sharpened her tone.

MELPOMENE'S DAUGHTER

"It's true." I craned my neck to look up at the distant ceiling. "From here, those stargems could be little LED lights."

"Although this is simpler than some I have seen, most *sidhe* have a receiving chamber," Jack murmured. "It is a place where visiting delegations can get themselves organised after a long journey. And where the host has the option of slaughtering them, if they decide they are not taking guests that day."

"Oh." My voice was raspy. I swallowed hard.

"There'll be weapons or soldiers behind those curtains then," Ryan said, eyes bright.

"Please don't," his mother breathed, hand fluttering to the pendant at her throat. Her gaze flicked from one curtain to the next, as she no doubt wondered where the attack would come from. On her shoulder, Welkin patted her cheek reassuringly; she didn't seem to notice. "This is hard enough as it is without thinking about—"

She stopped short as one of the drapes—different to the one the hob had left through—twitched. My breath caught in my throat, burning there until the curtain rustled aside and the same golden-eyed hob reappeared, straightening his shirt. The fabric was cut like a jester's motley, much as I remembered from my first dream of this place. Both the sackcloth clothes and the straw mask had to itch unbearably. As much as he big-noted himself, I couldn't help thinking Melpomene must not like him very much if she forced him to wear that outfit. Or maybe she just didn't care.

"Lady Melpomene will see you now." The hob inclined his head faintly, avoiding eye contact. "Follow me."

"Thank you," I said and then bit my lip. Jack glanced at me, and I whispered, "Sorry, it's a reflex."

"It is okay," he replied, giving my hand a brief squeeze. "That is one of the reasons I love you."

"Aww," Sarah said from behind us.

"Shush."

The corridor behind the curtain was elegantly furnished with more pale marble sculptures—a curling wave forever about to break, a wading bird holding a fish in its beak, a badger poised on its hind legs. The only colour in the corridor was from the black tiles forming half of the chessboard-like pattern we walked along.

Although Ryan would no doubt inform me that black was a shade, not a colour.

By the time we reached the end of the corridor, my hands trembled with nerves. I willed them to stillness, but couldn't stop my heartbeat from thundering in my ears. I was about to see my mother for the first time. What would she be like? Would my father be there? Could I convince her to let him go? What would I do if she said no? My plan basically consisted of asking nicely and, if that failed, demanding it.

And if *that* failed...?

The corridor opened up into a colourful room, startling after all the stark, black-and-white marble. Lush carpet the colour of a well-watered lawn cushioned my steps. Poplars formed an arcade on either side of us, lifelike until I looked more closely and realised their bark was carved timber, the leaves intricately dyed fabric. The air was thick and cloying with the scent of rose perfume.

In the centre of the room—although a golden sun hung above the trees, so maybe "room" wasn't the right word—stood a huge rose. Not a bush, but a single flower, thorns long and sharp, leaves angled downward to form steeply sloped sides around the stem. There, reclining on the scarlet petals as though they were the cushions of a throne, lounged Melpomene.

I'd have recognised her instantly, even if I hadn't seen Dad's hoarded photos or Ryan's painting. Her face was so similar to mine we could have been sisters. Not mother and daughter, though—she looked my age. Her glowing skin was so flawless I'd wager she'd never had a single pimple, and her glossy brown hair was so dark it was almost black.

She regarded me with dark eyes that smouldered with anger. Her aura, though, was as invisible to me as if she were one of her own statutes. How was she concealing it? "Who brought you here?" she demanded.

I blinked, startled by the question. "What?"

"Was it Helios?" Long, red fingernails drummed against the side of the petal, muffled clicks audible from where I stood. Her voice was cool, glittery and sharp, reminding me strangely of the champagne I'd tried last year. I hadn't liked that either.

Who? "No one brought me. I brought myself."

"To supplicate yourself to me?"

"To get my father back." An idea formed. "I realise us being here might be inconvenient for you, embarrassing with the other *aosidhe*. Give me Dad, and we'll head back to Australia. I'll make sure he never comes back here again." If he tried, I'd kill him myself.

"You mean David?" She ran a hand along the forest-green skirt of her satin dress, smoothing out an imagined wrinkle. The fabric whispered under her touch.

"Who else?"

"You are mistaken, girl. I do not have him."

"What?" The words left my mouth in a strangled gasp as my stomach clenched with sudden anxiety. She was lying. She *had* to be lying.

"Isla," Jack whispered. I glanced at him, and he nodded towards the base of the rose stem. "There is someone underneath, behind the leaves."

"Dad!" Before I could think better of it, I ran forward, towards Melpomene's throne.

Something thudded towards me from my right. A tall figure loomed: naked man from the waist up and bipedal deer from the waist down. He held a bronze sword out, blocking my path. His eyes were hard and dark as polished obsidian. "You will not approach my lady." The voice was soft and deep.

Fury snarled up through my throat. "Get out of my way." I shoved fear into him, sharp as the sword he wielded. It flared in his aura and widened his eyes but, although the sword wavered, he didn't budge.

"Fawn's fear of me is greater than his fear of you," Melpomene commented, faint amusement in her voice. I couldn't see her past the creature. "I am a lot older and more practiced at manipulating emotions than you are. Although I do commend you for bringing snacks along. Forward-thinking of you, especially for a half-human."

I ground my teeth together, inching to the left so I could see past Fawn's huge, well-muscled arm. "Snacks?"

"Your aunt and the red-haired girl." Melpomene's gaze flickered to the others. "Elizabeth. You have not aged well at all, dear. So many wrinkles."

"Melanie," my aunt replied, voice bitter with dislike.

"Never call me that name again." The *aosidhe*'s expression darkened. So did the light in the room, the sun above us dimming in response to her mood. Fawn trembled, the whites of his eyes showing. Fear—not the emotion I'd implanted but an older, deeper fear—crept like advancing shadows across his aura. "If only you knew how it galled me to have to pretend to be a human. To be your *sister*." She sneered, her hands curling like talons around the rose. Little shreds of red, scraped from the petal seat, drifting to the ground.

Uh oh. Time to get her attention back on me. "Was that why you were looking for us then," I blurted. "Me and Dad?"

"Looking for *you*?" The smouldering eyes turned back to me. The last wisps of my daydream about her greeting me with open arms and maternal warmth fled with that look. Hard, bright determination to save my father remained in its place.

"I heard you were looking for us. Years ago." That was the first clue Jack had found about my mother's identity— a rumour of a half-human baby being sought by an *aosidhe* mother.

"Yes. I was going to see whether you were useful. Whelping you cost me so much. But David—" she spat his name, as though it curdled on her tongue "—had taken you across the sea, out of reach."

"And if I wasn't? Useful?"

A cruel smile curved across Melpomene's blood-red lips. Her silence was answer enough. After several seconds, she tipped her head to the side; her hair swung, revealing delicately pointed ears. "The question, girl, is whether you prove useful now."

I glanced towards the throne's leaves. There was definitely something under there, something with pale skin, visible even in the deep shadows. I pointed at her throne. "If you don't have Dad, who's under the rose?" Narrowing my eyes, I willed the screening foliage to move aside.

The leaves trembled as though the rose itself didn't want to obey me. The trident sang, my skin flared yellow and white—and the flower raised its leaves like a dancer raising her arms to the heavens.

Underneath the flower, lying on a stone bier, was a young human woman. Despite her youthful face, the hair cascading around her, tumbling to the ground, was as white as snow. Her nightdress was old-fashioned, something from the start of last century, and her hands were folded across her chest. From this distance I couldn't see if she was breathing, but her aura swirled with pink amusement, flecked through with gold.

"That is my *aislinge*," Melpomene said. Her voice was surprisingly calm given I'd just rearranged her furniture to have a look underneath. "Her power manifests through dreams. I keep her hidden away, since it renders her defenceless." Chastised, the rose lowered the leaves again, screening the girl from view. Could she escape if she ever woke, or were the leaves also the bars of her prison?

"Fawn, stand down." The deer man lowered his sword and stalked away, heading back to lurk in the shadow of the poplar closest to the throne. His skin and pelt were the same mottled colour as the bark; no wonder I hadn't seen him until he moved. "I do not have your father," Melpomene said again, slow and thoughtful. She tapped one of her fingernails against her lips; the scarlet matched perfectly. "If I did, I would have killed him by now. Or had sex with him, for old time's sake." Oh, *gross*. "Perhaps both. But I expect I know who does, and why. I can help you get him back."

"Why would you suddenly agree to help me?" I put my hands on my hips.

She glanced down at the rose, which trembled faintly, like a kicked dog. "You just proved yourself interesting. Daughter."

CHAPTER TWENTY-FIVE

Melpomene and I sat at the strangest dining table I'd ever seen. A huge block of ice, it squatted, long and wide, on perfect, spherical legs. Each sphere had a white, opaque centre, like the random patterns you sometimes get in an ice cube—except these were shaped like roses.

A block of ice so large should radiate cold like an open freezer in all directions. But, as I sat beside this one, I felt comfortably warm. At first I'd thought the table was cut glass, but when I rested my hand on the surface, it quickly grew cool and damp.

"It is excellent for keeping food cold," Melpomene said, popping a strange piece of fruit into her mouth. She managed to look graceful even though the chair she sat on was a glorified stool; by comparison, I was awkward and ungainly, fussing over the back of my skirt, folding and unfolding my arms. Up close, she was even more beautiful—and as cold as the ice table.

I glanced at the wall behind me, where my family

stood, shuffling their feet. Jack was with them, narrowed eyes roaming the room; the others stared at Melpomene with varying levels of fascination and resentment. "Can we get seats for them?"

The *aosidhe* raised a disdainful eyebrow. "Your human heritage is showing."

I shrugged, twining my fingers together on my lap. Not wanting to reveal the trident by removing my gloves, I'd declined Melpomene's offer of food. The various delicacies on offer were brightly coloured and smelled sweet, but I didn't recognise any of them—so at least I didn't know what I was missing. "I'm quite proud of my human heritage. So can they have seats?"

She turned to her masked hob, who stood on the other side of the room with his hands by his sides and his head high: a soldier at attention. Although she didn't say anything, he bowed deeply and scurried through the double doors, which were wide open to show the poplars in the throne room beyond. "It is a weakness, and one other *aosidhe* will use against you."

"The way they're trying to use my father against you?"

"They are seeking to embarrass me, not manipulate any feelings I have for him. I have none." I couldn't see her aura, but her knuckles whitened as her hands clenched into fists.

"He still has feelings for you."

She smiled, teeth flashing white in the diffuse light. "Naturally."

"You manipulated him into loving you, didn't you?" I couldn't keep the accusation out of my voice.

"Of course I did. Helios was hunting me, and David was convenient."

"Can you undo it?"

"I could, but why would I bother?" She plucked a purple-skinned fruit from a bowl shaped like a cupped hand and peeled the skin off with sharp nails, dropping twists of rind to the floor. A citrusy smell reached my nose, making my stomach rumble. Fortunately, the noise was covered by the sound of the hob re-entering the room, three others behind him. Each carried a short wicker stool, placing it beside a member of my family. Jack declined the offer with a shake of his head and the hobs scurried out, each peeking from the corner of their eye at me and their mistress. Anxiety and curiosity warred in their auras. Hoping I wasn't going to double their trouble?

"Can the girl play?" Melpomene raked Sarah with a glance, taking in the guitar hanging down her back.

"Yes."

"Play for us, girl."

Sarah's face flushed with anger. I caught her gaze and shook my head. She inhaled, nostrils flaring, and unslung the guitar, plucking a few tentative notes to see if it was tuned. Then she started playing a soft melody, one of her band Drakeford's ballads—although she didn't sing. Beside her, Ryan had pulled out his sketchpad and was drawing swiftly, aura sparkling with gold glints like a mirror ball.

I hoped the vision was good news.

Turning back to Melpomene, I picked up our conversation where it had left off. "You should undo what you did to Dad because forcing someone to love you is wrong."

"According to whom?" She separated a segment of lavender fruit and placed it on her tongue, lips curving with apparent pleasure at the taste. Or perhaps she was laughing silently at me.

"Me."

"And you have never done it? Made someone love you?"

"No." I'd made Dominic trust me, but I wasn't going to admit it.

Melpomene's eyes drifted across to Jack. "The pretty hob loves you."

"She did not need to use her power to make me feel that way about her." Jack leaned against the wall, but his relaxed pose didn't fool me. He looked ready—eager, even—to spring into action. Being this close to an *aosidhe* left him quivering with tension; hatred and fear roiled in his aura. Emotions my mother could read as clearly as I could.

"Impudent hob," Melpomene scoffed. "Know your place. If you were mine, I would have you flogged."

"I love him too," I said, lifting my chin to stare at my mother.

She pursed her lips as though tasting something sour. "Would you like me to fix that for you?"

"What? No! He's my boyfriend."

She looked between Jack and me, frowning so faintly I could barely see the lines on the creamy skin of her forehead. "It is hardly an even-sided relationship, though, is it? With him sworn into your service and having to obey your every command. He is, isn't he? With such smooth skin, he must be."

My cheeks burned. "It's none of your business," I snapped. "Let's talk about who has Dad."

Before Melpomene could take offence at my tone, Ryan spoke. "It's this guy, isn't it?" He turned his sketchbook to show the outline of a face. Most of the picture had been hastily rendered with only a few lines, showing a strong jaw and long, wavy hair, but the eyes glared from the page with a fire that made me shiver. My hands gripped the fabric of my dress.

Melpomene studied the picture for several heartbeats, her eyes as intense as the sketched face was, as though she wanted to tear it into confetti—or kiss it.

"That's Helios?" I guessed.

"How did you know?"

"You've mentioned him twice. He must feature pretty strongly on the list of people you don't like."

She sniffed, her expression settling back into cool, emotionless lines. "Yes, that is Helios. Insufferable fool."

"And he's your enemy?"

She nodded. "For the last thirty or so years, yes. He is gathering oaths. Seeking to have enough *aosidhe* sworn into his service that he can proclaim himself ruler of all *aosidhe*."

A sharp inhalation of breath made me glance at Jack. His eyes were wide. "That did not work so well for Neptune," he said when I looked at him. "The other *aosidhe* would never stand for it."

"The ones sworn to him would not have a choice." Melpomene ripped another purple fruit in half with a twist of her slender wrists. Juice sprayed across the table surface, growing milky as it froze. "If he accumulates one or two more, he will have a majority. And there will be war."

"Let me guess," I said. "Everest was sworn to him?"

"Yes." She looked up from dismembering the fruit, surprised. "How do you know of him?"

"He came to Australia late last year, looking for Dad."

MELPOMENE'S DAUGHTER

"Isla killed him," Sarah declared with satisfaction. Beside her, on the opposite side to Ryan, my aunt sat back so abruptly she nearly fell off her stool. My cousin flinched, ducking her head back over her guitar. A cascade of red hair almost hid her blushing cheeks.

"Way to go, Sarah," Ryan muttered, rolling his eyes.

Melpomene didn't notice; her gaze bore into me. "Did she now? Not so human after all, are we, daughter?"

Jack's advice—to own Everest's death—rang in my mind, but I couldn't. Not when Aunt Elizabeth stared, grey-faced with horror. "He set himself on fire," I said defensively, looking between Melpomene and my aunt. I wanted to rush over, take Aunt Elizabeth's hand and reassure her I wasn't a monster. Instead, I pled with my eyes for her to trust me. Anxiety fluttered in my chest like a trapped bird. "I didn't do it."

"Did you precipitate this self-immolation in some way?" Melpomene grinned, shark-like, her teeth stained faintly purple with fruit juice.

"He was trying to force me to swear to him." I hated the defensive note in my voice, Melpomene's glee at my aunt's horror. "Probably to use me against you the same way he wanted to use Dad. It was self-defence. Now, can we *please* focus on Helios and getting Dad back?"

The room fell silent except for the faltering strains of Sarah's guitar and the renewed scratching of Ryan's pencil. A prickle of cold ran up my back as the *aosidhe* glared at me. *We're in her lair,* I reminded myself, *and need her help. Way to piss her off, Isla.*

"Very well," Melpomene said finally. "If I assist you, I will require an oath, and payment for the risk you are asking me to take." Out of the corner of my eye, I saw

Jack stand up straight, eyes widening with alarm. His expression mirrored my feelings perfectly.

"What payment, exactly?"

"You have an object of power on you," she said. Thinking she meant the trident, my heart leapt into my throat— but her eyes dropped to the opal on my dress, still glowing with stored energy.

I touched the stone lightly. It was smooth under my fingertip, even through the glove, and sparked as though with static. "And what's the oath?"

"I merely ask you to swear to that thing you already offered. That you will return to Australia and never leave again, and take your father with you." She flicked a piece of imaginary lint off her skirt. "If he is still alive."

I'd only just begun to experience the wonder of being a tourist in a foreign land, marvelling at the strange landscape and architecture, savouring the feeling of "same but different". Was I willing to give up the opportunity to ever experience that again?

To get my father back? Yes. Yes, I was.

"I swear to you: once Dad has been returned to me, I will return to Australia within a month—" better give myself more than enough travel time "—and never return." The oath settled like fine rain falling onto frozen metal, hardening as it bound me. I plucked the opal from my dress and held it out to her on the palm of my hand.

Melpomene considered my words with narrowed eyes for a long moment while I held my breath. Finally she nodded, plucking the stone from my palm with her long fingernails. "Good enough. Although if your father is dead and his body is returned to you, the oath will still hold."

I bit my lip and nodded, unwilling to dwell on the

possibility.

She turned to look at the golden-eyed hob again. "Write to Helios. Tell him I understand he has something that belongs to the *aosidhe* Isla and she wants it back."

"Is she throwing down the gauntlet?" the hob asked his mistress.

Melpomene turned to me. "Well, are you?"

The expression was vaguely familiar from my term spent studying medieval history in high school. But, not wanting to make assumptions, I glanced at Jack for clarification. "It means to issue a challenge to a duel," he said. "If you win, Helios must give you what you seek."

"And if he wins?" I squeaked.

"He will demand something from you in return when the duel is negotiated." Melpomene sounded bored. "Probably your oath, given his current preoccupation. Also, since you cost him Everest, Helios is likely to suggest you should replace him. Otherwise, he will remain one additional *aosidhe* short of his goal."

"And when you say duel...?"

"A contest of some kind. Not necessarily a sword fight, if that is what you are worried about. The terms will be agreed between the two of you."

"Not necessarily" wasn't very reassuring. But I'd come this far; I wasn't going to back down. Still, the back of my throat tasted of acid and I swallowed before speaking. "Then yes, I'm throwing down the gauntlet."

Melpomene nodded at her hob and he left to send the message. I wondered if they used carrier pigeons. Or *piskies* with tubes tied to their backs.

"I am risking a lot, organising this meeting." Melpomene stood, stretching with the grace of a big cat—and she was just as deadly. "I am calling you an *aosidhe* when you are not. You will have to prove your strength and earn the title for yourself. Do not disappoint me." She swept from the room in a cloud of rose perfume.

"God, I've only known her for a half-hour and I'm already disappointing her," I muttered as the doors swung closed.

"This is a terrible idea," Sarah said, laying her hands flat across the guitar strings to silence the instrument. "What if you lose the duel? You'll be stuck here forever, serving this Helios guy. We might get stuck right alongside you. Jack and Ryan definitely would be."

"And me." Welkin flew from my aunt's shoulder to Sarah's, tugging her hair. "Don't forget me."

"I can release you and Jack from your oaths if it goes badly," I said to Welkin, giving my older cousin an apologetic look. "I'm not sure if I can free Ryan, though." He didn't notice; his eyes were fixed on the paper before him.

Jack hurried to my side. I stood, wrapping my arms around him. "I would not let you release me," he said with steel in his voice. His fingers against my cheek were warm and gentle. "If you stay here, so do I. But I do not believe you will lose."

"We don't even know if Helios has Uncle David," Sarah pointed out with a sigh.

"Yeah, we do." Ryan looked up. With a flourish, he showed us the rest of his drawing. Helios glowered from the page as he had before; behind him, in his shadow, was a familiar figure, head bowed and a metal band around his throat. Dad.

I clenched my jaw as I stared at the drawing. I'd win the duel. I didn't have a choice.

CHAPTER TWENTY-SIX

*T*he carriage reminded me of something out of *Cinderella*, with a pumpkin-shaped central body and spindly, delicate-looking wheels that shouldn't be able to bear such a weight. Except it wasn't orange, but the black of a beetle's carapace, and there was no place at the front for a driver. Instead, harnessed to the front was an ebony horse.

"What's that strapped to its back?" I wondered aloud, approaching the creature. My eyes felt like they opened as wide as the carriage wheels when I realised that what I'd at first assumed must be a strange saddlebag was actually a pair of feathery wings. They were bound to the horse's back with a delicate golden chain that ran down the creature's side and under its chest, clinging so tightly I doubted I could get a finger between the metal links and that glossy fur.

"Oh, you poor thing," I murmured, holding out a hand for the creature to sniff. It rolled an eye at me, ignoring my outstretched fingers, and stared forward again. I could see its aura. It was bored.

"We aren't going to be flying anywhere, are we?" Sarah asked, a tremor in her voice as she regarded the creature. Welkin, back in his usual perch like a pirate's tiny parrot, patted her cheek.

"Of course not," the golden-eyed hob said with a sniff. His name—I'd learned by eavesdropping, because there was no way my mother would think to introduce him—was Hiram. He clicked his fingers and a second carriage rolled forward to stand beside ours. An identical winged horse was harnessed to its front, but the vehicle was heavy with ornate gold decoration; ours looked plain by comparison.

"We won't be riding with Melpomene?" I asked.

He looked down his nose at me. "No." That single word was so heavy with contempt it was a wonder he'd been able to speak it.

"Watch your tone," Aunt Elizabeth snapped. She'd recovered from her initial shock and stood beside us, hands on her hips as she stared at Hiram with blue-green eyes identical to her daughter's. "That is an *aosidhe* you're speaking to. Do you think your mistress would be happy at you, insulting her guest? Her daughter?" She let him think about it for a moment before adding, "Besides, it's rude." Pride swelled in my chest. And she'd only slightly mangled the pronunciation of *aosidhe*.

"Forgive me," Hiram replied, his tone stiff. "I simply meant one carriage would not be big enough for both entourages." He stalked away, head held high beneath that ever-present mask.

"Yeah, right," Sarah muttered. "He means Melpomene is too good to ride with us."

MELPOMENE'S DAUGHTER

"That's *Aunt* Melpomene to you." I folded my gloved hands in front of me primly. Sarah looked like she'd swallowed a bug.

"Nice wheels," Ryan said as he sauntered over to us, Jack at his side. "Are we ready to go?"

"Just waiting for Melpomene," I said.

"Why is she even coming with us?" Ryan adjusted the sketchpad in his tote bag. "I would've thought she wouldn't want to get within a mile of Helios, if she hates him so much."

I opened my mouth to answer, but snapped it shut again when I spied Melpomene approaching, striding across a broad courtyard that looked for all the world like part of a castle in a fantasy novel. A sun even beamed down from above, peeping between fluffy white clouds so picturesque that they looked fake. Which, of course, they were.

My mother had swapped her green, slinky dress for a full-skirted, sleeveless gown. Delicately embroidered peacock feathers fanned across the bodice in gold, blue and black, spotted with glittering jewels. The teal skirt shimmered as she moved.

"Nice dress," I said as she approached.

"Yes," she replied, raking her gaze over me in a way that made me embarrassed about my plain—by comparison—gown. "Let us go."

Jack assisted each of us into the carriage, even offering a hand to Ryan, although my cousin shrugged it off. Once we were all tucked inside the carriage, sitting on plush velvet seats, we heard Melpomene's carriage rumble into motion. Ours started soon after.

"I hope the pegasus knows where we're going," Sarah

said, "because no one is steering this thing."

"I'm sure it does," Welkin said. "They're very clever animals. Vain as anything, but clever."

"The poor things, though, having their wings bound." My cousin sighed, staring out the window at the passing tunnel walls. Sconces were set at intervals, flickering with blue flame. I squeezed her hand briefly, and she smiled back at me. She sat on one side of me on the broad bench seat. Jack was on the other.

"It's the only way to stop them escaping." Welkin's tiny face was grim, lips pressed into a thin line. "I feel bad for them. Winged things don't like to be earthbound."

"Maybe we could bargain for their release?" I suggested tentatively.

On my other side, Jack shook his head. "They are too valuable," he said, eyes wide with sympathy. "Not all *aosidhe* can afford such a prestigious slave as a winged horse."

We rode in silence for a while. Then Ryan leaned his elbows on his knees. "So why do you think she's coming?"

"I have two theories," I admitted, reaching over my head to rub one tense shoulder. Jack turned sideways on our seat and brushed my hand aside to take over. I sighed as his strong fingers massaged the knot of muscle; warmth flooded through me at his touch. Aunt Elizabeth pursed her lips.

"And they are?" Ryan raised his eyebrows.

"Oh. Right. One is that she wants to make sure I follow through on my oath and get Dad out of the country before we cause any more trouble."

"The other?"

Sarah spoke before I could. "She's got the hots for Helios and wants the chance to see him."

I nodded, twisting so Jack could reach my other shoulder. "Uh huh. Look how she changed into that fancy dress. What she was wearing when we met her was enough to meet any old *aosidhe*, or her long-lost daughter, but for Helios? She gets into the fanciest dress in her wardrobe." If she had a wardrobe. Wouldn't she just conjure her outfit every day to suit her whim? The idea was fascinating.

"Speaking of which, you need an upgrade. You can't let her show you up." Sarah gave my dress an appraising look. "It's pretty. Looks sort of like the ocean, with the ruffles down the back. Can you add some pearl beads into the train, and on little chains in your hair? And a finish like those shells. You know, the shimmery ones?" Her eyes widened with delight. "Oh, and you should totally add vents here, at your sides, to show off the gills. It shows you're powerful enough to change your body."

"Gills?" Aunt Elizabeth murmured. She barely looked startled anymore. Was that a good or a bad thing? I stared hard at her aura but it showed only surprise, not the confusion I'd seen in Dominic's aura when the *sidhe* had affected his mind. "Gills, Isla?"

I nodded slowly. "Jack and I kind of swam here."

"And does he, ah, have gills too?" She looked from me to him, as though wondering what else was hiding under those pinstripes. Scales, perhaps? Or wings?

I could have reassured her he was otherwise quite normal under his clothes, but the revelation that I had seen him naked might be one shock too many. "Only at the moment. Because I gave them to him."

"So you could swim. Across the Atlantic."

"Well, we took a shortcut. And hitched a ride. We didn't

do much actual swimming, really."

"Right. Okay."

Under Sarah's instruction, I modified my dress, turning it into something so ornate that, if it were white, it would fit right in at a bridal boutique, crusted as it was with beading in patterns reminiscent of waves breaking on the shore. Pearl and diamond bracelets encircled each wrist, around the gloves. The dress now had open, scalloped sides, revealing my ribs and the four gills under each arm. They resembled scratches until I flared them open for a second, showing off to make my cousins gasp.

After one intent look, Aunt Elizabeth turned to gaze fixedly out the window.

Ryan, though, couldn't help staring. "Do you think you could morph my body? I've always thought a monkey tail could be handy. I could use it to hold spare paintbrushes."

"No!" My aunt grabbed Ryan's arm with both hands. She took a deep breath and sat back, but didn't release him. "You know, your father and I worried when you were children that you might get into body modification. Piercings, for example. We never thought you'd become half-fish." I looked up from her clutching hands and smiled as the amusement crinkled around her eyes.

"It's temporary," I assured her. "But I *can* do some modifications for you. Within reason." I frowned at Ryan.

"I've been thinking I want to get rid of this blond streak in my hair," Sarah said, running her fingers through her fringe. I raised my eyebrows, surprised. That streak had become symbolic of my cousin's belief her band was destined to hit the big time. "What? It's so much effort trying to keep the roots dyed, and I can always redo it later when we're famous. Then I'll have my own personal hairdresser. Right?"

"Just think of the money we could save on hair dye," my aunt said with a grin that made her look a lot like her daughter. "No more grey hair to worry about!"

"Any time," I promised. "But for now, did you want anything...?" They shook their heads and we rode the rest of the way in silence.

CHAPTER TWENTY-SEVEN

O ur carriage slowed a half-hour later. We gathered around the window to peer out; the marble tunnels close to Melpomene's *sidhe* had transformed into honey-coloured stone, flecked with an extravagant number of stargems.

Jack stepped out of the carriage first, peering around before helping me down. My family followed behind, while I tried not to gawp like a tourist at the tremendous courtyard. Yellow sandstone bricks formed the outer edge of the *sidhe*, while the courtyard's inner wall was tall and smooth, with columns set at intervals. Carvings that reminded me of dancing flames wound around each of the columns, sinuous and strange. I shuddered, reminded of Everest's death. He would have fit in well here. Perhaps that was why he'd been attracted to Helios—they shared a love of fire.

Melpomene stood out like a flower in a field, her skirt almost glowing against the stone. She regarded my trans-formed dress, lips pressed together tightly with a displeasure that filled me with equal parts alarm and satisfaction. Had she wanted me to seem like her poor cousin? I fluffed my train, showing the waves of the ruffles to full advantage. Hatred flashed across her face for a fleeting second before it settled back into its beautiful, cold lines.

With a wink, Sarah moved between me and my mother, adjusting my hair so it sat properly beneath its new silver chain hairpiece. She leaned forward to whisper in my ear, "It looks like a crown. It's perfect." On her shoulder, Welkin gave me a thumb's up.

A hob dressed in bronze chainmail with an orange-and-white tabard over the top stepped forward and gave a shallow bow, first to Melpomene and then to me. "Would you be Isla, the..." he hesitated over the word "...*aosidhe* who has thrown down the gauntlet to my master?"

"I am."

"But you are not *aosidhe!*" the hob replied. His hair was a fiery orange, making my cousins' ginger look drab by comparison, and his eyes were amber yellow. The colouring matched his livery perfectly—no doubt a deliberate choice. My eyes stung with sympathy. I doubted the livery had been chosen to match the hob, after all. "You look human."

"Would a human's skin glow in the *sidhe*?" I said, holding my gloved arms out as though the soft glow weren't already obvious from my low-cut gown.

"Not usually," the hob admitted. He gave Melpomene a sidelong glance. "Not unless an *aosidhe* made it do so."

"I have done no such thing, Alexander," Melpomene snapped, voice sharp as razors. "This impudent girl is my daughter. Helios has agreed to see her. Do you block her way?"

"Of course not, Lady Melpomene. Please, follow me."

Melpomene swept forward, her entourage in tow, to follow immediately behind the hob as he passed through a huge doorway, ignoring the heavily armed *powrie* guards on either side. I scowled and followed after, hating that she expected me to trail behind her like a child. Jack's arm linked through mine and he set a stately pace, as though we had all the time in the world. I smiled at him and he winked back before schooling his expression to seriousness.

The corridor was long, set with huge, arched windows at regular intervals. At first I ignored the views beyond, more concerned with keeping my eye on the enormous guards who loomed between each one. They were dressed in armour and livery similar to the hob's, except their chainmail extended up and over their heads, concealing their faces. How could they see? Were they statues, like Melpomene had? But no, one of them shifted from one foot to the other as we moved into view.

It was Sarah's muffled gasp that drew my gaze to the windows themselves. Each one contained a sunlit view. One showed a bustling Hellenic marketplace at midday; the scent of strange spices tickled my nose. Another window framed a glittering sea at sunset, the lonely sound of a gull's cry clear over the sounds of our footsteps. Opposite, sunrise peeked over a snow-capped mountain-top, chill air raising goosebumps on my arms.

They weren't paintings or glassed windows, they were portals. If I stepped through, would I fall into the scene, carried far away from here? Or would I be trapped in a tiny pocket dimension?

Helios's throne room was massive, at least five times

the size of Melpomene's. A heavy scarlet carpet speared through its centre like a trail of blood. On either side, crowds of *duinesidhe* turned to stare as we entered. The *aosidhe* among them glittered, standing out amidst leather-clad *puca*, officious-looking hobs and even the occasional flittering *piskie*. *Powrie* lined the walls, dressed in the same armour as the ones in the halls. Although their faces were likewise covered, I knew what they were. Their auras were filled with bloody rage.

Voices murmured as Melpomene approached the throne, the rest of us in her peacock-feathered wake. Some voices were shrill, others deep, but all carried the weight of derision and all belonged to *aosidhe*; their attendants didn't dare speak. My mother wasn't liked. Because she'd brought me here? I looked around, judging the intensity of the feelings in those auras: hatred, cruel amusement, no little jealousy. These emotions were long-held. Because she dared to defy the *aosidhe* who owned them all?

Those who met my curious gaze regarded me with shock.

"Melpomene." A deep voice thrummed through my bones, making the hair on the back of my neck stand on end. It came from the other end of the room, where the throne would be. I couldn't catch more than a glimpse of it past Fawn, who loomed just behind Melpomene, his bare shoulders knotted with apprehension.

"To what do I owe the pleasure?" The voice drew out the last word, as though it was a promise. *Helios.*

"Did you not receive my message?" she replied, sounding bored.

"I did." His boredom matched hers. These two could be bored for their nation. "Show me this *aosidhe* I have never heard of before, then."

Melpomene turned to look back at me, gesturing for Fawn and Hiram to step aside so I could approach the throne. I did so, Jack glued to my side. I could feel the tension thrumming through him, vibrating up from the point where his arm looped through mine.

When my gaze settled on Helios, I bit the inside of my lip to stop myself from gasping. He reclined on a throne built from what I suspected was solid gold. Heavy metal rays flared from the back of the chair in a stylised sun, a halo around the head of the god sitting before it. For Helios resembled a god, an ancient Greek god like his namesake. A pure white toga hung from one shoulder, a sun-shaped clasp made of diamonds fastening it in place. The fabric did little to conceal the tanned, hairless skin of his chest, the defined muscles that would turn a gym junkie green with envy. A laurel crowned wavy golden hair that tumbled to his shoulders, so soft I wanted to run my fingers through it. Even the points of his ears somehow looked manly, less delicate than Melpomene's.

His eyes, piercing and fierce as an eagle's, were just as Ryan had drawn them—although my cousin's pencil hadn't conveyed the way they glowed even against the lesser backdrop of his skin, as though pieces of sunlight were trapped within.

"Oh my." Helios stared down at me, his aura blooming with scarlet lust. "Melpomene junior. How delightful." He looked back at my mother. "Now you come as a pair, I want you twice as badly."

Melpomene's chin lifted and her eyes narrowed. "She may bear a resemblance to me, but she is not of my court," she declared. "I care naught for her."

Once, the truth ringing in her words would have cut

me like a blade. Now it rolled off me; all I felt was relief as I finally understood why Melpomene had come with me to Helios's court. She wanted to denounce me in front of everyone, in case I failed in my challenge and ended up sworn to Helios.

She wanted to make sure I couldn't be used against her.

"The girl is not full *aosidhe*," Alexander murmured from Helios's side, looking up at his master with worshipful eyes. I hadn't even noticed him approach the throne. "Her ears are rounded and her flesh clearly mortal, though it glows as though she is one of my lord's people."

"The ears can be fixed." Helios's fiery gaze ran over my body, so intense my ears burned. "I shall enjoy sculpting this one."

Jack, his face as dark as thunderclouds, looked as though he wanted to speak. But he took a deep breath, nostrils flaring, and then released my arm with a deferential bow. "Make him respect you," he whispered so softly I could barely hear him, and stepped back, leaving me alone before Helios's stare.

I dug my hands into fists, nails pressing into my skin even through the gloves. "As Melpomene has already made clear, I am not sworn to her." My voice sounded loud to my ears. "She may enter your service if she wishes, but you do not own me."

Helios raised a single, amused eyebrow. Although he was so handsome my chest ached and my stomach tightened, I kept my chin raised and met his gaze as he replied, "Oh, little half-breed? And you think you deserve to be treated as one of us, rather than as a slave?"

He'd said slave instead of human. What a peach.

"As I said to your hob, my skin glows, right?"

He shrugged, dismissing that.

"I also have an *aislinge*," I said, gesturing to Ryan, who met Helios's gaze for several seconds before looking away, cowed. "And when Everest sent an elf shot to wound my father, I drew it from him with my power."

"And where is Everest?" one of the *aosidhe* to my left, a tall, spindly woman with feathers instead of hair, demanded. Her eyes ran over my family as though expecting the *aosidhe* to appear among them.

"He came to my court and tried to take over." I swallowed hard, hoping my nausea at the memory wasn't obvious. "So I dealt with him."

"*Dealt* with him?" The woman's voice was shrill.

I chose my words carefully, not wanting to be caught in a lie. "There wasn't much left, afterwards. My *duine-sidhe* had to sweep him up."

The roar of voices to either side of me was silenced by Alexander's narrow-eyed glare. As the right-hand hob to the most powerful *aosidhe* in the room—and in the world, for all I knew—it seemed he carried a lot of weight.

"Is that how it happened?" Helios said, looking down into the shadows of the throne to his right.

"Yes," a familiar voice said. My mouth fell open as Ariel stepped forward, his green eyes full of hatred as he glowered at me. He looked the same as he had several months ago, except his cheek bore a silvery-white scar where Sarah struck him with a haematite necklace after he threatened her. The same necklace she wore now. I wanted to turn and hug her, reassure her I wouldn't let him have her … but that would undermine me with Helios. "She tricked my master into burning himself to death," he added.

MELPOMENE'S DAUGHTER

"I was defending my court. Would you let another *aosidhe* come into your home and take what is yours?" I kept my voice level.

"No, I would not." Helios shrugged those magnificent shoulders, muscles rippling under silky skin. "However, is that not why you are here today? Ariel brought me this lovely human toy, and you have come here to take it from me. Have you not?"

My stomach churned with bile as Ariel tugged on a chain whose end was tucked into his belt. A figure lurched forward, out of the shadows and into the unforgiving glare of the throne room.

Dad.

He wore shabby jeans and a shirt that had seen better days. Although the clothes were clean, they were torn in places, revealing bruised flesh and slowly healing injuries. From when Ariel had captured him? Or had he been tortured since?

The fierce, satisfied smile on Ariel's face as he watched my reaction was answer enough. The shock drained all warmth from my face, leaving me as cold as marble.

Dad's gaze latched onto Melpomene and his eyes brightened, his depressed grey aura pierced with hope as though the sun had come out from behind a storm cloud. "Mel! You've come for me!"

"Hardly," she sneered. His face fell, heartbroken. "But she has." She nodded to me.

When Dad saw me, he began to weep. "Oh no, Isla. No, no, no. You can't be here."

"It's okay, Daddy," I said, trying to reassure him. "I'll get you out of here."

Around me, the *aosidhe* courtiers laughed. Fury surged

through me, roaring up through my chest and out of my fingertips as I jabbed a hand at the crowd. "Shut your mouths!" I snarled.

The trident clanged furiously in my mind. A dozen pairs of *aosidhe* teeth snapped together, biting off their amusement. Shocked silence fell.

Helios stared at me, steepling his fingers under his chin in a way that conjured up Everest's ghost—although I was sure Everest had acquired the gesture from his master rather than the other way around. "Interesting," he said. "How did you do that?"

I lifted my chin and stared him in the eye. "I am *aosidhe*."

"Not just any *aosidhe*." His voice warmed with approval, and his eyes flooded with the heat of desire. There was nothing personal about it, though—not like Jack's eyes as we made love, filled with feeling for me. Helios wanted to acquire me and my power to add to his collection of *aosidhe*. Nothing more. "So you have come to throw down the gauntlet, claim your father back?"

"Yes," I said, stepping forward past my dumbstruck mother. She made no move to stop me. "And I want him." I jabbed a gloved finger at Ariel, my bracelets glittering in the light. "He has taken from me. Not just my father but also my grandmother too. He killed her, and I want justice."

"I wish you could hear the way she screamed as her skull crunched under my blows," Ariel growled. Behind me, a voice moaned, low and sick. Aunt Elizabeth. His eyes skipped from me to my family. "I wonder if the skulls of her daughter and granddaughters will sound the same."

Helios regarded the hob, full lips curled in a sneer, before turning his eyes back to me. "So if you win the challenge, I let you leave with the human. Your father. If I win?"

"I swear an oath of service to you, become one of your court. But if I win, I want Ariel too."

Helios waved that away. "My dear, you can have Ariel whether you win or lose."

The hob stared up at the *aosidhe*, shock ripping through his aura. "No!" He dropped the chain and turned to flee. Two *powrie* lumbered in, grabbing his arms. His legs dangled, kicking the air, as they stood straight. Their chain-covered faces turned up to their master, silent and expectant.

"Just hold him there."

Dad, freed by the distraction, scurried across the tiled floor to where I stood on the carpet, clutching at me with hands that trembled with fear. The chains running from his wrists to his throat clinked with each movement; the leash trailed across the floor behind him. "Isla," he whimpered. "My Isla Rose. You shouldn't have come."

I kissed him on the stubbled cheek. His skin was wet with tears. "Of course I came." Sarah and Ryan hurried forward, wrapping their arms around him and drawing him away from me. "Look after him," I said. They nodded, faces pale. Sarah gathered up the chain so none of the *duinesidhe* could grab it and haul him away.

Helios didn't protest when my cousins flanked Dad. Aunt Elizabeth wrapped her arms around him, speaking in a whisper, keeping his attention on her.

If it stopped him from fixating on Melpomene, who still owned his heart, I was grateful.

"So we are agreed?" Helios said. "I will set a challenge that you must complete."

"Agreed." The oath felt like shackles, binding me as surely as they did Dad.

"You claim to be a true *aosidhe*, with your own court," Helios mused, his gaze taking in the gills at my side, the glow of my skin. "And you are powerful, perhaps more powerful than most *aosidhe* here." A murmur from the courtiers, swiftly silenced by the narrowing of his eyes. "However, I think that, at your heart, you remain flawed. Human."

"I don't regard being human as a flaw." I nodded to my clustered family. "They are as loyal to me as any of your servants are to you. More. And they serve me out of love, not fear of cruelty."

"Melpomene's *duinesidhe* serve her out of love too," Helios pointed out. "She forces them to love her, as I expect you could do if you wished. If you have not already. But she does not love them or feel compassion for them in return. She does not love your weak human father. *That* is where your weakness lies."

Melpomene drew her gaze away from Dad, looking back at Helios. She blinked as though drawing her mind back to the conversation. Was Helios wrong? Did she love my father, maybe a little bit? Did she love Fawn, or her *aislinge*? Could a creature who dealt in emotions truly keep herself distant from them, even if she was an *aosidhe*?

If Helios noticed her expression, he didn't say anything. "An *aosidhe* must be strong and, yes, cruel at times to defend what is his—or hers—from the predations of others. Can you be cruel, Isla, or has human compassion wormed its corrupt fingers into your heart?"

"I don't agree that compassion is corruption."

ʍELPOʍEΠE'S DΛUGʜTER

"You do not need to agree," Helios said, his voice strangely gentle. "I merely explain to you the logic behind the challenge I am about to set. You must win ... or forfeit." Anxiety roiled in my stomach. Helios's piercing eyes took in my reaction. Those lips curled into a smile. "There is no doubt you have defended your court once, but can you do it again? Can you protect your people when another *aosidhe* turns one of them against you?"

Fear cut through me, turning my knees to water. I willed them to lock in place, to keep me standing. "Yes," I whispered. "I can."

He turned to Alexander. "Give her your blade."

The hob approached me, drawing a long, bronze dagger from a leather sheath at his belt. The blade seemed to gather all the light in the room, trapping my gaze as he stalked towards me with it.

"The challenge is simple. Take the weapon. Stab your hob through the chest with it. Prove you can be as cruel as you need to be. Prove you are one of us."

Heart burning in my throat, I turned to look at Jack. His gaze met mine, eyes full of the compassion Helios wanted me to foreswear. "I..." The word stuck in my throat. *I can't*, I wanted to scream. But if I didn't, Dad would stay Helios's prisoner. I would have to serve him, and he could order me to torture Jack whenever he liked. Ryan would be trapped. The others might be too.

I looked at Melpomene. Her dark eyes, so much like mine, were as flat as chips of stone. Unsympathetic. "I did warn you."

She had.

"You seek to take one of my servants from me," I said, voice rasping as I turned back to Helios. "Jack is valuable."

"As Everest was valuable to me." Helios examined his fingernails. "However, I did not demand you killed the hob, just that you stab him through the chest. The weapon does not contain iron. He will heal."

"Probably," Alexander added, his yellow eyes glittering as he pushed the dagger into my hands. The hilt was slippery in my gloved fingers.

I turned back to Jack. Tears burned my eyes, flowed down my cheeks when I blinked. He came to my side, pressing his forehead against mine. "You can do this," he whispered.

"I can't." The thought of pressing the blade's tip against his chest made me want to vomit. Scream. Die.

"I *want* you to do this. I will be fine."

"You can't know that."

"I do."

Helios cleared his throat, drawing my gaze back to him. I wiped the tears away with the back of my glove. "You can choose not to accept the challenge, Isla. I would be delighted to instead take your oath of service. Then you need not harm a hair on your precious hob's head. Poor little human girl. I know how this must pain you."

Jack took a step back, hands unbuttoning the jacket, the shirt. His skin was pale beneath. I couldn't take my eyes from it. Just yesterday I'd kissed his chest. We'd made love. How could I do this? I couldn't.

"You must do this," Jack whispered, holding the fabric aside with both hands. "Isla, please. I beg you. It is a simple thing."

I raised the dagger in a hand gone numb with shock. He reached out and placed his fingers over mine, steadying the blade, guiding it over his heart. I'd lain my head there, listening to it beat.

"Not there," I croaked, moving the tip to my left, close to his right shoulder. "He only said I had to stab you in the chest. Not where."

"Good point." Jack's smile was sweet. "I love you, Isla."

"I love you too, Jack." My own heart shattered into a million pieces.

Together, we thrust the blade into his chest.

Blood gushed, hot and sticky, over our fingers. It soaked through my gloves in an instant. Jack guided my hands, and the blade, between his ribs. Sweat beaded his forehead. He grunted with pain, and I shook myself from my stupor. Spinning myself into his aura, I sheltered him from the agony, catching it like a fish in a net and drawing it into myself. It thrummed along my veins, searing, as hot as the sun.

Jack smiled, beatific.

"What the..." Alexander stepped forward. My free arm lashed out, catching him around the wrist.

"Here, Alex. I have a gift for you," I snarled, shoving Jack's pain into him. Alexander's scream rent the air. He fell back onto the carpet, clutching at his chest.

My only regret was that Helios was out of reach.

"What did she do?" the *aosidhe* demanded, stiff with outrage.

Melpomene stared at me, mouth hanging open.

I turned back to Jack. Bloody foam flecked his lips. Did that mean we'd punctured a lung? I struggled to recall my high school first aid course. "What do I do?" I whispered, eyes begging for an answer. For forgiveness.

Jack clenched his fist around the blade, yanking it from the wound. Blood sprayed, spattering my face and chest. He staggered back. Suddenly Sarah was there, catching him, pressing her hands to the injury. Her eyes were wide, her face ghostly pale, but all she said was, "I've got this." Welkin, ever-present on her shoulder, spoke to her, gesturing urgently.

Face wet with tears, I turned back to Helios. The bloody dagger was in my hand; I tossed it onto Alexander's writhing body. "Thanks for the loan." My voice was hard, strange to my ears, as I looked up at the throne. "So I did as you asked. I'll be taking my people and leaving."

Melpomene had recovered from her shock. "Did you drain his pain?" She sounded almost petulant.

"Why, mummy dearest?" My expression felt twisted and wrong as I grinned at her. "Can't you do that?"

Helios clapped his hands together, the sound a gunshot in the quiet room. He threw back his head, laughing. Golden hair tumbled across his bare shoulders like something out of a shampoo commercial. "Oh, I like you. Isla. Isla Rose? You are, as the humans say, a keeper."

"That may be, but I did as you demanded. The oath is fulfilled. We're leaving now."

"I can see why you might think that." His amusement dropped away like a blanket, falling to the floor to reveal the steel underneath.

"You swore you'd let us go." I hated the strident note that crept into my voice.

"I did, and I will not stop you. But I imagine Alexander might feel differently, given how you just hurt him. Alexander?"

The hob clambered to his feet, pale and trembling. He clutched the bloodstained bronze dagger in one hand, jaw clenched as though he wanted to ram it through me.

Hatred seethed in his aura, the colour of Jack's blood on my skin. "*Powrie!*" he roared. "Do not let them leave." The room shook as the heavily armed soldiers ran forward.

"You cheated!" I screamed at Helios.

He shook his head slowly. "So very human."

My family—including Dad—rushed towards us, gathering around Jack and helping him stagger towards the door. I stood between them and the onrushing *powrie*, hands spread wide. As the first approached, I flicked my fingers at it as though I wielded a whip, lashing out with my power. My skin blazed, as bright as Helios's eyes. The *powrie* screeched, falling back. Its rage was gone, fear gnawing at its heart.

Another *powrie* took his place. That one I filled with grief, leaving it sobbing on the floor.

The third received shame. The fourth, despair.

And still they came.

"Isla!" Ryan's voice cried from behind me, at the entrance to the room. "They're back here too!"

The trident flared, its distinctive shape visible through the soiled glove. Its chime had grown clamorous, demanding. I stripped the ruined fabric off, tossing it aside, and touched the tattoo with my other hand.

With a sound like a church bell pealing, the trident separated from my flesh, resuming its normal form. The shaft was heavy and warm in my hand. The *powrie* hesitated. Alexander frowned, confused.

Behind them, Helios leapt to his feet, eyes wide with recognition. "Let the girl go. I do not care. *Just get me that trident!*" He leapt from the throne and hurried towards us, sandalled feet thudding on the floor.

The trident chimed, insistently recalling to my mind

our walk through Helios's palace. The courtyard, the portals. The ocean, with its perpetual sunset.

Closing my eyes, I imagined the ocean churning, rising up out of the portal. Saw it spilling into the corridor, spraying sea foam on the heavy drapes and filling every crevice. A breeze tugged my hair, carrying the briny scent of the sea. The sound of that lonely gull.

The hissing, rushing sound of the merfolk tongue reached my ears; the clicking, furious chatter of the *cecaelias*. With the trident in my hand, I understood their words. They were confused, furious. Forced to obey.

I opened my eyes. Water ran past my feet, my calves, my knees—the current so strong it nearly swept me off my feet. The back of my dress swirled around me. Chaos erupted in the throne room as the *duinesidhe* scurried back from the onrushing tide. Were they afraid of getting their toes wet? As the water reached my waist, a glance over my shoulder revealed the true cause of their fear. Swarming through the open doorway, moving around my family and Jack as though they were a boulder dividing a river in two, was a host of sea creatures. Merfolk and tentacled *cecaelias* I'd expected, but there were sirens too, and other, stranger beings I didn't recognise. Even a waterhorse swam below the surface like a shark, teeth bared and ready to bite.

The trident had called the creatures of the sea to defend its mistress. And they had answered.

Helios alone surged forward through the water towards me, furious, blazing eyes fixed on the trident in my hand. The sea steamed around him, hissing as it struck his burning flesh. "Give the trident to me, girl, and I will let you go!" he bellowed over the ocean's roar, his hands curled into fists.

"You have to let me go or be foresworn," I yelled back, stepping backwards through the water without looking, grateful for the even footing. Merfolk bristling with weapons moved in front of me, torsos raised up out of the water as they brandished spears tipped with coral and sharp flakes of stone. "We're leaving. Don't try and stop us."

Standing on top of a heavy table amidst trays weighed down with delicacies, Melpomene met my gaze. She nodded once, respectfully.

"What about Ariel?" Helios said, his voice wheedling. "I will trade him for the weapon."

I shrugged. "Kill him. I don't care." I narrowed my eyes, glaring at the *aosidhe* across the heads of my scaly defenders. "But know this. If any *aosidhe* attempts to come to Australia, I will destroy them."

Ariel's scream followed us down the corridor and through the ocean window.

CHAPTER TWENTY-EIGHT

Twenty-four hours later, we struggled up out of the Pacific onto an empty beach, exhausted by our last swim from the underwater tunnel entrance to the shore. The sun hung below the horizon, painting the sky a greyish pink. Dawn. Steadying myself with the trident as though it was a walking stick, I ran my gaze over my family, making sure they were okay. Each wore a wetsuit, hiding the gills I'd given them as we plunged from the portal window and into the waves below. Dad moved stiffly, but when he met my gaze, the corners of his eyes crinkled in a smile.

Jack stood beside Dad, refastening his ever-present bandana. He was pale—paler than usual—but his hob regenerative powers had almost completely healed the dagger wound. He met my gaze and smiled. "I am fine," he insisted in a low voice, answering the unspoken question.

"Promise?" I whispered back. Every time I recalled that horrible moment in Helios's court, my heart almost stopped.

"Of course I do," he said, taking my free hand.

MELPOMENE'S DAUGHTER

Together, we turned back to the surf.

Visible between each rolling wave were dozens of heads. Each was low to the water so nothing below each smooth or scaly chin was visible. Every pair of eyes—except one—narrowed with hostility as they wondered what I would do next.

Their master.

They weren't the same sea creatures who had saved us from Helios. We'd left those behind on the other side of the world when, after Jack had healed sufficiently, I used the trident to teleport us back to King Moana's court. We made our way home from there, followed by this silent crowd of sea creatures. The king was among the watching crowd, as were the queen and Marin. Pania's hair, flowing golden around her, intermingled with her father's.

She was the only one who smiled, pretty face full of trust.

My family watched, tense, as I dropped Jack's hand, squared my shoulders, and moved forward. When the waves rolled over my dive boots I halted, bracing myself as the retreating water stole the sand from under my feet.

"King Moana." I inclined my head towards the merfolk monarch. "I want to make you an offer. And also the rulers of the other ocean folk who live around this continent."

He moved forward slightly, as did a *cecaelias* and a siren I didn't recognise. "What is your offer, Isla?"

"I told Helios if any *aosidhe* tried to come to Australia, I'd make sure they were destroyed. I can take care of the land, but I'd like to ask you to take care of the sea for me."

"Ask?" the siren said, baring a double row of teeth in a snarl. Its voice was bitter. "You don't have to *ask*."

"I do," I said, "because I want to make you a trade." I glanced at the trident in my hand. It was silent, quiescent.

Because it was on land in the human world? I doubted I'd tired it out.

Moana realised what I was suggesting before the others did. His eyes widened with incredulity. "We agree and you'll give us the trident?"

I nodded. "But only to destroy it. If you swear you and your people will stop *aosidhe* from travelling across the ocean through either the *sidhe* or on earth, so they never reach Australia's shores, I will give you the trident and you can break it. That way, no one can ever enslave you again." I held my breath and waited for an answer. *Duinesidhe* rulers could bind their people with an oath; that was how the sirens had been bound long ago not to eat live humans. Would they agree to do it now?

I didn't have to wait long. "Done," Moana said, nodding regally.

"Agreed," the siren said.

"We agree too," the *cecaelias* hissed in its own tongue. Trident in hand, I understood it.

As soon as the oaths were sworn, I waded into the surf until the water lapped at my chest, holding out the trident. Each of the three placed a hand upon it. As I released my grip, the weapon realised the peril it was in, and clanged an alarm in my mind. When I stepped back, relinquishing it to the sea creatures, the notes turned sad, shifting into a minor key. Tears burned my eyes and a hard lump formed in my throat. I was betraying a friend, and the trident had saved our lives more than once. I should leap forward, claim it back, save it from this final end—

I was being manipulated. Digging my fingernails into the palms of my hands, I watched as the three rulers between them shattered the trident into thirds. The mournful song fell silent, cut off at last. Moana lifted the three-pronged head into the air, while the *cecaelias* and siren each had half of the shaft. The other sea creatures cheered, splashing the water with delight.

"Thank you," King Moana said as the *cecaelias*, siren and their people disappeared below the waves. "First you saved our daughter; now you have forever freed us from the fear of enslavement."

"Make sure you don't let the parts get reassembled," I replied, eyeing the coral-shaped tips of the trident. It looked dormant, dead—but I didn't trust such a powerful weapon to stay that way.

"Do not fear," Marin said, an amused gleam in his eye. "That would require our races work together."

"Besides," said Queen Nerida, swimming forward with her daughter at her side, "we'll take it to the nearest undersea volcano and toss it in."

Moana looked at the beautiful workmanship of the trident head for a regretful moment before nodding. "So we will, my pearl."

"Will we see you again?" Pania said, sadness in her sea-green eyes.

"Sure," I said, smiling at her. "You'll be queen one day. I'm sure there'll be all sorts of things that will need negotiating. Trade deals and whatnot."

"Boring." She rolled her eyes, and I laughed.

A sliver of sun peeped above the horizon; it was time for the merfolk to go, before the first jogger or dog-walker came down to the beach and got the fright of their lives. As they turned in the water, Marin nodded at me, relief and gratitude warring in his aura. "Thank you," he said. "I doubted you. I'm sorry."

"Don't worry about it," I said, smiling back at him.

Back with my loved ones on the beach, we started the walk across the damp sand to the familiar headland containing the *sidhe* entrance. "I can't wait to get out of this wetsuit and into some dry clothes," Sarah said, glancing back at me over her shoulder. It looked empty without Welkin perched there, but he'd refused to travel underwater no matter how much she begged, deciding to travel home the same way he'd arrived. "Do you think you could conjure me up some brand-name jeans?"

"Probably not without a reference," I admitted ruefully, remembering my attempt to recreate my sneakers in England.

"Later, once we get home?" Her eyes sparkled with delight. "You could do a huge trade in counterfeit goods! You know, if you wanted to."

Aunt Elizabeth, raking her hands through her wet hair, clicked her tongue with disapproval.

"Hey, can I keep the gills?" Ryan said. "When you put everything else back the way it was?"

"I, uh—" I avoided my aunt's furious gaze.

"No, you may not," she barked.

He wilted. "But—"

"No!"

"Fine," he grumbled.

Jack's hand slipped into mine. Warmth bubbled up in my chest as I looked across at him. Framed by the rising sun, the wisps of hair that escaped the bandana made a halo around his head. "You know the *aosidhe* could still send their *duinesidhe*," he cautioned, his voice quiet. The wave of alarm surging through my family's auras told me they'd heard him anyway.

MELPOMENE'S DAUGHTER

"I know." I frowned. "Unfortunately, the alternative would stop all *duinesidhe* coming here. Refugees like you and Evie. That would be worse. We'll just have to risk it."

Aunt Elizabeth sighed. "I just wish we had our documents and clothes," she said, not for the first time. We'd left some of our possessions in the Edinburgh hotel room, others at Nana's house.

Well, they had. Jack and I hadn't had any possessions to speak of.

"Maybe you could ask the hotel staff to bag everything up and ship it over," I suggested. "If not the clothes, at least the passports and stuff."

Dad looked sheepish. "I'm sorry you guys had to leave everything behind."

"As if it was your fault Helios chased us out of Dodge," Sarah said, stepping over the first of the rocks scattered around the headland. "Or that he kidnapped you in the first place."

"Well, no," Dad said, looking at my aunt. She grimaced back at him, and I bit my lip to keep in a laugh; the exchange was so like the ones between Ryan and Sarah. "But it is going to be a long walk home."

"Stop here a second," I said just as we reached the headland. Its bulk screened us from the view of anyone approaching from the sand dunes. "There's something I want to do first."

"What?" Sarah raised her eyebrows, radiating impatience. I knew how she felt; I was as keen to get out of my wetsuit as she was.

But this was important.

I turned to face Jack, taking both his hands. He gazed back at me, sapphire eyes luminous in the dawn light.

"Something Melpomene said has been bothering me," I admitted. "About how our relationship is one-sided."

"Do not worry about it," Jack said. "She was just trying to upset you, to throw you off balance."

"Except she was right. You're sworn to obey me. How can you be my boyfriend like that?" Someone gasped. Heart in my throat, I ignored the distraction. "I want to release you from your oath."

"No."

I'd known he would say that. "In that case—" I drew a wavering breath "—I am Isla Blackman, and I swear I will speak only the truth to you, and devote myself to you, Jack, for all of my life."

The oath settled over both of us, resonating through my soul in a way the trident's chords never could: a majestic note like a grand harmony played on the world's hugest piano. It rang on and on, like wedding bells, in time with my thundering heart.

Eventually, when it fell into silence, I grew aware that beside me, Sarah was squealing and clapping with glee. "I always wanted to go to a beach wedding!"

Jack gaped at me, eyes wide with shock. "You did not have to do that," he breathed.

"I know," I said, stepping forward to kiss him on briny lips. "I know I didn't. But I love you, and that's just how it is."

"I love you too," he murmured back, lips against mine.

"Good." I beamed at him. "Now, let's go home."

THE END

ACKNOWLEDGEMENTS

Melpomene's Daughter wouldn't have been possible without feedback, support, hugs and/or coffee from the following people.

Firstly, and most importantly, thank you to Nathaniel, for your bright-eyed enthusiasm and determination to make me laugh. Being your mummy has helped me see the world with fresh eyes, and it's pretty awesome.

Thank you Peter, friend, alpha reader and evil genius, for telling me when you thought my bad guys weren't being bad enough. Thanks also for that epic plotting (and scheming) session during our caving holiday. As you can see, I stuck to the plan. More or less. To Jennifer Anderson, editor extraordinaire, for encouraging all that Australian slang: cheers, mate! Also, thanks and high fives to my friends Mikey and Cass for showing me it could be done. You were my inspirations when I sat down to write *Isla's Inheritance*. True story.

For their full-throated support and enthusiasm, I'm

grateful to Craig, Ali, Karen, Nicole, Barbara, Stacey, Lauren, Kim and the rest of the Pageinators. And, as always, thanks to my family and work colleagues, the BC09 gang, the rest of the Aussie Owned crew, and all my writing friends on Twitter: you guys are my safety net.

The cover and internal design for *Melpomene's Daughter* are by the super-talented Kim from KILA Designs. Bask in her talent. I know I am!

And finally, thanks to Isla, Sarah, Jack and the others, for letting me spend time in your world. It's been a blast.

Also by Cassandra Page

LUCID DREAMING

*W*ho would have thought your dreams could kill you? Melaina makes the best of her peculiar heritage: half human and half Oneiroi, or dream spirit, she can manipulate others' dreams. At least working out the back of a new age store as a 'dream therapist' pays the bills. Barely. But when Melaina treats a client for possession by a nightmare creature, she unleashes the murderous wrath of the creature's master. He could be anywhere, inside anyone: a complete stranger or her dearest friend. Melaina must figure out who this hidden adversary is and what he's planning – before the nightmares come for her.

ABOUT THE AUTHOR

Cassandra Page is a mother, author, editor and geek. She lives in Canberra, Australia's bush capital, with her son and two Cairn Terriers. She has a serious coffee addiction and a tattoo of a cat—despite being allergic to cats. She has loved to read since primary school, when the library was her refuge, and loves many genres—although urban fantasy is her favourite. When she's not reading or writing, she engages in geekery, from Doctor Who to AD&D. Because who said you need to grow up?

www.cassandrapage.com